GAME, SET, MATCH

GAME, SET, MATCH

JENNIFER IACOPELLI

REQUITED
New York Boston

Interior design by Carla Weiss.
Edge design by Sandra Chiu.

Requited
Hachette Book Group
1290 Avenue of the Americas, New York, NY 10104
Requited.com

Originally published in 2013 in ebook by Coliloquy in the United States and originally published in paperback in 2015 by JCI Books
Simultaneously published in 2026 by Hachette UK in the United Kingdom
First Requited Trade Paperback Edition: February 2026

Requited™ is an imprint of Hachette Book Group, Inc.

Library of Congress Control Number: 2025941855

ISBNs: 978-0-316-59787-6 (special limited edition trade paperback), 978-0-316-60331-7 (standard edition trade paperback), 978-0-316-59790-6 (ebook)

Printed in Dongguan, China

APS

10 9 8 7 6 5 4 3 2 1

To everyone still here, thirteen years later.

This one's for you.

Prologue

Estadio de Tenis
Madrid, Spain

"ONCE YOU HAVE HER DOWN, YOU CAN'T LET HER UP AGAIN," Penny Harrison whispered to herself as the noise from the sold-out stadium crowd washed over her. "Never give an opponent hope. Finish her, Penny. Finish her now."

Blinking down at the red clay and the formerly white tips of her sneakers, she swiped her wrist across her forehead and brushed away rivulets of sweat. She tucked the wayward strands of dark brown hair escaping her braid behind her ears.

She needed to be steady to win this. But steadiness was difficult with everyone still roaring after her last point.

"One at a time," Penny told herself. "One at a time."

With a deep breath and then another, she filled her lungs

and exhaled, slowing her heart rate, bringing herself back under control or at least trying to—it was a lot harder than usual. Then again, she'd never been in a situation this big before. Three points from a win against Zina Lutrova, the best tennis player in the world, this would easily be the biggest moment of Penny's career and she would prove all the naysayers wrong. All the so-called experts had blasted her after her loss in Australia. They said she wasn't ready for the big time. Three more points and they would be eating their words.

She couldn't help the rush of excitement that flowed through her body, and the shiver that followed, goose bumps rising across her skin. The last time she'd felt like that she wasn't on the court, she was with *him*. A flash of blue eyes and tanned skin and a well-earned cocky grin invaded her mind, undoing all that breath work in an instant.

Penny had been striving for this moment her entire life, and now she was here, on the precipice of something great. She was not about to let anything get in the way of that, certainly not some guy.

Focus, she needed to focus.

Across the net, Lutrova waited, bent at the waist and crouched low like a cobra ready to strike. Most people facing Zina completely lost it the second they caught the icy-blue gaze of the Russian superstar, but Penny wasn't scared, at least not anymore. She was about to prove she was as good as the world number one.

The crowd murmured, an anxious wave of sound, equal parts hope and dread.

The umpire, high atop his chair, shushed them. "Silencio, por favor."

Penny approached the baseline; the crowd's collective voice faded to a distant hum, but they were behind her, pulling for her, willing her to win. Everyone loved an underdog. Her body was loose now, almost relaxed, and the world slowed down around her, nice and easy.

"Time to finish this," she whispered.

One bounce, then two, three, and four in perfect rhythm. Her body weight shifted forward and then back, arms up, racket ready, the ball suspended above her head. She pushed into the ground, then sprung up and out, racket face hammering a clean stroke, skimming it off the white chalk T in the center of the court.

Penny's feet hit the ground together, balanced and ready for a return that never came. The ball whistled by Lutrova's desperate lunge and pounded into the wall behind her.

An ace.

Thirty–love.

Santa Monica Community College Library
Santa Monica, California

"So, I told them I'm an entrepreneur and as soon as the app goes live I'm going to be rich," the flushed-face, lanky guy said, leaning forward with one elbow on the library table and his other hand jabbing at the air. "I'll sell it to the highest bidder and my parents will finally stop being on my ass about this school shit. I mean look at all these people, it's pathetic."

Pathetic wasn't the word Indiana Gaffney would have used

to describe the students around her. The library was crowded for a Sunday morning, and when the guy from her bio class spotted an empty seat at the table she'd claimed for herself, he sat down without invitation, started talking . . . and hadn't stopped for nearly an hour. She couldn't remember his name and he hadn't paused long enough for her to ask or, really, for her to say anything at all.

Occasionally, she would flick her eyes up from her laptop, hoping he would get the hint that she didn't have time for his shit. She was *mostly* working on her final bio lab report of the spring semester, but also keeping an eye on her phone, propped up against the screen, where a young tennis player, barely older than her, hair pulled back in a neat brown braid, walked across the screen bouncing a ball against her racket into the red clay surface of a court in Madrid.

Rolling her neck, Indy flipped her long blond hair over her shoulder, revealing the earbud firmly in place and raising the volume on her phone, completely drowning out her tablemate since he wouldn't take the hint. If Penny Harrison was going to beat Zina Lutrova, Indy wasn't missing it for some deluded tech bro who talked shit about community college students working hard on a weekend while *also* enrolled there.

The commentator was shouting over the raucous crowd. "Penelope Harrison, just twenty-one years old, is up a set, a break, and thirty–love. Another serve like that and she'll have three match points."

"It's amazing," the other announcer chimed in. "If you didn't know who Penny Harrison was before today, you sure do now. She's going to take down the number one player in the world and defending champion in the final of the Madrid Open—a huge win in her young career."

Indy felt a small pang inside her chest. Two years ago she and her mom had watched this tournament on TV together. Her mom had been sure Indy would be playing there one day on that court in Madrid or Paris or New York, winning a major tournament. After she died, winning tennis matches really didn't matter much to Indy anymore. Nothing mattered except she was gone and wasn't coming back.

Though she'd probably be pissed as hell at Indy for giving up.

The thought came unbidden from a place in her mind she'd locked away for far too long. Was it time to start again? It was what her mom would have wanted, wasn't it?

The camera zoomed in on the stands where Dom Kingston, Penny's coach, sat, his hands clasped together like he was praying. He was one of the best coaches in the world and he'd wanted Indy to come play at the Outer Banks Tennis Club, his training facility in North Carolina. If she had, that could've been her standing across from the number one player in the world right now. Or maybe she would've been number one already. Indy bit her lip, wondering if Coach Kingston's offer would stand more than two years later.

A hand pushed at her laptop, forcing the phone to slip onto the keyboard and send a scrawl of unintelligible text across her document. Her eyes snapping up, she glared at the guy, who immediately sat back in his seat, hands up in surrender, with a smirk that he probably thought was attractive but only gave smarmy creep.

"Could you not?" she whispered to be sure she didn't disturb the other students around them.

"Your loss," he said when he *finally* got up to leave as she readjusted her setup. By the time the phone was in place, the camera was focused on the court again as Penny tossed the ball into the air. Her serve was up into Lutrova's body, an attempt to handcuff the Russian, who managed a sharp return, grunting with the effort, sending Penny scrambling.

It was a furious battle, a blistering exchange from the baseline, as they pounded away at each other like heavyweight boxers, neither giving an inch. Then Penny seized upon a short backhand and sent a rocket into the corner, perfectly placed. All Lutrova could do was watch the ball cut through the air as it passed her by.

"Yes!" the tiny version of Penny bellowed from the screen, pumping her fist, a rare show of emotion from her on the court, now just a point away from the championship.

"Yes," Indy echoed under her breath. If she wanted it, if she wanted to be on that court in Madrid, then Bio 101 and scaring off college guys wouldn't get her there.

Maybe she'd put in a call to Dom.

After all, what did she have to lose?

Forty–love.

Harrison Residence
Ocean Hill, North Carolina

"And Penny Harrison has three championship points!" The announcer's voice roared through the television set.

Jasmine Randazzo grabbed the bottle of Jack Daniels by its neck and tried to yank off the cap. As much as she was rooting for Penny, it still stung a little that the other girl was off winning a huge pro tournament and she was sitting at home after losing in the first round. A warm hand surrounded hers and pulled the bottle away from her.

"Easy there, Jas," Teddy Harrison said, twisting the cap off and handing it back.

"How are you not drunk?" she asked, narrowing her eyes at her friend. "*I'm* drunk."

Teddy snorted softly. "I'm not drunk because I do this more than you. Some of us have actual lives off the court, you know."

"I have a life, sort of," she muttered, pouring herself another shot. The whiskey missed the glass, spilling over the table, and Teddy took the bottle away again. He poured out two glasses and handed one to her.

"Yep, sort of."

"To Penny." Jasmine saluted the TV set, then sent the burning liquid down the back of her throat.

"You gotta stop worrying about my sister," Teddy said, settling back against the couch beside her, his arm coming around her shoulders, squeezing tightly.

"I'm not worrying about her," Jasmine argued. "I'm happy for her and she better watch her back once I get on tour."

"How many have you had?" Teddy asked, snickering through another shot.

The television camera zoomed in on the player's box. Their coach, Dom Kingston, was there, applauding with the rest of the crowd, and one row behind him were Jasmine's parents, sitting beside the Harrisons and cheering on Penny.

"God forbid we make it through a match without my parents being on camera," Jasmine grumbled, leaning her forehead against Teddy's shoulder. He was so solid and warm. She snuggled closer.

"It's good for publicity," Teddy said, probably for the hundredth time that week. "When people see Mr. and Mrs. Tennis out there, they want to come to OBX and train at the place they founded."

"They aren't nearly as cool as everyone thinks."

"They're pretty damn cool, Jas."

"They're my parents. Totally dorky like everyone else's."

"Nah," Teddy said, taking another shot. Jasmine frowned. When had he poured that? "Your Grand Slam–winning, Olympic gold medalist parents are awesome and so are you."

"Damn right I am."

"You want another shot?"

She shook her head and the world spun a little more than it should have. "No, I think I've had enough."

Teddy smiled widely, the dimple that routinely tortured her appearing in his cheek. "No such thing."

Jasmine leaned forward, wrapping her arms around his shoulders. Her nose trailed over his neck, inhaling deeply. He smelled good, really good, like spices and ocean water and soap and Teddy, her best friend. It was nice to be that close to him. She should do it more often.

Vaguely, from the TV across the room, echoed the *thwack* of the ball against racket faces, a final desperate scream from Lutrova, and then an answering joyful shriek from Penny.

Jasmine knew that sound—she'd been on the wrong side of it more than once. The crowd moved from a heavy anticipatory silence to a raucous cheer as the announcer shouted over them, "Game, set, and match, Harrison."

"Teddy," she whispered against his skin.

A grunt rumbled through Teddy's throat. "Yeah, Jas?" he asked, his mouth suddenly really close to hers, close enough to feel his breath against her lips. She answered by leaning forward ever so slightly until there was no space between them at all. The kiss was heavy and deep. She could feel it in her fingertips, in her toes, and in a lot of other less innocent places, and then he was gone, flinging himself to the opposite end of the couch, staring at her, mouth agape.

For a moment the only sounds in the room were their breathing and the announcer screaming over the crowd. "Penny Harrison has won the Madrid Open and American tennis has found its newest star!"

"Jas," Teddy started, but she shook her head. "Shit, Jas, I'm…"

"Forget it," she mumbled, leaping to her feet, her shin brushing against the table, sending the now-empty bottle of Jack over on its side. She stumbled to the doorway and broke into a run. She heard Teddy call her back over the buzzing in her ears, but she didn't turn around. She just kept going.

Game, set, match.

Chapter 1

PENNY WAS BURNING FROM THE INSIDE OUT.

That was the only explanation she could conjure at the sensation of pure fire coursing through her veins. She reveled in every flame as she arched up off the cool slip of silk sheets, the firm grip of his palm at her hip, calloused thumb gently circling the rise of it as his other fingers left imprints that would bruise in the next few days down her thigh.

His mouth at her breast, the scratch of his stubble on her skin, his hips driving into hers, then the nip of his teeth against the sensitive line of her neck. His body long and firm above her, thick and heavy inside her. Strokes dragging, deep and deliberate, to hit the spot he found that made stars explode behind her eyes. She rose to meet him over and over, rocking into a punishing rhythm of their sweat-soaked skin and his raspy groans and filthy words and a note, high and desperate, from the back of her throat, that pulled her soul from her body while she shook beneath him and he talked her through it.

That's right, love, take me with you. You're so fucking perfect. Finish me off.

Her only answer was a jumbled mess of incoherence and distantly she heard his voice catch on one final word before his arms gave out and he fell into his own release, collapsing down into her, his weight a satisfying, crushing thing.

Penny.

And then . . . consciousness.

A beam of sunlight shining through her window warmed her cheek and she pressed her nose into the cotton sheets, not silk, and inhaled. The fresh, clean scent of the laundry detergent that her mother used—not sweat and sex and a hint of warm spiced cologne that led to so many bad decisions—was a reminder that, for the first time in four months, she was home.

That was a dream.

Just a dream.

But a vivid one, like she was back there, back with *him*.

"Penny!" Her brother Jack's call carried up the stairs and into her bedroom, a repeat of the sound that pulled her from her sleep and a very different voice that said it. "Delivery for you!"

Groaning, she rolled out of bed, banishing the last fleeting images of burning blue eyes and the sound of his voice when he called her name.

That dream had turned into a nightmare in real life, and she no longer had time for it. She had work to do.

When she got downstairs, both her brothers were in the

kitchen. Jack, five years older than her, who pulled double duty as her big brother and her agent, was digging through the fridge. Her twin, Teddy, was sitting atop the central island, shoveling a spoonful of cereal into his mouth. Beside him was a long white box wrapped with a bright blue ribbon.

"You want some?" Teddy asked, his mouth full of the sugary crap he called breakfast, but honestly she was just impressed he was up this early. Normally you wouldn't see him out of bed before noon on summer break.

"No thanks."

Penny pulled the ribbon free of its bow and folded it neatly, setting it aside. She lifted the lid to reveal a dozen long-stem roses. There was a note tucked inside the sea of petals.

To many more victories.
Your friends at Nike

She breathed in the aroma of the fresh-cut flowers. Nike was upping their game. They'd been dangling a sponsorship deal since she'd won a few lower-level tournaments during her first year on tour, but they'd backed off slightly after she'd lost in the quarterfinals of the Australian Open. Penny wrinkled her nose. *Lost* was a bit of an understatement. She'd been eviscerated. A total embarrassment and something she'd never let happen again.

"The flowers are a nice touch," Jack said, pouring himself a glass of orange juice.

"A car would've been a nicer one," Teddy quipped.

"I already have a car," Penny said, tucking the note back

inside the box and then pushing his legs out of the way to find a vase under the island.

Teddy smiled, his dimples appearing, making him seem far more innocent than he'd ever been. "Yeah, this new one could be for me."

"Spending too much of that NIL money on beer, man," Jack said.

Teddy's name, image, and likeness deal with Duke had netted him a decent amount of money over the years, particularly after Penny had started making waves on tour. But it definitely wasn't enough for a car.

"Speaking of cars, though, can I borrow yours real quick?" he asked, ignoring their brother and turning to Penny.

"Nope. I'm going to OBX," she said. "You could come with me?"

"Wait, why are you going in today?"

"I have to train. The French Open is in less than a month. I can't just walk into Roland-Garros unprepared."

"Yeah, and you just won a million dollars in Madrid. You're not going to take a day to enjoy that?"

"I did," Penny said. "When Jack and I stopped over in New York to talk to potential sponsors I took the whole afternoon off and went shopping."

"You're a real wild woman."

"I try."

"C'mon, please? I don't have time to wait for you to finish training to drive home, and I've already walked back once today."

"What do you mean?" Jack asked.

Teddy smirked. "I stayed over at OBX last night and I left my phone by accident. I just need to pick it up."

"A new girl?" Jack's eyes narrowed. "You just got home." Teddy went to Duke and had wrapped up his junior year a couple of weeks before. "Who was it this time?"

"Katie Nelson."

"Katie's sweet," Penny said, looking up from arranging her flowers. "She deserves better."

"*She* doesn't think so. In fact—"

"Don't finish that sentence," Penny said, reaching for the bowl of car keys on the counter. "Take my car. I'll hitch a ride with this one." She motioned toward Jack.

"You're the best."

Teddy jumped down and took the keys from her, then strode out of the kitchen toward the front door.

"So, Nike," Jack said, taking the card from the box. "Looks like your win in Madrid made them rethink things."

Penny wiped some of the last sleep from her eyes. "Looks like it."

"You know this isn't just an outfitting deal. They want you to be the new face of their tennis brand. You can't go into a major tournament and bomb out again. Things have to be different in Paris."

"I know that," she said, crossing her arms over her chest. They'd had this conversation a million times since January. "I'll be ready."

Jack slung an arm over her shoulder and squeezed. "I know, but I wouldn't be doing my job if I didn't remind you."

Rolling her eyes, Penny said, "What was I thinking hiring my brother as my agent?"

"You were thinking that your big brother is brilliant and that he'd always do what's best for you, even when that means kicking you in the ass. Now go get dressed."

She stood tall and saluted him. "Sir, yes, sir."

"Brat."

Twenty minutes later, they sped down Ocean Trail toward OBX, windows open, the morning sun sparkling against the water, salt air crisp against her skin. Pulling into the parking lot, Jack navigated into her designated spot.

RESERVED FOR PENELOPE HARRISON
WORLD #33

The sign had been updated after her run at the Aussie, as well as some decent finishes in a few other tournaments. Now, after last week, she'd popped into the top twenty for the first time in her career. They'd have to update it again. Rankings were determined by a points system that reflected the results, good and bad, of each player at every tournament. Some tournaments were worth more than others and Grand Slams were worth the most. When Dom recruited her, convincing her parents to move their family from Chicago to this tiny town on the North Carolina coast, he promised she would someday be a top-twenty player. Now, here they were, a few weeks away from the French Open, where she could hopefully push into the top ten.

Penny grinned, thinking about that last match in Madrid. She'd worked for that win for a very long time. A breakthrough. A crucial step that brought her closer to winning her first Grand Slam.

As she stepped out of the car, the sounds of the game she loved filled her ears from over the high fences surrounding the forty-five-court complex, the solid *thwack* of balls hitting racket strings, sharp instruction from coaches, the pounding of feet on the hard courts. Jack went to the trunk to grab his bag, but Penny headed straight in.

She and Jack managed only a few steps into the main building, which housed the offices, a few indoor courts, and the training rooms, when Roy Whitfield caught sight of her.

"Penny Harrison!"

"Hey, Roy."

The old security guard was at his usual post in the atrium, his stack of daily newspapers ready, the collar of his navy-blue polo shirt starched, and his ever-present walkie-talkie on his hip. He greeted her with a bright smile, just like he always did when she arrived home from tour.

As usual, not much had changed in her absence.

The air smelled the same, rubber from the soles of all the sneakers, the distinct aroma that popped out of every newly opened can of tennis balls, and the sharp scent of the floor cleaner. This was home, too. OBX was the place that made her dreams a reality.

"Coach asked to see you as soon as you got in," Roy said, nodding up at her coach's office.

"I'm not in trouble, am I?" she asked as she walked to the stairs.

"I wouldn't call it *trouble*," Roy said, his cheeks wrinkling as he smiled.

"I'm gonna head out there, Pen. I'll see you later. Roy," Jack said, walking off toward the back exit. After playing tennis at Harvard, Jack had sometimes helped with the coaching when he was back at OBX between law school terms. And even once he'd graduated and started representing Penny, he kept at it. He insisted he did it to keep himself in shape, but Penny figured he must miss playing—she couldn't imagine giving tennis up cold turkey.

She took the stairs two at a time up to Dom's office and found him standing at his window, which overlooked the rest of the facility, and in the distance, the coast with tiny umbrellas dotting the shoreline in various shades of the rainbow.

"Hey," she said, tossing herself into the seat across from his desk.

Dom turned and moved around his desk. "P, welcome back. You ready to go?"

"Yep. Roy said you wanted to see me. What's up?"

"I wanted to talk through our training plan."

Penny pursed her lips and waited for him to continue. As nice as it was to be home, there were two tournaments between now and the French Open she could be playing in, both of which Zina Lutrova was headlining. It had been Dom's idea to skip those tournaments in favor of coming back to train.

"I've brought in an old friend of mine to be your hitting partner. He's just getting back into full-time training himself, so it'll be the perfect fit for the next few weeks."

Penny raised an eyebrow. "Yeah?"

Dom nodded. "Yeah. I want you to focus on your defensive game and building up your endurance. You saw what it was like in Australia this year. Two weeks of tennis is no joke. You can't fade at the beginning of the second week.

You need to be peaking for the semis and finals, not for the round of sixteen."

"Right," Penny said, clenching her teeth. She wanted to tell him that endurance or lack thereof had nothing to do with the end of her run at the Australian Open. It was the only time her mental focus had slipped. At the highest levels, the mental game was even more important than the physical.

"I am still the world's number one." Zina's Russian accent reverberated through Dom's office. Penny's head snapped to the video screen in the corner and everything else flew straight out of her head. It was an interview from the tournament in Rome where Zina was playing this week. "Harrison played a good match, but I did not play my best. It was a fluke," the young superstar said from the press conference desk.

Dom paused the video as the interview ended. Penny focused on the smirk Lutrova managed to wear even while discussing a decisive loss at the hands of a player she was claiming to be better than. That expression alone was enough to make Penny want to grab a racket, fly to Rome, and take Lutrova's ego down a notch or fifty again.

"These next weeks are critical. Zina will be gunning for you in Paris. You're going to face her down and you're going to win," Dom said.

"I'll be ready."

"Good. Now go. I'll be out in a few. I've got to pull together the Classic rankings by this afternoon."

A wave of nostalgia hit her. For the first time since she'd arrived at OBX, Penny wouldn't be competing in the Classic, a tournament Dom arranged every year for the best up-and-coming young stars tennis had to offer. Since it was his tournament, the player rankings were up to his sole discretion. Penny had never not been ranked number one.

And she'd never not come out on top.

"It's that time of year again, huh? Feels like yesterday I won my first one."

"Yeah, well, three in a row was a good run, but looks like we'll have to find a new champ this year."

Penny was halfway to her practice court, one of the very few clay courts on campus, before she realized she hadn't asked Dom who her new hitting partner was. He'd said it was an old friend, but Dom had been in the tennis world for nearly thirty years. That didn't exactly narrow down the field. Whoever it was, they were sure to be damn good. Her coach would only let her train with the best.

She opened the gate and dropped her bag against the fence before tilting her head in confusion. There was a man sprawled across the court, eyes closed, face to the sun, completely relaxed, except for his hands, which were firing through the air, drumming along with the music she could hear buzzing through his headphones even from the other side of the court.

"Excuse me," Penny said sharply. "This court is reserved."

The man didn't move. He was tall and broad, making the large playing surface seem much smaller than it actually was.

"Excuse me," she repeated when he didn't so much as twitch in response, "this court is..." Frowning down at the court squatter, she immediately recognized him, especially since the last time she'd seen him he'd been in a similar state, totally relaxed, eyes closed—though he'd been wearing much less clothing.

Alex Russell, the best men's player in the world—or at least he used to be—and the guy she'd been dreaming about, remembering, really, just this morning.

Seven years before, when he was only seventeen, Alex Russell was the first English man to win Wimbledon since 1936 and the youngest man *ever* to do it, breaking a record from 1985. By age twenty he'd added French, US, and Australian Open trophies to his mantel, completing the career Grand Slam. Then, in the handful of years since, his game had gone to hell. Too much partying and not nearly enough training sent his ranking free-falling from number one in the world down into the mid-twenties, and only that high because of his insane natural talent.

He also held the distinction of being the only thing to distract Penny Harrison from tennis and the last person she ever wanted to see again.

Chapter 2

"WHAT THE HELL ARE YOU DOING HERE?" PENNY KICKED AT the sole of Alex's sneaker and his eyes flew open.

He pulled the headphones off, the notes even clearer now as a heavy bass beat echoed against the court.

"Sorry, what was that, love?" he asked with a wink, his eyes lighting up in recognition and then slipping over her form quickly, his tongue darting out against his bottom lip. And shit, she could practically feel his mouth against hers, stealing her breath and her sanity.

The air crackled between them as the low timbre of his voice sent shivers down her spine and her mind reeling back nearly four months, to the Nike event at the Australian Open she hadn't wanted to attend in the first place.

She was midway through the most important tournament of her life and not in the mood for a party, but Jack insisted it was a chance to mingle with her potential sponsors and get her face out there. Plus, it was all for a good cause as proceeds were going to the fight against pediatric cancer. Jack had pulled that last part out of his hat after she flat-out refused to go.

Twenty minutes in she'd been ready to go back to the hotel. She'd lost Jack in the crowd and was steadily making her way to the exit when she ran headlong into a chest and narrowly avoided the drink that sloshed out of its accompanying hand.

Penny blinked herself back to the present and looked at the same chest now as Alex stood, running a hand through his sandy hair, his jawline covered with stubble, just enough to give him an edge. His eyes shined down at her.

"What the hell are you doing here?" she repeated through clenched teeth, crossing her arms. Her throat started to close because she suspected she knew the answer already. He was wearing a white T-shirt streaked with red clay stains, and dark shorts that hugged around his thighs in a way she definitely wasn't thinking about.

"Dom didn't tell you?"

Suspicions confirmed.

He was *technically* an old friend of Dom's. When Alex started on tour, Dom was finishing up his long career. They'd met up on the court more than once, and Dom's final match—in the second round at the US Open—was against the much younger man, who was on his way to his very first championship.

"I'm your new hitting partner or you're *my* new hitting partner, whichever you prefer." An easy smile spread across his face.

Penny's eyes narrowed. That was the same smile he'd bestowed upon her that night in Australia. He'd smiled and asked her to dance.

"You're training again?" she asked, raising an eyebrow. "No, forget it. I don't care. This is not happening."

"And why's that?" His eyes sparkled, actually sparkled, like he was some damned cartoon prince in a Disney movie.

"I don't play against has-beens."

The smile wavered and then disappeared completely. "A has-been?"

"Everyone knows the LTA dropped your sponsorships and your agent left you, but besides that..." She trailed off, her eyes lingering on his knee, an angry-looking scar surrounding the top of the joint. He was recovering from knee surgery and hadn't played in a tournament since Australia, but she couldn't bring herself to use that against him. It was every player's worst fear, an injury that pulled them out of competition, maybe forever. He'd supposedly been lying low in London, rehabbing his knee and what was left of his reputation.

"Besides what?" he asked, forcing the issue. His expression darkened as he stepped closer, his chest nearly brushing against hers.

"Your knee...they said...everyone said that your knee was..."

Completely fucked.

"You should know better than to listen to *everyone*."

Penny swallowed. The implication was obvious. The tour had buzzed incessantly about how they'd left the Nike party together in Australia, but no one knew the truth. The stories ranged from outrageous to obscene, but the reality was even more embarrassing.

He'd asked her to dance, and staring into those eyes and that grin, it had been easy to say yes. They'd danced; their bodies pressed together, the bass of the music pounding through them, his hands trailing paths of fire over her skin, and she knew he was feeling what she was, an intense physical connection, burning hot on the dance floor, that would become an all-encompassing inferno somewhere more private. His mouth had pressed against her ear, pleading with her to leave with him. Taking a risk for the first time in her life off the tennis court, she agreed, and it had been one of the most incredible nights of her life. She snuck out the next morning, half out of embarrassment—she didn't do one-night stands—and half because she had a training session.

The next night on the news came reports of a motorcycle accident. An Australian supermodel with an insanely high blood alcohol level had been treated for minor injuries and the man people once thought could become the greatest tennis player of all time had torn his knee to shreds.

Penny brushed off everyone's questions, even Jack's. Alex had given her a ride back to the hotel, she said, nothing more, and she was pretty sure Jack had believed her, even if no one else did. Rumors and gossip didn't matter. It stung a little that Alex was with someone else the next night, but what really struck her to the core was that it just as easily could have been her in that accident. She could've lost everything, and at the time, the risk hadn't even crossed her mind. That was the thought she'd taken with her onto the court for her quarterfinal match, and that was what distracted her enough to go out in straight sets against a player not fit to carry her racket bag. Then Nike had pulled back their interest, and her reputation on the court—the only reputation that really mattered—took its very first ding.

She'd been working her way back ever since.

"Grab your racket." Alex's voice broke through her thoughts.

"What?" she asked, blinking up at him.

He walked to the bench just off the court and tossed his headphones and phone into the racket bag sitting atop the bench before pulling out a brand-new racket, still covered in the clear protective plastic. The distinctive red *W* was easily visible against the tightly wound white strings. A Wilson racket, what he'd been playing with since he was a junior, not that Penny would ever admit she knew that.

"Grab. Your. Racket," he said again.

"Why?" But she knew why, and the thought of facing off against him was both exhilarating and terrifying.

"I'll show you exactly how much of a has-been I'm not. Let's go. You and me, right now."

"No."

"Scared?"

Penny glared at him. He was pushing her buttons, yet her pride won out over the logical part of her mind that told her this was a bad idea.

"Warm up and you serve first."

The confrontation had her blood pumping. Alex ran in place, swinging his arms around, stretching them over his head and behind his back before going through his serving motion, whipping it through the air. Penny slowly went through her measured stretches starting with her ankles and wrists, then working her way inward. She kept her eyes focused on the clay, allowing each muscle to loosen up before moving on. Finally, she looked up at him. He was waiting at the opposite end of the court, racket in hand, bouncing a ball.

Penny pushed up onto her toes as she waited for what had once been the world's best serve to catapult at her but then fell to her heels as a looping volley traveled over the net.

She straightened and caught the ball on her racket. "Has your game really regressed to this level? If it has, I'm not going to waste my time," she called out, offended he was going easy on her.

"All right, then. Fifteen–love."

Shaking her head that he counted that ridiculous serve as a point, she again bounced on the balls of her feet, preparing to receive a real serve.

He stood up straight and ran a hand over the back of his neck. "You sure about this? I figured we'd save it until you improved defensively, like Dom wants."

Penny's eyes narrowed. "Just hit the damn ball."

"Your funeral," he muttered, but loud enough for her to hear, before his body coiled and exploded through the ball.

She got her racket on it and blocked it back, but the combined speed of the ball and the tight strings of her racket sent it sailing long.

"Thirty–love."

That was the best serve she'd ever seen. She'd played against men who could hit as hard, but this was in another category altogether. A wicked spin combined with the velocity, even with the clay slowing it down a little, made it sheer luck she got her racket on it. Apparently, reports of his knee injury were grossly exaggerated. No one could blast a serve like that on a blown-out knee. Crossing to the other side of her court, she prepared again, taking a step back this time to compensate for the velocity. His face was stone, no emotion—all business.

Alex fired another serve out wide, sending her lunging. This time her return landed in play. Her feet caught up underneath her and she changed direction, knowing he would counter crosscourt.

She hit the ball in stride, launching it back across the court. For a split second, she watched the gorgeous backhand fly to the opposite corner for a winner. Then her momentum sent her sprawling into the clay. She rolled over, tucking her shoulder and landing on her back, knocking the breath from her lungs. Penny lay there a moment, gasping at first and then breathing slowly in through her nose and out through her mouth. Everything felt okay, so she rolled onto her side and stood up, brushing the clay from her hands.

Alex was on her side of the net by the time she regained her footing. “Are you all right?” he asked, one hand cupping the back of her head, the other running down her side to check for injuries.

A tremor slid through her as his calloused fingertips traced her jawline, tilting her chin upward, forcing her to look at him. She shouldn’t be feeling like this. Her body ignored her mental reprimand, and she ever so briefly leaned into the touch. It was just like that night, magnetism unlike anything she’d ever felt before. His eyes left hers and drifted down to her lips. She wet them unconsciously and he sucked in a harsh breath. It was enough to break the spell.

"Don't touch me." She pulled away, her skin immediately mourning the warmth of his hand. "I'm fine."

"Are you sure? Dom will kill me if you're hurt."

"Thirty–fifteen." She ignored the pain in her hip—only a bruise—hoping to both reassure him and reignite the competition. She wanted to play, even more now than before.

Alex studied her and Penny kept all emotion off her face, not giving away even a hint of discomfort. "Thirty–fifteen," he agreed before retreating to his side of the court.

A half hour later, they were thrashing each other, holding their serves, and despite the bruise still blooming on her hipbone, she was pleased with her effort. The respect she saw in his expression after she returned one of his serves for a clean winner wasn't a figment of her imagination. She would never admit it out loud, but playing against him every day *would* help her prep for the French.

She was drenched in sweat, and adrenaline thrummed through her veins, so the sound of the gate opening didn't register. She was too caught up in the thrill of the match, of having a fierce opponent, and she relished every point she won, a small revenge for the little part of her that still resented him for hooking up with someone else the night after Penny was in his bed.

"Got going without me, huh?" Dom's voice rang out, startling Alex as he tossed the ball up. It fell to the ground, bouncing away.

Penny cringed. Dom had instructed her to start on her conditioning, not get roped into a full-on grudge match.

Her coach stood at the edge of the court, the breeze ruffling his dark hair. He looked every inch the elite athlete, still in great shape, even in retirement.

"Couldn't help ourselves," Alex quipped, retrieving the ball, and she contained the urge to glare at him.

"Well, next time, wait for me. I'm your coach. Can't analyze anything if I'm not here to watch," Dom said.

"Right," Alex said, laughing. "Haven't had a real coach in a while. Might take some getting used to."

Shaking his head, Dom turned his attention to her. His eyes caught the red clay stain on her white tennis shorts and blue T-shirt. His thick black eyebrows lifted into his hairline, asking the question without having to voice it. *What the hell happened to you?*

"Can I talk to you for a second?" Penny asked, inhaling deeply through her nose, trying to keep from exploding at her coach. He didn't know about her and Alex. This situation wasn't his fault. It was hers. "Privately."

"Say whatever you like, love. I'm a big boy."

Her back teeth ground together and she turned to her coach. "Roland-Garros is in a few weeks and I don't have time to waste helping him get back into match shape or whatever. I'm not training with him."

"I don't know. It looks like you two got in a pretty good workout. Any other reason?" Dom asked, narrowing his eyes and crossing his arms over his chest. It was his battle stance. She hadn't seen it in a while.

"She thinks I'm a has-been," Alex said as he started kicking around one of the stray tennis balls, picking it up with his foot and bouncing it off his knee then down, catching it with his toe, showing Dom exactly how seriously he took her opinion.

Penny pressed her fingertips against the side of her head, trying her best to ignore him as she led Dom a few feet away, giving her a little more privacy. "I can't train with him, Dom," she said, her voice quieter this time. "He's too…I just… can't."

Words failed her. She couldn't tell her coach she wouldn't train with Alex because he was a smug prick who already managed to seduce her once. That no matter how much playing with him could help her game, he would be nothing but a distraction at a time when she could least afford it.

Dom lowered his head, keeping his voice low. "Listen to me—he's the perfect training partner for you." She tried to interrupt him, but he cut her off. "This is the best thing for you going into Paris: someone who can keep up with you, challenge you on a daily basis. Even not having played in months, he's better than everyone here. And he won't admit it, but you'll be good for his recovery."

"He seems fine," Penny groused, looking up at the sky and sighing in defeat as his words echoed her own thoughts.

"Good, then, so there's no problem?" Dom asked, but it wasn't a question, and he was already walking away from her, gathering up the stray balls from their impromptu match.

"What's the verdict?" Alex asked, suddenly right beside her, and despite everything, as his body hovered mere inches from hers, her skin started to hum at the proximity. She spun on her toe, nearly losing her balance, and Alex's hands came up to steady her, but she slipped away from his grasp.

"I told you not to touch me." She moved back out onto

the court and he matched her stride, their arms brushing as they walked. She pulled away immediately and stepped in front of him. Looking up, she squinted into the sunlight shining behind his head, reflecting off the golden streaks in his hair. "Outside of this court, you stay the hell away from me, understand?" she whispered so Dom wouldn't hear.

Alex grunted, a sound deep from within his chest, a sound she recognized. He'd made it once with his lips buried between her shoulder and her neck, his weight pressing her down into the bed, skin against skin.

"Understood," he said, but Penny knew the real test wasn't if he could stay away from her, but if she could keep herself away from him.

Chapter 3

"SHIT. SHIT. SHIT," INDY CURSED TO HERSELF. SHE PULLED HER long blond hair into a ponytail, not even sparing a glance for her reflection, as she raced past the mirror hanging inside the closet door.

The closet was still empty, its future contents still in the suitcases and boxes lining the floor of her dorm room. The walls were bare, no posters or pictures to brighten up the sterile ecru cinder block. The dorms at the Outer Banks Tennis Club were functional, used as a place to sleep and that was about it.

Decorating was the least of her worries. After arriving the night before and unloading the back of her yellow Jeep Wrangler, Indy had collapsed into bed, feeling like she could sleep for a week. Unfortunately, her travel-slogged mind hadn't remembered to set her alarm, and her body was still operating on California time.

California, where, if she hadn't dropped out of school last week, she'd still be sound asleep with nothing more to wake up for than getting to class in the afternoon.

Now, she was supposed to meet her new coach, Dom Kingston, at eight, which meant she had five minutes. Indy grabbed her tennis bag, shoved her room key into a small pocket, and slammed the door behind her. Then the real panic set in. Looking left and then right, she realized she had no idea how to find Dom's office. Her brain had barely registered her room number the night before when the night security guard showed her the way, let alone memorized the zigzag pathway they took to get here.

A few hours of uneven sleep later, she definitely had no idea where to go. Then, miracle of miracles, the door across the hall cracked open.

"Thank God," she said as a tall guy with a dark tan and even darker hair slipped from the room, pocketing his phone.

He whipped around to face her, his eyes wide in obvious panic. Lifting a finger to his lips, he eased the door closed behind him. A bright pink paper daisy was pasted in the middle of the solid wood with the name Katie written across it in glitter. Indy smirked. Apparently, Katie, whoever she was, had had an overnight guest. The guy standing across from her smirked back, a dimple appearing in his cheek.

"Morning," he said, and then turned, starting down the hallway.

Indy sniffed out a short laugh and then followed. "Wait," she called out, catching up quickly. "I'm late."

"That's nice," he said, but didn't break stride.

She cringed. "I'm late for a meeting with Dom and I have no idea how to get to his office. Please, it's my first day."

That made him stop, the smile creeping back onto his face. He stepped up to her. "A deal, then. I take you to Dom's office so you're not late on your first day, and you never saw me here."

Indy grinned. "Saw who where?"

"Atta girl," he said, his green eyes lit with mischief. He tossed his head in the opposite direction. "This way. It's faster."

He led her out of the dorms and through a maze of practice courts. OBX had courts in all surfaces, though the blue hard court was the most common, and many of them were already in use.

"This is as far as I go," he said, drawing to a halt outside the main building. "Good luck, New Girl."

Then he was gone, jogging to a very shiny black Audi and speeding out of the parking lot before she could even thank him.

Indy glanced up at the main entrance. OBX was written in huge block letters painted navy blue, darkly contrasting the light sand-colored stucco exterior of the building, except for the *O*, in neon green with white stripes, like a tennis ball. Outer Banks Tennis Club, the best training facility in the world.

It looked exactly as it did the last time she'd been there, two years ago with her mom, and starting today, she would be a part of it. It was perfect timing. The spring tennis season was starting to heat up, and if she could make a splash in OBX's invitational in a couple of weeks, she'd be well on her way to the pro career she and her mother had always dreamed of. That is, if she qualified.

It had been a long time since she'd played at an elite level. The last major trophy she'd won was well over two years ago. She was crowned the West Coast Regional 18 & Under Champion a few weeks before her mom got really sick, too sick to even fight her on pulling out of Nationals.

Indy was back now and really, she'd put this off for too long. Watching Penny Harrison kick ass in Madrid was the tipping point. Indy knew her mom wouldn't have wanted her dreams to be put on hold forever. She wouldn't have wanted them to be put on hold at all. And thanks to Dom's actually taking her call after so much time had passed, she had another chance.

Swallowing back the lump in her throat—one that wouldn't go away no matter how much time had passed since her mom died—she reached for the door handle and stepped into her new life.

"Welcome to OBX," an older Black man dressed in a dark suit greeted her as she stepped through the main entrance. He put down his newspaper and stood from behind a reception desk at the center of the large atrium. Shining gray-speckled tile lined the floor and there was a large wall of windows up on the second level. "I'm Roy Whitfield, head of security. You must be Indiana Gaffney. The night security guard told me to expect you this mornin'."

His accent was a little jarring to her ears. Despite the beaches and warm sun, the distinctive twang in his voice was a stark reminder of exactly how far away she was from home.

"Indy," she said, "just Indy."

"Well then, nice to meet you, Indy. Running a little late this morning, darlin'? And was that Teddy Harrison I saw you walking with?"

"I, um, I guess so. I don't know. I was lost," she fumbled.

Was that who he was? Teddy Harrison, twin brother of Penny Harrison, the one the tennis world called "the normal Harrison" because he was only on a full athletic scholarship at Duke and not racing up the rankings of the pro tour?

Roy nodded. "Hmm, all right, then."

"I'm supposed to meet Coach Kingston..." she started to say, but Roy's attention was drawn behind her.

"Ah, speak of the devil."

Indy couldn't help but smile when she turned and saw her new coach striding toward them from the other end of the atrium. Dom Kingston was tall and tan, his dark hair a little too long and graying at the temples. As a player he had won both the US Open and the Australian Open twice, and he was going to help her get there, too.

"Indiana, happy to have you here *finally*," Coach Kingston said, shaking her hand firmly. His dark brown eyes met her blue, letting her know without a doubt that he meant it.

"Thanks."

She was truly grateful that he hadn't given up on her and had enough faith in her abilities to bring her on. She'd basically called him up out of the blue, hoping the old cell phone number she had for him was still good. It was, and it turned out he was thrilled to hear from her, even after so much time had passed.

"Have a little trouble with the clock this morning?" Dom asked, raising his eyebrows.

Indy laughed nervously and shrugged. "Yeah, the Eastern time zone and I aren't friends yet, and then I got lost."

"Teddy Harrison was nice enough to show her the way," Roy cut in, his mouth turning down unhappily. "The second time I saw him leave campus today already, by the way."

Dom pressed his lips into a thin line and hummed. "Indeed." Then he focused back on Indy. "You should start getting used to time changes. Success on tour is half talent, half being able to adjust to new time zones, and here at OBX we have a policy: On time is fifteen minutes early."

"It won't happen again," she promised, a twinge of excitement shooting through her at the thought of being on the pro tour and that Dom saw her living that life one day.

"See that it doesn't. Now, Roy, would you be kind enough to show Indiana to the locker room and then drop her off at the training courts?"

Roy nodded and Indy quashed down the stab of disappointment that Dom wouldn't be taking her around himself. He must have read it on her face.

"I've got a lot of paperwork to catch up on this morning. It all piled up while I was in Spain." He strode to a side staircase near Roy's security desk, then turned back. "Welcome to OBX, Indiana. I'll see you out there. I leave you in Roy's capable hands."

"Now, Indy," Roy said as Coach Kingston climbed the stairs and let himself into his second-floor office, "come on, girl. We'll get you set up with a locker and then off to practice. I've been here since the day OBX opened its doors. You have any questions or need anything at all, you can come to me."

He led her down a hallway off the atrium. OBX had state-of-the-art indoor facilities, both for training and recovery, a full spa, video analysis rooms, and indoor courts. She'd seen it all before, but that didn't make it any less impressive. Then, at the end of the hallway, a large mahogany wall littered with small brass plaques caught her eye. It stretched from the edge of the locker room door all the way to the exit that led to dozens of practice courts.

"The Title Wall," Roy said when he saw the direction of her stare. "Walk past this every day, Indy, and it's easy to stay motivated."

Indy squinted at the plaques, catching names and dates any tennis fan would be familiar with, incredible athletes who came through the doors of this training facility just as she had, with the same dreams and aspirations.

The newest plaque was still shiny and bright, one barely a week old.

PENELOPE HARRISON
MADRID OPEN

"They got that up there fast."

"Dom doesn't waste time," Roy agreed, but it felt like he wasn't just talking about plaques on a wall. Dom wouldn't be wasting his time with *her*.

"I'll be up there soon."

She was already picturing her name on a brass plate with a huge tournament name next to it.

Roy's eyes twinkled at her. "You win a tournament, Indy, and that's where it goes, up on the Title Wall."

She repressed the urge to hug the old man. She barely knew him.

"Come on, now," Roy continued. "Let's get you out to the training courts. Workout's started and Coach D'Amato hates tardiness. Especially on the Classic rankings day."

"Lead the way," she said, giddy at the thought of her standing in the center of OBX's main court holding a trophy aloft as the crowd cheered her victory. Now she just had to go out there and prove she belonged in the Classic.

Indy's breath came heavy and hard. The knot crept back up her throat, choking her as she scrambled to keep up with the dozen or so other athletes racing back and forth, sideline to service line, sideline to alley line, and then finally sideline to sideline. Assistant Coach Giulia D'Amato watched them like a hawk as their sneakers pounded from ad to deuce and back again.

"All the way through." The smooth Italian accent echoed off the hard surface. "Do not stop, run through the line. Andiamo!" The tiny woman barked orders like a drill sergeant.

Their feet skidded to a halt near the fence that surrounded courts eleven through fifteen. According to Roy, these were the training courts for all the female athletes who hadn't yet given up on the idea of playing on the pro circuit, either at the lower Challenger level or, like Penny Harrison had, making the jump straight to the top.

Indy knew it was an honor to train on these courts, but right now they were being used for torture.

"This is ridiculous," she mumbled under her breath. As soon as she arrived, fifteen minutes later than Coach D'Amato had expected her, the entire group was instructed to complete fifteen *Einsteins.*

Nothing had ever winded Indy so fast, not even the drills her former coaches made her do. She thought she'd kept herself in decent shape over the last couple of years, running, lifting weights, swimming, but apparently it wasn't enough.

"Eccellente," D'Amato called. "Take some acqua and then rackets for serving drills."

They jogged to the fence behind the far baseline to grab some water. It seemed no one walked anywhere at OBX. Everything was done at a run. Indy's one consolation was that most of the others looked as out of breath as she felt.

That was her first goal, then: step up her conditioning so she could surpass everyone purely on an endurance level.

They drank greedily from their water bottles and waited in a cluster for Coach D'Amato to call them back to practice.

"Why does she call them Einsteins?" she asked the girl next to her. Shorter than Indy, she had a natural tan, and her long dark hair was pulled back in a sleek ponytail. Strikingly pretty, she was one of the very few athletes *not* panting.

With a roll of her brown eyes, she said, "Einstein's definition of insanity, not that Einstein ever actually said it. Doing the same thing over and over again expecting a different result. She makes us do one for every minute anyone is late."

"Sorry," Indy muttered, and the other girl's cool facade wavered a little.

"It happens. Just don't let it happen again."

"I'm Indiana Gaffney, by the way, but everyone calls me Indy."

"Jasmine Randazzo. Welcome to OBX."

It took Indy a moment to realize why she recognized that name, but then it clicked. Jasmine Randazzo was the daughter of John Randazzo and Lisa Vega, serious tennis royalty and founders of this facility.

Jasmine wasn't quite as tall as she looked on TV and her frame was a lot slighter.

"Oh, you're... That's so cool."

"What?" Jasmine frowned.

"That you're..." Indy began, but then realized her mistake. "I'm sorry. You probably get that all the time, your parents being who they are."

Parents who cared about their daughter's career. Indy had that once, with her mom. Her dad couldn't give less of a shit—he barely remembered she existed most of the time, only ever popping up into her life when it was convenient to have a daughter, usually to make himself seem more human to whoever he was doing business with that week.

Jasmine shrugged. "They're my parents, no big deal."

The group standing near them buzzed. Clearly Indy'd said the wrong thing.

"Right, and you're totally following in their footsteps. You played in Madrid last week."

"The Spanish Federation asked me to play."

"Wow." Indy smiled. "That's such an honor."

"It was nice of them, but the competition wasn't all that great."

"I mean it must have been pretty good, you were out after one..." The words slipped from her tongue before Indy even fully thought them. The others gasped. "Shit, I'm sorry. I didn't mean—"

"Wow, bitch," Jasmine muttered, and stalked away, racket in hand. Silently, the others followed her, like little drones trailing their queen bee, most of them without enough guts to meet Indy's eye—except the last two, a short blond and a tall redhead, who stared at her hard, then turned and pointedly walked away.

Indy pursed her lips. Her mouth always got her in trouble, but it wasn't like she was wrong. Jasmine *had* lost in the first round.

"Allora andiamo!" Coach D'Amato called. "Line up for serves. Indy, you first."

Indy caught the ball the coach threw in her direction.

"Power it up the T," Coach D'Amato said, moving off to the side to observe.

Indy bounced the ball a few times until she felt comfortable, tossed it in the air, and put everything she had into firing the ball up the middle of the court. Her serve wasn't quite at the level it had once been, but it felt really good to let it fly.

Indy stood tall as someone let out a whistle and another added a "whoa." She turned, let her eyes linger on the line of girls behind her, and smirked.

Coach D'Amato cleared her throat, drawing Indy's attention back around. "Again."

She obliged, grunting with the effort of her serve. It had been clocked at speeds averaging around 115 miles per hour, sometimes more. It was the most dominant part of her game and what convinced her mother she could become a professional tennis player. When she started playing big junior tournaments a few years ago, she'd never been broken on serve. It's what caught Dom's eye at a regional championship when she was eighteen and the reason he'd invited her to train at OBX.

Hopefully that would be enough to get her apparently out-of-shape ass into the Classic.

Five more serves and the line behind her buzzed again, the worker bees getting agitated.

"Grazie, Indy. Jasmine, next."

Jasmine sent her a snooty glare. Indy ignored her and moved to the back of the line. She watched as Jasmine hit solid, steady serves. Indy recognized the technique from Jasmine's mom, Lisa Vega, two-time French Open Champion. Her serve was good, really good, and suddenly Indy couldn't wait until she and Jasmine went head-to-head. Tennis royalty or not, to prove to everyone she was the best, Jasmine Randazzo was who she had to beat.

Chapter 4

"EASY, AGEVOLE, EASY," COACH D'AMATO CALLED AS JASMINE jogged around the practice court with the rest of the group, cooling down from their practice session. "Va bene, va bene. That is all, eccellente."

Leading the line, Jasmine slowed to a walk and then went for her racket bag resting against the fence. She'd had a decent practice and her muscles were tingling, a good hurt. It was the perfect way to start off Classic rankings day.

"Good practice," Coach D'Amato said as everyone began to leave the court. "Indiana, uno momento, per favore."

D'Amato pulled the new girl aside and seemed to be explaining something about her footwork, demonstrating a simple crossover step.

Jasmine smirked. Indiana had a massive serve to go along with her ridiculous name, but not much else. Her footwork was a mess. Her forehand was okay, but her backhand was so weak, decent players would attack that instead. And of course she was starting at OBX just before the Classic. She wasn't the first player to try that strategy. They would show up thinking Dom would be so floored by the talent oozing out of their pores he'd hand over the Classic trophy and all prestige that went along with it, though Indiana was the first to actually show up on ranking day. It didn't make her any less delusional, but still, it was a gutsy move.

No, Indiana Gaffney wouldn't be giving her any trouble. Jasmine let her eyes wander over the rest of the training group gathering up their things, almost all of whom looked ready to drop. In truth, none of them would give her a problem. Since Penny started full-time on tour, Jasmine was easily the best player at OBX. Years of hard work had brought her to this point, and now it was her time to shine. Time to live up to her parents' legacy.

"Lookin' good out there, Randazzo." A voice carried from the other side of the fence, breaking into her thoughts. She would know that voice anywhere. Teddy Harrison. Her eyes flew open wide, looking around for an escape route, but the fence surrounding the courts only had one other exit, and it was four courts away. She briefly considered sprinting in that direction, but it was too late.

"What's up?" she asked, forcing a smile onto her face before turning to look at him. He was outside the court, both hands up against the top of the fence rail.

"You ready?"

"For what?" she asked, stalling, looking around for someone, anyone to latch herself on to and give her a plausible excuse to leave, but everyone else was already off the court, headed for the locker rooms. The only one left was Indiana, and hell would freeze over before she asked her for anything.

"It's Monday, Jas," he said. "We have a hitting session."

"Oh, right, I uh, I forgot."

It was only half a lie. She hadn't thought about him at all during practice, but when she woke up this morning, she'd hoped he'd forget about their weekly session. They'd had one stilted and altogether awful conversation after their kiss last week. It was all about how much better they were as friends and how they shouldn't let one silly kiss change all that. Or at least that's what Teddy said, and she'd gone along with it, because the truth was she'd rather have him in her life—even just as a friend—than not at all. She loved him. It wasn't a stupid kiss for her. It was everything she'd wanted for the last four years, even though she knew Teddy didn't do relationships—ever.

But that didn't stop her from feeling what she felt, not even after getting firmly rejected. She still wanted him, especially now that she knew what it was like to kiss him, how good he was at it, even in their drunken stupor. It wasn't hard for her mind to make a leap from that kiss to what else his mouth could do, what the rest of his long, lean body could do.

Except he didn't want her, not that way at least.

"Right. So, are we going to train?" he asked, bouncing on the balls of his feet, expelling some of the excess energy he always carried around. It seemed like he was willing to move on and ignore the tension that still lingered, if he even felt it at all. Jasmine felt like her body was encased in quicksand, being crushed under the pressure of loving someone who wouldn't love her back.

Keeping her expression schooled into indifference, Jasmine nodded and moved off the court.

"Hi, Teddy," Indy said as she followed right behind Jasmine.

"Hey, New Girl," he said, flashing her a brilliant grin, one that made Jasmine's stomach flip, even if it wasn't for her. "How'd you find out my name? You asked around, huh?"

Indy laughed, yanking her long blond hair out of its ponytail and shaking it out. "More like Roy recognized you through the window."

Teddy laughed and winked. "Sure he did."

Jasmine stood, gaping. How the hell did Indy know him? She'd been here for like three seconds.

"You two know each other?"

"Yeah, *someone* was lost and late this morning, so I showed her the way to Dom's office."

"Right, only after I swore—"

"Sorry, Indiana," Jasmine cut in, "Teddy and I have a training session. See you later."

Jasmine pushed past her and started down the path to the practice court she and Teddy always used. She heard him mumble a quick goodbye to Indy and then heard the sound of his footsteps as he jogged to catch up.

"That was rude."

She stopped short and turned to him. He nearly crashed right into her but caught himself in time, taking a quick step back. "Do you always have to do that?"

"Do what?"

"Flirt with every single girl who smiles at you?"

"I was being polite."

"You were flirting."

"Jas," he said, his bright green eyes looking into hers. Jasmine pursed her lips, not impressed that he thought her name and an apologetic expression would be enough.

Running a hand through his short hair and huffing a frustrated breath, he began again. "I'm sorry. I thought we said we were better off as friends."

The panic was laced through his voice, like he was being backed into a corner.

"We did."

She tried to pretend she didn't hear his sigh of relief.

"Then why are you freaking out?"

"I'm not freaking out. I—wait, what were you doing here this morning?"

"I, uh..." His eyes grew wide, and she knew he was fumbling around in his head for an excuse.

"Who?"

"Who what?"

"Who did you screw last night, Ted? Don't play dumb."

"Shit," Teddy muttered, his eyes locking onto something over her shoulder. She could hear the chatter of female voices from the path behind her. "Teddy?"

"Walk with me this way." He grabbed her arm and led her down a smaller path, away from the practice courts, near the edge of the property that ran along the beach.

"Teddy, what the hell? Why can't you answer the question?" Jasmine yanked her arm free and turned in time to see a girl with long blond hair, a lot like Indy's, stride past on the main walkway where they'd been standing. Katie Nelson, probably on her way to the late-morning session with Coach D'Amato, just back from her freshman year at UCLA and hoping to play in a few Challenger tournaments in the summer.

"Sorry, I—"

"Didn't want Katie to see you." She finished his sentence for him.

"Yeah, I didn't want a scene," he said, looking away from her, keeping his eyes trained above her head.

"Why would there be a—oh, it was her?"

He shrugged carelessly. "It didn't mean anything."

"It never does," she muttered.

"What?"

She deflated, the anger seeping away. They were just friends, nothing more. That's what they'd agreed to, and if she kept pushing this, she'd lose him.

"Nothing, let's go hit, okay? I need to get another good workout in before Dom posts the rankings. I know my mom and dad will want to go celebrate afterward, so I probably won't be around for afternoon session." She was at her wit's end, and if she didn't have a tennis ball to hit soon, she was going to use his head for one.

"Jasmine, come on!" Lara Cronin yelled from the locker room door. "Dom's going to post the rankings in five minutes!"

Jasmine gathered her racket bag and met the gaggle of girls waiting for her at the locker room door. They were twittering with anticipation as they all followed her down the hallway, past the Title Wall and out into the main atrium.

"What's all this?" Roy asked from his desk, looking up over the edge of his newspaper. "You ladies all here for me?"

A ripple of laughter echoed up into the atrium's high ceiling.

"We're here for the Classic rankings," one said, and Jasmine rolled her eyes.

"Ah, it all makes sense now. Dom's still up in his office. Should be comin' down the pike any minute, though." Roy chuckled, going back to his paper.

They all looked up and saw Dom through his office windows. He was in the corner of his office, where his printer sat on a table. He reached for a piece of paper and studied it for a moment before nodding and disappearing from view.

He was so melodramatic, printing out an old-school list when he could have just sent it out to everyone.

Even still, it was like all the air was sucked out of the room. Everyone pulled in a breath and held it, waiting for their coach to appear on the stairwell, rankings in hand.

"I think I'm gonna be sick," one girl muttered.

"Gross, then get away from me," another chimed in.

"Are they out yet?" a voice asked. Jasmine turned and saw Indy jogging up to the edge of the crowd, hair still wet from her shower and hanging halfway down her back.

"Not yet—"

Jasmine cleared her throat, a firm *ahem-hum*, cutting off whoever was responding. She squinted in that direction, but it was impossible to pick the voice out of the group.

"Oh God, I can't handle this," Lara said, gripping Jasmine's wrist. Dom descended the last few steps and surveyed them silently before turning to the wall beside the stairwell.

Jasmine pulled away and moved forward, feeling everyone hesitate and then crowd in behind her.

Dom pinned the single sheet of white printer paper to the corkboard and then faced them. "Ladies, behind me is a draw ranking for the OBX Classic. Remember, not everyone will make the tournament. Some of the best up-and-coming players in the world will be attending as well. If you have any questions, I expect you to come see me in person. I will not be taking any calls from agents on this one. Is that understood?"

They all nodded.

"Good. Now, one more thing. Some of you might've heard that Penny's back on campus and that Alex Russell is here as well, getting himself back into match shape. He and Penny will be training together leading up to the French Open."

Jasmine's focus shifted from the white sheet of paper behind her coach's head to Dom's face as a few gasps and nervous giggles came out of the crowd around her. People were used to Penny being around, although some of them liked to suck up to her, like her talent might rub off on them if they got close enough. But Alex Russell? That was insane. Her own parents were a big deal, but more for their relationship off the court than anything else. Alex was only twenty-four and already had the same number of Grand Slams as her parents did combined.

"I expect you all to behave professionally. No hovering

around their practice court and making nuisances of yourselves. Do I make myself clear?"

Everyone nodded again.

Dom eyed the crowd like he didn't quite believe them, but he continued anyway. "Excellent. I'll see you all tomorrow."

He turned around, escaping up to his office, and the crowd pressed forward immediately.

For a moment, Jasmine's vision blurred as she took in the names. She took a deep breath, blinked, then looked again.

OBX CLASSIC RANKINGS

1. Jasmine Randazzo (USA/OBX)
2. Cara Pagnini (ITA)
3. Tatiana Belova (RUS)
4. Indiana Gaffney (USA/OBX)
5. Stella Almanzar (ESP)
6. Jessica McCormack (NZL)
7. Aliya Polina (RUS)
8. Ellie Forester (AUS)
9. Jelena Petrović (SRB)
10. Yulia Markelova (RUS)
11. Laura Wiltvank (NED)
12. Cassie Raker (USA/OBX)
13. Lara Cronin (USA/OBX)
14. Katarina Odette (GRB)
15. Daciana Raducan (ROU)
16. Katie Nelson (USA/OBX)

Behind her Lara squeaked in delight at making the cut, and Addison Quinn, who hadn't, started sobbing, but none of it really registered for Jasmine. Her eyes were glued to the top of the list.

How was it possible that after one day of training Indiana Gaffney was fourth? Dom even put her above Stella Almanzar, who'd already won a couple of Challenger tournaments and was a player Jasmine had lost to on more than one occasion.

She pushed through the crowd and saw Indy hovering at the edges, her weight shifting back and forth, eyes focused on the board but not moving any closer to it. It almost seemed like she was scared to look. Their eyes met, but Jasmine strode past her, across the atrium and straight for the door. As she was about to open it, someone pulled it from the outside.

A slim woman dressed in a flowing white dress down to her ankles, secured at the waist by a large brown leather belt, and a tall man in jeans and a collared shirt stood just outside the door.

"Mom, Dad, what are you guys doing here? I thought we were going to meet up later," she whispered, glancing back over her shoulder to see if anyone else had noticed the appearance of the famous couple.

"We came for you." Her mom, Lisa, practically skipped the last few steps between them, bracelets jangling at her wrists, before pulling her into a hug. "Number one ranked in the tournament. Mija, I am so proud of you."

Jasmine lifted her head from her mom's shoulder and saw her dad, John, standing behind them. Her parents were her biggest fans. Tennis was never something she was expected to do. They never even brought up the subject of her playing until she begged for lessons when she was seven. Yet, despite all the success they enjoyed in their own careers, the smallest things, like a number one ranking in an invitational, had them beaming like she'd won a Grand Slam. The problem was, it was still a number one ranking in an invitational and *not* a Grand Slam victory. But she was going to eventually get one—that was the plan—and the OBX Classic was a necessary stop on the path she'd wanted to travel since she was old enough to understand exactly who her parents were.

A lock of salt-and-pepper hair fell onto her father's forehead. "Dom called me when he put the rankings together. I wanted to be here when you found out."

"Oh my God," a breathy voice said from behind her. "They're here."

The crowd behind Jasmine converged around them. Though her parents had founded OBX, they pretty much gave Dom free rein to run the facility as he saw fit and stayed out of his way. Whenever they showed up on the grounds, it was a pretty big deal and incredibly annoying that no one could ever have an ounce of chill about it.

"Can I have a picture?" Lara asked, holding her phone out and sidling right up to Jasmine's dad, snapping a picture before he could answer one way or the other.

"I watch the video of your French Open win all the time," Katie said to her mom, leaning around Jasmine's shoulder. Jasmine fought down the urge to snap her elbow into Katie's stomach.

"Wait, will you sign my racket bag?" Cassie asked, digging through the bag for a pen.

Lisa shot Jasmine an apologetic grin but then turned to her admirers and patiently responded to them one by one.

A small shriek from over by the rankings list echoed over the din of autograph and picture requests, and Jasmine's eyes flew to where Indiana Gaffney stood, hand over her mouth, staring at the board. The blond girl turned around, her hand falling away, a huge smile on her face. Apparently she'd worked up the courage to look at the list. Jasmine averted her eyes. She was ready to live up to her parents' legacy, and if she beat Indiana Gaffney along the way, so much the better.

Chapter 5

FOURTH.

Dom ranked her fourth in the Classic.

Sure, after coming to OBX, Indy had every intention of taking everyone by surprise in the tournament, battling her way into the final and winning the whole damn thing. She hadn't expected Dom to rate her so highly. He hadn't even watched her train before he put the rankings out—and thank God for that, because he probably would've changed his mind. It was all she could think about during lunch, right through the afternoon workout in the gym, and during dinner, just before he posted the list—that and the word Coach D'Amato had used during morning practice. *Inaccettabile.* That's what the tiny Italian coach called her footwork, and now, the day was almost over, but the word was still ringing in Indy's head. She was ranked fourth, even with her inaccettabile footwork.

Indy didn't speak Italian, but that was easy enough to translate: unacceptable, not good enough, weak. That meant more practice. So, after dinner she headed straight out to the practice courts to start addressing that weakness.

Tossing her bag against the fence, she leaned down and grabbed the small orange cones sitting on the ground. She'd start out simply. Moving to the middle of the court, she placed them about ten feet apart and stood in the center. One crossover step to the right and then back to the middle, another crossover to the left and retreat again. Over and over, keeping her feet moving and then faster and faster, like she'd seen Jasmine Randazzo do this morning at practice, like Penny Harrison did against Zina Lutrova. Time flew, the spring sun beginning to set, and as the scuffing of her sneakers against the hard court sped up, so did her breathing, coming in short puffs. Her legs were tired after a long day of training, but that was all the more reason to push through. She couldn't just take a little break during a match if her legs got tired. Finally, she had to stop to catch her breath, hands on her knees, sucking in as much air as she could.

There were eyes on her. Indy could feel the stares burning into her skin like white-hot laser beams, making the hair at the back of her neck, now sticky with sweat, stand up on end. She turned and saw Addison Quinn and Lara Cronin, who'd giggled when Jasmine snubbed her that morning. Lara was her first-round opponent in the Classic and Addison was the one who'd collapsed into sobs when she hadn't made the cut at all. Indy bit back a sharp comment and ignored them, hoping they'd go away. She started up her drill again, focusing more closely on keeping her footwork crisp and her strides long.

They were still there. She could feel them, and anytime her drills took her close to the fence, their hushed, biting whispers, unintelligible but clearly about her, would stop.

"Look," Indy said, finally unable to ignore them any longer. She slid to a halt and whipped around. They stood at the baseline of the court, a few feet behind her, hands on their hips, looking ready for a fight. "I don't have time for this crap. If you want to train, you're free to join me. Otherwise leave me the hell alone."

Addison huffed and Lara's eyes narrowed, but a stony silence was their only reply.

"That's what I thought," Indy said, turning back to her cones.

"It's not like you have any chance, anyway. I'm going to destroy you in the first round, bitch," Lara muttered.

"Is there a problem here, ladies?" a voice called beyond the gate, getting closer with every word.

Indy whirled around again and stared at the guy the voice belonged to as he made his way onto the court. She hadn't even seen him approach—he was easily the best-looking man she'd ever set eyes upon. Tall, dark, and handsome didn't even begin to cover it, but it was a good start. He was built, not super skinny like some really tall guys tended to be, dressed in jeans and a crimson T-shirt with HARVARD TENNIS emblazoned across his chest—his very broad, very firm-looking chest, from what she could tell.

"Yeah, there's a problem," Lara spit out, flinging a hand out toward Indy. "She's using our practice court, Jack."

His name was Jack, but... Jack what? He looked sort of familiar, and as Indy tried to place his face, he said, "Last time I checked there were over forty courts around here. Why don't you go claim another one as your own before I bring Dom down here and tell him about this misunderstanding."

Lara's jaw dropped and it looked like she was about to say something else, but Jack crossed his arms over his chest, stretching his T-shirt over the muscle there and making Indy swallow hard. He was too fucking hot for words.

OBX's self-appointed court police let out twin, long-suffering sighs, and when Jack raised his eyebrow, probably daring them to protest, they marched away from the courts entirely, clearly having no intention of training anyway.

"Thanks," Indy said, pulling her gaze away from his body and into his eyes, hopefully before he noticed her staring. It wasn't a sacrifice. His eyes were bright green, an interesting shade considering his dark, thick curls and tanned skin.

"No problem," he said, closing the gap between them with confident strides. "If there's one thing I can't stand, it's bullies."

Indy laughed. "I wouldn't exactly call them bullies. More like annoying little gnats."

He chuckled softly. "Glad to hear they didn't do any lasting damage."

"Nope, still in one piece," she said, smiling back at him.

"I don't think we've met before. I'm Jack Harrison." He held out his hand and she took it immediately, hoping hers wasn't too sweaty. His fingers wrapped completely around hers. It was like holding on to a mug of hot chocolate after coming in from the cold. Jack Harrison. Penny Harrison's older brother and agent. She remembered seeing shots of him in the stands during the Madrid tournament, but her phone screen did not do him justice.

"I'm..." She paused, her voice catching in her throat. "I'm Indiana Gaffney. Indy."

His smile widened. "Indiana. I like that."

Anyone else in the world and she would have corrected him. No one called her Indiana except her dad, and it grated on her nerves whenever he did, but the way Jack said it, his voice soft and deep, she wanted to hear him say her name all day long. His hand released hers after a gentle squeeze.

"So, how have I not seen you around here before, Indiana?" He didn't step away, invading her space in the best way possible.

"Today's my first day."

"I didn't think I could miss someone like you." She blushed, but he nodded in the direction in which the terrible twosome had marched off. "And you've already made enemies. Impressive."

She shrugged, unable to help the grin spreading across her face. "They're pissed because Dom ranked me ahead of them for the Classic. I mean, I was hoping Dom would think I was good enough, but I was shocked when he ranked me fourth. I've only been here a day. It probably wasn't the best way to make friends, but that's not really the point of training here, right—"

Then a voice cut her off, thank God, or she would have rambled forever.

"Jack! There you are!" Teddy Harrison strode toward them, hopping the low fence by the gate with such ease Indy supposed he did it all the time. The resemblance between the brothers was astounding, though Jack was far more muscular.

"I've been waiting forever. You said you just had to..." He trailed off as his eyes flashed to Indy. "But now it all makes sense. Hi again, New Girl."

"Teddy," she said.

"You two know each other?" Jack asked, looking between them.

"Indy was lost this morning and I was gentleman enough to show her the way."

"Yeah, after he snuck out of some poor girl's dorm room."

He went silent, and she wondered if she'd said something wrong *again*, but Teddy laughed at her calling him out. "So, what were you working on out here by yourself?" Teddy stepped into the space Jack had just vacated beside her, but his closeness didn't quite have the same effect.

Indy grimaced in frustration. "My footwork," she said, nodding at the cones. "I was trying to—"

Teddy *tsked* at her. "You aren't going to get anywhere with two cones and no one to watch you, right, Jack?"

"What?" Jack asked, and Indy's eyes shot to the older brother, catching his gaze briefly before he looked away. Had he been looking at her? He'd definitely been looking at her.

"Focus, bro," Teddy scolded, but his smile was back in full force. "Don't you know some epic footwork drill we can show Indy?"

Jack's mouth opened and then closed again, his shoulders stiffening, like he was preparing for battle. "I'm not sure if..."

Teddy shook his head as he picked up the cones she'd set out and tossed them to the side. "Yeah you do. The batshit one that Penny loves, what is it called?"

Indy felt her calf muscles spasm at the thought of another running drill. "Not Einsteins?"

An unexpected guffaw slipped out of Jack's throat.

"Do you want to show her or should I? I know you're retired now, old man. You might pop a hammy or something," Teddy teased from the center of the court, a clear gauntlet laid down for his brother, who couldn't possibly be more than a few years older than they were.

Jack lifted an eyebrow and then did not disappoint.

"I got this," he said, his eyes not leaving hers as he swapped places with Teddy. Jack moved to the center of the court, balanced on the balls of his feet for one moment, and then he was off, a few crossover steps to his left and back, then to his right and back. Indy felt a small grin of satisfaction inch over her lips. She'd been on the right track with her own drills. Then her face fell as Jack's legs started covering more ground, pivoting at the corners of the service lines, sprinting to the net in diagonals and then back again.

"See, tough, right?" Teddy said from beside her as Jack literally ran circles around them, those strong thighs flexing with every shuffle of his feet, the twist of his T-shirt against his abs showing off tiny slivers of tan skin—and for the briefest moment, a line of cut muscle at his hip disappearing into his shorts. He moved with all the fluidity and grace of an elite athlete, retired or not.

He drew to a halt back where he started. "Got it?"

Indy bit her bottom lip to hold back what she really wanted to say before she nodded and rasped, "I think so."

"Let's see it, then," he said, moving out of the way for her.

She set herself, but as she started her crossover step, Jack's voice rang out. "No, no, stop."

"What?" she asked, spinning around to face him, hands landing on her hips.

"You're totally off-balance. Come back here," he said, moving in closer. She complied while every inch of her skin tingled pleasantly at his sudden proximity. "Okay, now stand with your feet a little more than shoulder width apart—I said a *little* more, Indiana, not like the earth is tearing apart beneath you." He tapped gently at the outside of her leg, his hand warm and large, and she jumped, or at least her heart did. She managed to keep her feet on the ground while trying not to wonder exactly how his fingers would look wrapped around her thighs, as she slid them a little closer to each other. His hand moved away and she mourned the loss of contact immediately. Maybe she should screw up the next drill and he'd touch her again?

"Good. Now keep your weight on the balls of your feet, not your toes. It's all about balance and staying in an athletic position, knees bent slightly, perfect, shoulders over your toes. That's it," he said as she followed his instructions, and something about that, the soft but commanding timbre of his voice and the approval when she did something right, was almost as heady as his touch. "And now the pièce de résistance, relax your joints. You're stiff as a board." His hands landed on her shoulders and the muscles there tightened reflexively. "Relax." With a deep inhale and slow exhale, she tried to do just that, but it was nearly impossible with him standing so close. He must have sensed it because he stepped back with a knowing glint in his eyes, or maybe that was just the setting sun, and said it again. "Relax, stay loose."

"Okay," she said, allowing her shoulders to drop ever so slightly.

"Good. Now try it." Then he was gone, the warmth hovering behind her giving way to chilly solitude. She began, her feet speeding through the exercise he'd demonstrated. Her stride was smoother, the flow of her feet easier.

"You feel that?" Jack called out as she pivoted at the edge of the court and raced for the net.

"Yeah," she shouted back, and finished the drill. It was like an Einstein on steroids, but this little drill was exactly what she needed as she prepped for the Classic.

"Aw, Pen, you didn't have to wait for us," Teddy said from the sideline, and Indy whirled around, slamming back into the real world as Penny Harrison stepped through the gate, not over it as her twin had, and onto the court. She was showered and dressed in a mint-green sundress dotted with wildflowers. Indy had never really pictured Penny as a sundress kind of person. Then again, she probably didn't wander around in tennis clothes all day.

"I wasn't waiting," Penny said. "You have my car keys and Jack has his, so cough 'em up, Ted." Teddy reached into his pocket and tossed her a set of keys. Then she turned the green eyes that matched her brothers' to Indy. "Hey, I'm Penny."

Indy's mouth went dry at finally being noticed. Penny

Harrison had said hello to her. Praying she wouldn't mess up like she had in the morning with Jasmine, she said, "I'm Indy."

"Nice to meet you," Penny said before looking over her shoulder at Jack, who stood off to the side, still as a mountain and silent.

"Indy's training for the Classic," Teddy said. "It's her first day today and Dom seeded her fourth."

One perfectly shaped eyebrow lifted and Penny pursed her lips. "So, you're the one they're all bitching about in the locker room?"

Her eyes narrowed and Indy felt like an insect under the microscope of some scientist who was about to dissect it. The silence dragged on and Indy could practically feel something ridiculous building on the tip of her tongue when Penny grinned and said, "Good luck at the Classic."

A flush spread across her face. Penny Harrison wished her luck. So fucking awesome. "Thanks."

With a nod, the other girl spun on her toe and strode off the court, totally ignoring her brothers as she left.

"I better go, too," Indy said.

"We were just going to get dinner," Teddy said, smiling at her winningly, dimples flashing. He rocked toward her with his hands in his pockets. "Why don't you join us?"

"Ted, she said she had to go," Jack cut in, looking at his brother meaningfully. The implication was clear: He didn't want her to go. Indy felt like someone had slapped her. Where was the guy who'd cheerfully rescued her a few minutes ago from OBX's queen bitches?

"He's right. I do and plus I already ate." She tried to ignore the clear relief that spread across Jack's face at her words. "Thanks so much for your help. I'll see you guys around."

Indy left the court, trying to focus on the good. She had a great ranking for the Classic. That's what she'd come to OBX for, to win the Classic, but despite that, her thoughts kept drifting back to Jack Harrison and the way his voice sounded when he said her name...and the way her body reacted to it.

Chapter 6

THE NEXT MORNING PINK SLIVERS OF LIGHT CREPT ABOVE THE waterline far in the distance, giving the beach an unearthly glow. Indy stretched her arms over her head, muscles suddenly so much heavier than they'd been the day before, as she clomped down the wooden stairway leading from the practice facilities down to the sand. Each step made every fiber of muscle in her legs throb. After only one day, her body was in shock. She'd forced herself out of bed that morning knowing the sooner she moved, the less it would hurt—eventually.

Gingerly she reached the bottom of the stairs and landed in the sand, and suddenly, even standing still was painful as she tried to keep her balance on the soft surface.

"This wasn't a great idea," she muttered to herself. She wanted to turn around and crawl back into bed. She could run tomorrow, when her body was more accustomed to OBX's training regimen.

She grasped the handrail of the stairs to pull herself back up them, but as she looked up, she saw Penny Harrison, long dark hair piled at the top of her head and headphones plugged into her ears, jogging down the stairs.

Indy froze. It was one thing to be introduced to one of your idols, especially with two other people around as a nice buffer, but what the hell was she supposed to say now? Should she wait until Penny said something, or say hello to her like it was no big deal? She probably had people acting like crazed fans around her all the time and Dom had said not to bother her while she was training, but they knew each other now, so…

"Hey," Penny said, cutting into Indy's mental ramble as she jumped down the last couple of steps into the sand.

"Hi," Indy finally managed, and her resolve to limp back to bed crumbled. She'd come here to train at the place that made Penny Harrison one of the best tennis players in the world. If that meant pushing through the soreness, then that's what she would do.

Penny raised her eyebrows and nodded down the beach. It was probably the closest thing to an invitation Indy was going to get, so she nodded back, and they set off, their pace even and measured.

The smell of the ocean air wafted up from the shore, filling Indy's senses, forcing the last traces of sleepiness from her. She quickened her pace slightly as her muscles loosened and energy began to flow through her limbs.

"Easy does it," Penny cautioned from a step behind her. "You want to warm up, not tire yourself out for training later."

The sun finally burst out from the horizon, the ocean a sea of orange, purple, and pink as the light reflected off the water. They ran for about ten minutes, turned at the edge of the OBX property, and followed their footsteps back toward the practice courts.

"Shit," Penny muttered as soon as they turned and saw a figure jogging in their direction.

"What?" Indy asked, squinting into the distance. The little part of her that would always be a tennis fan first recognized the silhouette. Alex Russell was headed straight for them. Indy had no idea how that could be a bad thing, but she kept her mouth shut.

"Nope," Penny said simply, and turned, sprinting in the opposite direction, and Indy followed suit, her legs burning as she tried to keep up. She thought back to last night, watching Jack demonstrate the footwork drill and the way his shirt had stretched against his broad shoulders and the power in his thighs. Athleticism obviously ran in their family.

Finally, Penny led her through a small alleyway off the beach, and somehow they were back on OBX property. She pulled to a stop on a deserted walkway between two of the outer practice courts.

"Are you okay?" Indy asked, wheezing, not really sure what else to say. A wave of guilt slid through her for letting her mind wander to Jack, when his sister was clearly upset. Especially since he'd gone completely cold at the end there for reasons beyond her understanding.

Shit. She'd done it again. She forced herself to refocus on Penny.

"I'm fine," Penny snapped, and then cringed. "Sorry."

"It's okay," Indy said.

"No, it's not, but thanks."

"You're welcome?"

"You're not going to ask why I ran away from him?"

"It's none of my business."

Penny studied her carefully and Indy figured she was trying to see if there was some ulterior motive, the new girl trying to get close to the star. And yeah, maybe a part of her was freaking out that she was standing there with *the* Penny Harrison, but mostly she was just glad to have maybe found another girl who didn't hate her on sight.

Finally, Penny nodded. "C'mon, let's grab breakfast."

Indy followed her, thankful to have passed whatever test she unknowingly took and grateful her muscles weren't quite as sore anymore, thanks to their mad dash across the property. They walked in silence through the maze of practice courts, past the back doors to the atrium, and they both turned left at the edge of the main building toward the entrance of Deuce.

Open twenty-four hours a day, Deuce served as a dining hall for the live-in athletes, staff, and any tennis vacation guests, plus it was open to the public for lunch and dinner. With vaulted wooden, whitewashed ceilings and contrasting dark-stained floors and tables, plus an outdoor eating area that overlooked the beach, it was the place people gathered before and after training, and that morning it was bustling.

"Why's it so crowded?" Indy asked, looking into a sea of faces she'd never seen before. It hadn't been nearly as packed during lunch and dinner yesterday.

"Some of the international Classic players started showing

up last night and this morning. Athletes, coaches, families—it adds up to a lot of people here for a couple of weeks," Penny said, leading the way to the breakfast buffet at the far end of the room.

Indy recognized the two people in line ahead of them, Lara and Addison, and as they made their way through the buffet, she heard her name muttered more than once as the pair kept glancing back and then whispering again.

She tried to focus on the food instead as they each grabbed some scrambled eggs, turkey bacon, fruit, and toast, and after they paid, she saw Jack and Teddy already sitting at a table, waving Penny over. Indy hovered uncertainly for a moment at the empty chair between the Harrison twins, her eyes lingering on Jack, confirming that he was actually as hot as she remembered from the night before. He, however, was looking anywhere except in her direction.

Then Penny looked up at her, eyebrows drawn together. "Are you going to sit?"

"Right," Indy said, putting her plate down and sliding into the chair beside Teddy. He immediately smiled, gently nudged her with his elbow, and stole a strip of turkey bacon.

"Teddy," Jack warned from across the table, sending his brother a withering glare, but still seeming to make the deliberate choice *not* to look at her.

"What? She doesn't mind, do you?" he asked.

Indy shook her head. "Not as long as I can steal some of your potatoes. They were out when I went up."

Teddy immediately pushed his plate toward her and she grinned, popping one into her mouth. "Thanks."

Her joy was short-lived.

Across the room, Lara and Addison were holding court at another table filled with most of the top young players at OBX, including Jasmine Randazzo.

If looks could kill, Indy would've expired as soon as Jasmine's eyes locked onto her. Indy couldn't help herself. She tilted her head, half question, half challenge, until Jasmine broke eye contact and her table dissolved into fierce conversation.

Her ears burned, imagining the shit they were talking, sinking any chance at all of her recovering from the disaster that was her first encounter with Jasmine. Apparently simply making a new friend was another unforgivable crime when that friend was Penny Harrison.

All three Harrisons seemed oblivious to the attention, so Indy decided to ignore it. Having them with her was like having a solid wall that could keep out any crap anyone wanted to throw at her, but it was a temporary fix at best. She couldn't use them as human shields once she headed to training.

"Got confirmation last night that Harold Hodges'll be here covering the Classic, Pen. He wants to do a feature with you and Alex if that's okay?" Jack asked, dumping an unhinged amount of sugar into his coffee.

Penny's mouth twisted into a pout, but she nodded.

Teddy laughed and then, using his fork for a microphone, said, "You're like so famous, Pen. What's it like to be so awesome?" He nudged his sister with his elbow, making her drop the knife she was using to butter her toast, but Penny laughed with him.

It was weird. Indy hadn't really expected them to be so... normal.

"Indy!" Roy called out from the edge of the dining hall, approaching the table quickly. The entire place, buzzing with activity seconds before, fell into total silence. "Coach wants to see you. Come on with me back to his office."

"Oooh," Teddy said, chuckling, as panic hit her hard.

"Shut up, Ted," Jack said, glaring at his younger brother.

"What crawled up your ass today?" Teddy muttered, but Indy couldn't worry about whatever was going on with either Harrison brother right now.

Why the hell did Dom want to see her? It felt like being called to the principal's office, only a million times worse. Had she done anything wrong? He hadn't even coached one of her training sessions yet. Did he think she'd run into Penny this morning accidently-on-purpose after he'd warned them to stay away? How would he have even known about it?

She nodded to Penny, who smiled encouragingly, and left with Roy. Her joints were stiff, her feet dragging like lead and her throat tightening against the panic that tore through her.

When they reached the atrium, Roy nodded at the staircase leading up to Dom's office and she scaled the steps slowly, only to find the office empty. Indy took a seat in front of his desk and waited. Eyes on the clock, she watched the seconds tick by slowly. If he didn't show up soon, she might throw up. Her stomach grumbled, protesting that last thought. There was barely anything to throw up. She wished she'd grabbed a slice of her toast before leaving Deuce with Roy. At least then she wouldn't be starving.

Then two sets of footsteps echoed on the stairs. Indy

stood, wiping her sweaty palms against her shorts, then smoothed back her hair.

Dom stepped into the room, followed closely by a tall blond woman in her mid-thirties.

"Indiana, good, you're here." Dom quickly strode away from the woman, frowning over his shoulder at her. His eyes darted around the room and he wiped his hand over his entire face. Indy's stomach sank. That couldn't be a good sign. "I'd like to introduce you to Ms. Morneau."

The blond smiled, showing off two rows of perfect white teeth. She wore a white pencil skirt and a blush-colored silk sleeveless blouse, cut high at the neck. "Caroline, please." She said her name in a soft French accent, like "Cah-row-lean." Approaching Indy, she ignored her extended hand and pressed a faux kiss lightly on each cheek.

Indy pulled away sharply and looked back and forth between Dom and this odd woman who thought it was okay to kiss her.

"I take it your father didn't call you," Dom said, reading the confusion on her face.

Indy shook her head. "Dad doesn't have the time to call me. He's far too busy with work. Hedge funds don't manage themselves."

Dom cleared his throat. "Well, Caroline will explain, then. I'll just go."

Before Indy could ask him what the hell was going on, he was already out the door and down the stairs, leaving her alone with Caroline.

"Why don't we sit down?" Caroline motioned to the chairs in front of Dom's desk.

"I'm sorry," Indy said, ignoring the suggestion. "I don't mean to be rude, but who are you exactly?"

"Caroline Morneau. Your father has hired me as representation."

"Representation for what?"

"For you."

"I don't think I understand."

"I'm your agent, Indiana."

For the next twenty minutes, Caroline rattled on, but Indy barely heard a word. Only a few things stood out. Caroline worked for a company called Trinity Agency that specialized in representing athletes. They were a subsidiary of the law firm that her father had on retainer, and as soon as the news of her ranking had dropped, her father had put Caroline on a plane to North Carolina.

It was typical. Her dad was always doing things like this, barely speaking a word to her for months and then having a car delivered to her driveway for Christmas. Her mom used to say it was his way of showing affection. To Indy it screamed of a guilty conscience. She wanted to go pro and sign with an agent, but hell would freeze over before she let her dad have anything to do with it.

"Indiana, are you listening to me?" Caroline finally asked, pulling her from her thoughts.

"No, I'm sorry."

"That's all right, I can start again."

"No, that's not what I mean. I'm sorry you wasted your time coming all this way. I haven't even gone pro yet, not officially, and anyway, when it's time, I'll pick my own agent."

Caroline smiled, a small rise of the corners of her mouth that made Indy feel like she was five years old. "Perhaps you should call your father."

"Perhaps," Indy agreed. But if he wanted to talk about this, he could pick up the phone. She had zero intention of telling her dad anything. "If you'll excuse me, I'm late for a training session."

"Of course," Caroline said. "Take this with you. It is your contract. There is no need to decide today, but your father wishes to protect your interests."

"Sure." She took the papers and sped out of the office, down the stairs, and back into the atrium.

"Everything okay, Indy?" Roy asked, laying aside his newspaper as she nearly flew past his desk.

She stopped dead and turned to him with a smile. If he knew her better, he probably would've been able to tell the smile was fake. "Do you have a recycle bin behind your desk?"

"Sure do."

"Could you throw this out for me?" she asked, holding out the contract.

"No problem," Roy said, taking it and glancing down at the cover page. "You sure you don't need this?"

"Positive."

Chapter 7

PENNY LEANED OVER, HANDS ON HER KNEES, GASPING FOR breath, and glanced over at the sideline of the court where Dom was observing. She was dying and she and Alex had only been training a little over an hour. They were playing a mock match and were supposed to be working on each other's weaknesses. Alex's was his tendency to go for a winner too early in a point, and hers was reverting to a defensive game while dealing with the clay surface instead of staying aggressive. Instead, all they'd managed to do was exhaust each other.

Playing tennis against Alex Russell was almost exactly like having sex with him. No awkward fumbling of a first time or a short, unsatisfactory encounter, but the mind-blowing kind of sex most people dreamed of and very few actually had. It was intense and a constant struggle, a push and pull, every point a battle of wills, taking all of her physical and emotional strength and leaving her body suspended in a constant state of pleasure bordering the edge of pain—a really good pain.

Alex wasn't faring much better than she was. On the other side of the court, he was hunched over, each breath coming heavy and hard as he stared at her. His gaze was beyond unnerving. Not creepy, but not totally pleasant either. It was like he was looking deep inside of her into places she'd never let anyone see—not Jack, not Dom, or even Teddy. Penny kept her eyes locked on his. Then he sent her a cheeky wink and quickly pursed his lips in a phantom kiss before looking away.

"What the fuck is going on with you two?" Dom marched onto the court from the sideline, confident that they'd sucked in enough oxygen to catch their breath and were ready to take a total tongue-lashing.

His face was shifting from lightly tanned to bright red, and the vein in his forehead was beginning to protrude. "P, why the hell are you letting him dictate the pace? Stop hesitating and hit the fucking ball."

She tried to respond, but Dom was on a roll.

"And Alex, what is wrong with you? The way she's playing, you should be thrashing her. What happened to the Alex Russell who would step on the neck of a player he had down? Just finish the point when she leaves you an opening! If either of you thinks this shit is going to fly in France, you've got another thing coming. We're going to have media crawling all over this place in the next few days for the Classic. You don't think they're going to sneak a look at your training sessions while they're here? Take a tour, clear your heads, and come back ready to play."

Penny's legs were already carrying her to the gate, an instinctive response to orders issued by the man who'd had total authority over her training regimen for years.

A tour, as Dom put it, was a run around the entire campus through the maze of courts and then around the perimeter. She rolled her neck and broke into a jog, getting halfway down the pathway lining the practice courts before she heard Alex's long strides in a flat-out sprint as he tried to catch up with her. For half a second, she considered picking up her own pace and trying to lose him, but Dom would probably be pissed at her and make her do another tour.

Their strides matched, the rubber soles of their sneakers pounding the concrete in unison. She was perfectly happy to lead him around the complex in silence, and for a little while, it seemed he was, too, but as they rounded the corner at the outer edge of the practice courts, he broke it: "How much farther?"

"Winded already?" she said, keeping her eyes trained ahead.

"Hardly, just making conversation."

"Well don't. I have nothing to say to you."

Alex chuckled, his stride breaking a bit. "I don't know, I think we have a lot to say to each other. Last time we were really alone together we didn't exactly exchange a lot of words, though if I recall, my name was a favorite of yours."

Her nostrils flared as she tried to tamp down her reaction. They'd been operating under an unspoken agreement for the last two days not to talk about that night. Why the hell was he bringing it up now? "Just shut up and run."

"Hit a nerve, did I?"

She didn't answer but instead glanced up and sideways, taking in his profile, the strong jawline, a glittering blue eye, a nose slightly crooked, probably broken in a bar fight or something equally reckless.

"I wonder what Dom would think."

That stopped her, both her mind and her feet. It was a few seconds before he stopped as well and jogged back to her. She wanted to scream, to blast him and let him know that that night was the biggest mistake she'd ever made. But as he towered over her, his eyes softer than before, she couldn't.

"Please don't say anything," she said, avoiding his gaze.

He lifted a hand and ran it through his hair. "He doesn't know?"

"No, I told him nothing happened."

Alex pursed his lips and a muscle in his jaw clenched. "And of course he believed you. No wonder he offered me a spot here. If he knew I'd fucked his star player—"

"Nice," she said with a snort, stepping around him and breaking into a measured run.

Again, he caught up with her in a matter of seconds. "Don't take offense. Despite what they say, I'm rather choosy, as I'm sure you are. And you can't deny we were fantastic together."

"You were fine," she said, a smile quirking up at the corner of her mouth. "I was fantastic."

Alex raised his eyebrows but didn't take her bait. Instead, his eyes sparkled at her and for a moment she almost forgot she hated when he did that. "You were at that."

They fell back into silence, though a much more comfortable one than before as they approached the last and most difficult part of the tour, running on the sand. They were halfway across the beach when his pace started to slow. Penny glanced down out of the corner of her eye and saw his gait was a little labored, favoring his left leg.

She stopped and looked up at him, the sunlight shining behind his head, making her squint. "Is your knee okay for this?" The sand was soft now that the tide had rolled back out, much looser than their clay practice court or the low-impact rubberized paths they'd run on. The unstable surface could be hell on a recovering joint, especially after all the work they put in.

"Concerned? I'm touched."

"Purely selfish. I'll never be able to find another hitting partner this close to the French."

"Right, of course," he muttered. "I told you, the knee is fine. Or do you need me to kick your ass on the court again to prove it?"

They ran together, his strides as smooth as her own. The practice courts came into view as they passed the last of the vacation homes beside the OBX property.

Penny let out a tiny groan and then muttered, "Time to face the music." She was not looking forward to whatever lecture Dom was about to deliver post-run.

"Wait, hang on a tick," Alex said, coming to a halt as she was about to tackle the long wooden stairway that led up from the beach.

"What? We've already taken too long."

"C'mon, wait," he said, touching her arm.

She froze at the way his hand immediately set her skin alight and looked up at him.

"I asked you not to touch me."

"Right. Sorry," he said, pulling away. He shifted his weight back and forth, looking at her but not quite meeting her eye. "I won't say anything to Dom."

She stood, stunned, not really sure what to say, so she settled for "Thanks."

His eyes sparkled at her again. What kind of cruel God would give a man like him the ability to look at her like she was the only woman in the world?

"Purely selfish," he said, throwing her words back at her and breaking the moment. "Don't want him to kick me out."

Penny rolled her eyes and snorted out a breath. "Come on. Let's go."

They took the stairs together and then, through unspoken agreement, sprinted the last twenty meters or so to their practice court. Dom was waiting for them, leaning up against the exterior fence. "You two ready to get back to work?"

"Let's do this," she said, heading out onto the court.

"What she said," Alex added.

"Excellent." Dom followed them through the gate and took a seat at center court. "Penny, you serve."

"Defensive game, right?" she asked, picking up her racket and taking a quick swig of water.

"Forget what I said earlier, both of you," Dom said. "You're thinking too much. Just play."

Penny furrowed her brow, but then shrugged.

Dom was her coach—if he asked her to stand on her head, she would.

Alex, on the opposite side of the court, lunged from side to side, and for a split second, she thought his face scrunched into a wince, but a moment later, it was gone. He twirled his racket in his hands and then nodded. He was ready.

She served out wide, hoping to catch him expecting her usual first serve down the center of the court, but his body reacted instinctively, striding left and returning the ball back to her as she raced up to the net and put away his return with a short volley.

"Good job, P," Dom called. "Much better. You didn't force anything, even when he got that serve back. Good. Alex, let me see one from you."

Alex kicked at one of the balls at the back of the court, lifting it with his toe and popping it up into the air before catching it on his racket.

Penny sent him a disapproving glare, but set herself. He stretched his neck back and around before settling his feet, bouncing the ball on the clay. A quick inhale and he sprung into the serve, straight up the middle of the court.

She stuck out her racket and managed a return, taking a crossover step to the center of the court as he chased it down. They kept the rally going, neither of them backing down, not giving the other even the slightest opening. Penny hit a slice backhand over the net, hoping to catch him off-balance, but instead, he ran around it and fired a forehand down the line, well out of her reach, for a winner.

"Damn good job, Al!" Dom yelled from the sideline. "Perfect shot selection and you waited for the right moment to strike. Okay, that's it. I'll see you two in the gym this afternoon."

Dom left the court with a spring in his step.

Alex leaned against the net. His hair, damp and darker with sweat, was longer than it'd been in Australia. Penny flexed her hand and then clenched a fist, digging her nails into her palm while trying to quash the urge to run her fingers through it and maybe give it a not-so-gentle tug. If she remembered correctly, he liked that.

He smiled at her and asked, "You want to grab lunch?"

Penny smiled back and said, "No" before walking straight off the court, not having to look back to relish the shock on his face.

She imagined he didn't hear that word very often.

Instead of heading for the locker room, she made a sharp left as she entered the atrium and made straight for one of the smaller video rooms. Penny turned on the television and quickly found the stream airing the matches from Rome. The tournament was in full swing and Zina Lutrova was making mincemeat out of her opponents, looking a hell of a lot better than she had in Madrid.

The world number one was up a set and two breaks on her opponent, Giselle Beauchamp of France, the eighth-ranked player in the world. Lutrova's famous high-pitched shriek echoed through the speakers as she powered a forehand past a lunging Beauchamp. Penny shook her head. Even on clay, Lutrova's forehand was super strong. It was why she could almost forgive Dom for bringing in Alex. He was the perfect practice partner if she wanted to take out the Russian on clay. Obviously, his shots were more powerful, but he was even more accurate than the women's number one player, forcing her level of play higher with every rally. If she could get her head together, she would be fine. Easier said than done, though.

Her thoughts were cut short when the scent of melted cheese and pepperoni wafted into the room. Her mouth watered. She craned her neck backward and saw Jack standing in the doorway, a pizza box balanced against his hip.

"I hate you," she muttered, turning back to the screen. "Did you bring that in here to torture me?" It was one of the last things she grasped about being a great player: You could train as hard as you liked, but if you filled your body with crap, it all pretty much went to hell.

"No you don't. You love me," Jack said, plopping down next to her and holding the pizza box in his lap. The smile plastered across his face bordered on clownishly big, his dimple popping out and his eyes nearly closed.

"Why's that?" she asked, keeping her eyes trained on the TV, where Lutrova had three match points.

"Why don't you check the pizza and you'll find out," he said, shoving the box into her hands.

"Fine, but it's not like I can actually eat any..." Her voice trailed off as she took in the pie, pepperoni across the center spelling out the word *NIKE*. She looked up at Jack then down to the pizza and then to Jack again. "Are you serious?"

"Got the phone call a half hour ago. They've upped their offer and totally blew away everyone else's. It's exactly what we've been hoping for. They want you to be the new face of their tennis line. They're calling you America's Sweetheart, and if you fulfill even a few of the incentives in this contract, it'll be worth close to fifty million dollars."

It took a moment for Jack's words to sink in. Nike wanted her and they were willing to invest a huge amount of money to get her. Suddenly Alex Russell and his twinkling eyes and Zina Lutrova and her powerful groundstrokes didn't matter.

"This is... I can't..." She trailed off, tears starting to burn at the corners of her eyes. This deal wasn't only about her; it was about her family, too. If she was careful and invested wisely, that kind of money would ensure her children's grandchildren would never have a financial worry a day of their lives, her parents could retire comfortably, and Teddy could have whatever kind of car he wanted. "Thank you, Jack. Thank you so much!"

"Don't thank me. This is all you," he said, picking out a piece of pepperoni from the pie and smirking at her as he chewed.

"Oh, shut up," Penny said, grabbing him into a huge bear hug, the pizza forgotten as it slid off her lap and onto the floor.

Chapter 8

THE MUSCLES IN JASMINE'S FOREARM QUIVERED AS SHE HIT yet another backhand. The practice courts echoed with the sounds of balls hitting rackets, feet scrambling to set up shots, and Dom's voice as he paced back and forth, shouting corrections at each and every one of them. The sun was setting and a cool breeze came in off the water, a little relief from the heat they'd been working in all day. Jasmine watched as across the court, Indiana set herself for a backhand and returned the ball over the net.

"Better, Indy, better," Dom called from the sideline, and Jasmine felt his focus shift to her as Indy's shot traveled toward her. "Now, Jasmine, step into this one."

Another backhand. That was the point of this drill, forcing them to use their worst strokes, fine-tuning them until their weaknesses became strengths. That was the idea anyway, but mostly it was a struggle. Jasmine crossed over and attacked the ball, but her shot felt the same as the last, a little uncomfortable and not nearly as powerful as she wanted it to be, even against someone whose footwork was as bad as Indy's.

Jasmine frowned as the new girl took a crossover step and lined up another slice. Okay, so her footwork wasn't quite the mess it was a few days before, but it was still miles from where it should be.

"Don't drop your shoulder, Indy!" Dom yelled as Indy's shot landed well short of where it should have. "Come on now, Jas. Don't let her get away with that shot."

Jasmine took three small steps forward, keeping her shoulders aligned with her hips, and hit a crosscourt backhand past the tall blond girl.

"Nice job, ladies," Dom said, and then raised his voice over the shuffling feet and racket *thwacks* echoing from the attached practice courts where the others were performing the same drill. "That's all. Hit the showers, and don't forget—the Classic Coaches and Players Reception is tomorrow night. I expect everyone to be there by seven sharp to greet our guests."

Jasmine spun away from the court and went straight for her bag. It had been a long, grueling day and she was glad it was over.

"Great shot, Jas," Addison said as she jogged over from her court and started digging through her bag. Lara was right behind her.

"Thanks, I really feel like my backhand is getting there."

"It totally is and we're going to kill at Classic," Lara said, holding out her fist for Jasmine to bump.

They knocked knuckles and Jasmine glanced quickly at

Addison. She had a pinched look on her face but shrugged when Jasmine met her eye.

"Just kick Gaffney's ass off the court," Addison said to Lara, who'd be facing Indiana in the first round.

"Don't worry. She's not going to know what hit her," Lara promised. They looked over to the other side of the court where Dom was talking to Indy about something.

"Have you been working on your returns during free session?" Jasmine asked. Lara was a good player, but it wouldn't matter how good she was if she couldn't get Indy's serve back.

Lara was about to answer when Dom called out from across the court. "Jasmine, hang out for a minute, okay?"

She nodded. The other girls gathered their things and left. Jasmine hitched her bag over her shoulder and approached Dom and Indy.

"The footwork is getting there, but you need to keep at it. Do you understand what I mean, Indy?" Dom was asking as Jasmine approached.

"Yeah, I get it," Indy said, but she stopped talking as soon as Jasmine got closer.

"What's up?" Jasmine asked, looking at Dom.

"Harold Hodges from *Athlete Weekly* is here to do a feature on Alex and Penny. He's going to cover the Classic, too, and he's agreed to interview the both of you."

Jasmine's mouth dropped open and she looked back and forth between her coach and Indiana. "Both of us?"

"Yep, he wants to paint a picture of the rising talent in American tennis. He wasn't sure if it would fit into the schedule, but he's got Penny and Alex down at the beach for a photo shoot right now, so he's got time to talk to you two." Dom rocked back on his heels.

Jasmine's mouth was suddenly dry and she swallowed quickly, trying to understand what was happening. Dom wanted Harold Hodges to talk to her… *and Indy*?

What the fuck? The bitch just got here.

Dom led them from the practice courts and down to the beach, where the shoot was in full swing. Wind kicked up from off the water, swirling sand around the two objects of the photographer's lens, Penny Harrison and Alex Russell. The photographer's angle was obvious. Penny was in an all-white tennis dress with a gold Nike swoosh logo across her chest. Alex stood right beside her in a black T-shirt and black tennis shorts, no logos, no sponsors, just himself.

Standing at the bottom of the stairs was Caroline Morneau, one of the top agents in the world. Jasmine recognized her from parties her parents used to drag her to when she was little.

"Dominic, you did not even let them shower?" Caroline asked now, shaking her head.

Dom ignored her and turned to them. "Stay here, ladies." Then he strode down the beach a little closer to the photo shoot.

Caroline began digging through her large bag. "Men, they never think of these things." She pulled a hairbrush out and handed it to Indy. "Fix your hair so you do not look like a mess for your first big interview. Think of all the buzz this will create. Everyone will be talking about you!" Then she left them as well, kicking off her stiletto heels and carrying them down the beach with her, heading straight for Dom.

Jasmine took a deep breath and then turned to Indy. "Is Caroline Morneau your agent?" she snapped.

Indy yanked her hair out of her ratty, sweaty ponytail and shrugged. "She thinks she is."

Jasmine tried to keep her reaction off her face, not sure how successful she was. One of the best agents in the world wanted to rep this girl with the terrible footwork and zero track record.

"That's great," Jasmine managed to choke out.

"Yeah, well, we'll see," Indy said, her eyes focused down the beach as she pulled her new ponytail tight. Jasmine followed the direction of her stare and it landed on Jack Harrison, who was watching the photo shoot intently, like he did everything in his little sister's career.

"You want Jack Harrison instead?" Jasmine asked.

"What?" Indy asked, turning toward her, confusion written clear across her face.

"You want Jack Harrison?" Jasmine repeated herself.

"To be my agent? No." Indy's nose wrinkled. "I think Dom's calling us."

Dom was waving from down the beach, standing next to a short, balding middle-aged man in a golf shirt and khakis, Harold Hodges, who had Caroline at his other arm and was listening to her intently.

There were lots of people around—makeup artists, the photographer's assistants—and they all seemed really busy, but it barely registered for Jasmine. Her mind was still reeling. Nothing had ever gutted her quite like this before, except maybe Teddy's rejection. No, even that paled in comparison. Her whole life, her entire tennis career, had been leading up to these next few days when she'd take on the best the world had to offer, and now, suddenly, she had to share it.

"Okay, I think that's it," the photographer shouted, drawing her from her thoughts.

Penny marched away from Alex without a word, straight up the beach. Alex watched her go for a moment and then, with a shake of his head, turned and walked toward Caroline.

"Hey, they've got you doing this, too?" Penny asked when she finally reached them.

It took Jasmine a second to realize that Penny wasn't talking to her, at least not *only* her. Then she remembered breakfast yesterday. Indy showed up with Penny and then sat with the other Harrisons. Obviously they were friends, though she had no idea how that had happened. Except Teddy knew Indy from her first day, so of course the new girl would use that angle to get in cozy with OBX's best player. She'd reeked of ambition from the moment she stepped on the practice court a week before the Classic. Trying to buddy up with Penny Harrison definitely wasn't beneath her.

"How was shooting with him?" Indy asked, a smirk lifting at the side of her mouth.

Penny rolled her eyes and groaned. "He's just...he thinks he's God's gift to women. He pretty much latches on to anything female in his line of sight." She waved her hand back down the beach where Alex was leaning into Caroline and smiling widely as they headed away from OBX. "Case in point. I'm gonna get going before the photographer sucks me back in. See you guys later," she said as she started up the stairs.

"Penny, hold up!" Jack called as he, Dom, and the man Jasmine recognized as Harold Hodges finally walked away from the photographer and toward them. "Ladies."

Jack followed Penny up the stairs, but Dom stopped in front of them with the reporter. "Jasmine, Indy, this is Harold Hodges." Then he stepped back, giving them some room to talk.

"It's a pleasure to meet you, Mr. Hodges. I love your column," Indy said, shaking his hand.

"Thank you, Indy, and, Jasmine, we've met before, though I doubt you remember it. I did a profile on your father during his last year on the tour. You were only a baby at the time."

Jasmine smiled tightly. Competing with both Indy *and* her dad. Just great.

"Well, it's all going to be very straightforward. Just a few questions, nothing too difficult, I promise."

Jasmine rarely took reporters at their word, but Hodges's reputation was pretty solid.

"Let's get started, shall we?"

Hodges took out his phone and started to record.

"Both of you have a real shot to make a splash on tour next season. Why don't you tell me a little about how you got to where you are? Jasmine?"

"It's been a long, hard road. I sprained my ankle at last year's US Open qualifying, but I just got back from Madrid, my first real tour-level event, and that was super exciting, and now we're prepping for the Classic and the French Open."

She'd learned the pivot technique from her dad. It was best to give answers that didn't really answer the question. It kept reporters from putting together whatever narrative they wanted to write and forced them to write what you wanted.

"And Indy?"

"The last few days have been so crazy I don't even know where to start. A month ago, I was trying to figure everything out, decide whether to stay in college or try tennis again. Now I'm seeded fourth at the OBX Classic, and how did you put it? I have a chance to make a splash on tour next year. It blows my mind."

"Who are your inspirations?" Hodges asked, moving his phone back to Jasmine.

"Definitely my parents." Short, sweet, and to the point. There would be no way for Harold to take it out of context, but instead of moving on, his eyes lit up. She cringed inwardly. She'd opened the door to questions about her parents.

"Do you feel extra pressure to perform well given the high standard your parents set, particularly your father, during their pro careers?"

Jasmine smiled, wide and entirely fake. "No," she said from between her clenched teeth. "I'm not them."

"And what are your goals this year? Your mother won the French Open when she was your age," he said, as if she needed reminding. The trophy was in her living room for Pete's sake.

"My goal is to play my best. That's the only thing I can control."

Hodges nodded and then turned to Indy. Jasmine let her smile fall.

"And you, Indy, who is your inspiration?"

"Tennis inspiration or plain old awesome inspiration?" Indy asked, twirling the bottom of her ponytail around her finger.

Hodges tilted his head. "Whichever you prefer."

"My mom, then. This was always our dream. She inspires me every time I walk out onto the court."

"And where's your mother now?"

"She passed away. Cancer."

Jasmine's stomach sank. She hadn't expected that.

"I'm so sorry to hear that," Hodges said. "Is that why you've put off playing at a higher level until now?"

"Partly," Indy said. "If you don't mind, I don't really like talking about it."

"I'm sure she'd be very proud to see how far you've come in such a short time. Why don't you tell me about training at OBX, the best thing and the worst thing."

"The worst thing is that I was in such terrible shape before I got here, so the conditioning's been rough, but the best thing by far has been working with Dom and the other coaches here. It's a whole new level for me, but they've been really supportive."

"I spoke to your coach," Hodges said, glancing behind him to where Dom was still standing, "and he said, and I'll quote, 'Indiana Gaffney has the most natural talent I've seen in a player since Penny Harrison.' What's your reaction to that?"

Jasmine felt her knees buckle, like someone had come up from behind her and slammed them with a baseball bat. That was an incredible comparison. Penny was one of the best players in the world. She turned to Dom, wide-eyed, but he wasn't looking at her. He was focused on Indy. If that was true, if that was what he really thought, then where did that leave her?

Finally, Indy found her voice. "I'm not sure I have a reaction. Being compared to Penny is an honor I hope I can live up to someday."

Jasmine's stomach twisted and a lump slid up into her throat. She could see the article in her mind already. Penny Harrison, the star. Indy Gaffney, the one to watch. And Jasmine Randazzo, the daughter of two tennis legends. That was just great.

"Thank you, that's wonderful," Harold said, fiddling with his phone before pocketing it. "I think that about covers it, ladies. Thanks so much for your time. I know you probably have practice to get to. Good luck in the tournament to you both."

"I'll walk you back," Dom said to Hodges, and they went back to the photographer, who was nearly finished clearing up his equipment.

"I guess I'll see you tomorrow at training," Indy said as she began walking away, back up the beach.

"Yeah," Jasmine said, still staring at the men as they walked away. Had that really just happened?

She heard Indy climbing the stairs, leaving her behind.

"Hey, Indy," Jasmine called."Do me a favor?"

Indy turned. "Yeah?"

"Kick Lara's ass in the first round, okay?"

Indy tilted her head, a small grin tugging up at one corner of her mouth. "I plan on it."

A swell of courage roared through Jasmine's body. "Good, then I'll have the pleasure of beating the hell out of you in the final."

"We'll see, won't we?" Indy shouted back.

"Damn straight we will," Jasmine said to herself. "Damn straight."

Chapter 9

After dumping the last bucket of ice into the tub, Indy slid out of her training clothes with as little movement as possible. She let them fall to the floor. Bending down to pick them up wasn't an option; it would hurt way too much. It didn't matter, though. She had her dress for the Outer Banks Classic Coaches and Players Reception hanging in her locker.

Her body protested with a violent jolt, joints unbending, as she lifted one leg then the other, her calves spasming as she lowered herself into the tub of icy water. She huffed out a breath, and her entire body tensed as the frigid water saturated her skin, shocking her muscles into submission.

Less than a week and she was in constant agony. Every workout was harder than the last, every mistake magnified and dissected by her new coaches. Her strengths were twisted into weaknesses; her limitations were highlighted at every opportunity.

She knew going in it would be hard. She never imagined it would be *this* hard. Then again, she wasn't sure what exactly she'd imagined. Whatever it was, it definitely hadn't included daily ice baths.

Groaning as her head fell back against the edge of the tub, she tried to force herself to think about anything other than the numbing cold surrounding her body. It would get better soon. It had to get better soon or she was going to crack.

Fifteen minutes later, she lifted herself out of the tub, teeth chattering and gooseflesh spreading over her skin. She wrapped herself in a towel and moved into the main locker room.

As soon as she passed each row of lockers, the girls there dissolved into whispers and stares. She turned into her row, and across the aisle Lara and Addison were putting the finishing touches on their outfits for the night, Addison pinning her long red hair into a bun at the top of her head and Lara sliding bangles onto her wrists. Both girls ignored her, which was an improvement as far as Indy was concerned.

"Hey," Penny said, emerging from the other end of the row, wrapped in a towel as well. "Enjoy your ice bath?"

"Hilarious, but I'm too cold to laugh," Indy said, her teeth still chattering as she spun through her locker combination. The shivers outweighed any nervousness she still felt in front of OBX's star player.

"You'll get used to it." Penny pulled on a pretty pale yellow sundress, clearly not what she was planning to wear to the party, which was a formal affair held every year prior to the beginning of the Classic. OBX students were supposed to mingle with the press and sponsors and welcome the other players. The only welcome Indy wanted to give her competition was a serve into the body, but it was a mandatory event for all OBX players and staff, Dom's orders.

"Doubtful," Indy replied. She pushed the metal clamp up on her locker and opened the door. It was empty—the garment bag with her dress in it was gone.

"Did you bring your dress here?" Penny peered into the locker, too.

"I thought I did." Indy leaned in, as if searching the empty space would somehow make it appear again. "What the hell? It was right here when I went out to practice."

Penny frowned and glanced across the row to Addison and Lara, who were putting on a badly acted show of indifference but glancing at Indy every few seconds. "I think I know."

Indy closed her eyes. Those bitches. "I'm going to kill them. Both of them."

"No," Penny said, grabbing her arm. "Put on whatever clean clothes you have and come to my house. I have way more dresses than I know what to do with, and we're close to the same size. We can find you something."

"I can't just let them get away with this," Indy whispered through gritted teeth.

"Yeah you can," Penny said, and then lowered her voice. "They're only doing this because they're terrified of you. The tournament starts tomorrow and you're going to kick Lara Cronin's ass all over the court in front of everyone. That is so much better than cat fighting her in the locker room."

Indy nodded. “You’re right.”

“Of course I’m right,” Penny said. “Get dressed.”

Five minutes later, they walked shoulder to shoulder out of the locker room, pointedly ignoring the stares and whispers of the girls surrounding them.

Indy didn’t know what she expected from the Harrison home, but the pretty blue-shingled house with the basketball net in the driveway and two SUVs with Harvard and Duke magnets on the back bumpers definitely wasn’t it.

Penny led her inside, dropping her car keys on a table next to the front door. Indy followed her past a comfortable-looking living room and up a flight of stairs lined with photos of the Harrison kids at various ages. It was all so normal. Indy’s eyes caught on the last picture. It looked pretty recent, maybe last Christmas, if the brightly lit tree in the background was any indication. All three siblings standing beside their parents, the perfect family.

“Come on,” Penny said from the doorway to what Indy assumed was her bedroom. “We don’t have a lot of time.”

“Sorry, I was…” Indy trailed off and followed her into the room, her words failing her as the idea of being inside Penny Harrison’s bedroom hit her full force. They were separated by less than a year in age, but Penny had accomplished so much of what Indy wanted for herself. She’d thought that maybe the room would be lined with trophies and ribbons, evidence of her ridiculously successful career, but the walls were painted a soft lavender, a patchwork quilt rested across her bed, and the only indication that the room's occupant wasn't a normal girl was the end post of her bed, where dozens upon dozens of tournament player passes hung. It looked like Penny had kept every single one.

"Okay, I'm wearing this one," Penny said from her closet, pulling out a hanger with a gold silk dress, "but take your pick from the rest."

Indy hesitated. "Why?" she asked, suddenly not quite sure this was for real.

"Why what?"

"Why are you doing this? You barely know me."

Penny raised an eyebrow. "You think you're the first girl to show up at OBX and piss people off just by walking on the court?"

"Oh," Indy said, feeling awful for questioning Penny's motives.

"Now pick something out," Penny said, letting her off the hook.

"Seriously?" Indy asked, approaching and staring into the closet in awe. "Where did all these dresses come from?"

"Sponsors and events. There's a red carpet at all the big tournaments, and designers will give you a dress for free if you get your picture taken in it."

Indy snorted. "You mean they'll give *you* a dress for free."

"Just pick one out."

"Penny, this is a fucking Versace," Indy said, pulling out a silver strapless minidress intricately designed with crystal patterns across every inch of the fabric.

"Oh," Penny said. "Yeah, I wore that one in Australia this year." Indy bit her lip, wondering if that meant she couldn't wear it. "Go for it. It'll probably look better on you than it did on me. I left my eyeliner in the bathroom; I'll be right back."

As soon as the door clicked shut, Indy shimmied out of her shorts and yanked her tank top over her head. Carefully, she stepped into the Versace and slid it up over her hips. She managed to get the zipper up most of the way but couldn't quite reach the clasp at the center of her back. Still, it fit perfectly, hugging her like a second skin. She moved in front of Penny's mirror and smoothed down the satin against her thighs.

"Penny, let's go. We're . . . Indiana."

In the mirror, she saw Jack standing in the doorway, staring at her.

"Hi," she said, not turning around, but keeping her eyes locked on his through her reflection.

"Where's . . ." Jack cleared his throat. "Where's my sister?" He took a step into the room.

"In the bathroom."

He moved closer until he was right behind her. Reaching forward, his hands ghosted over her shoulders before sliding down to the line of fabric across her back.

"What are you . . ." she started to ask, but stopped as the dress tightened across her breasts. She breathed deeply at the brush of his fingertips against her skin and shivered. His eyes still held fast to hers even as his hands fell away. This wasn't the same man who'd ignored her on the beach during the *Athlete Weekly* interview and at breakfast the other day. It couldn't be, not with how he was looking at her.

His eyes wrenched away from hers suddenly and he

stumbled back a step. "You missed a clasp," he said, shoving his hands into the pockets of his dress pants.

She turned to face him. "Jack," she said.

"Wow, Indy, you look great," Penny said, emerging from the bathroom dressed for the party, looking more ready to walk the Paris runways than grace its tennis courts.

Jack looked stricken, but Indy stepped around him and smiled at his sister. "Right? Thanks for the loan."

"No problem," Penny said, and then turned to her brother. "You ready to go?"

"Absolutely," Jack said, storming out of the room.

Jack Harrison was the most confusing guy Indy had ever met. Scorching hot and then ice cold. She should just leave it alone, concentrate on her game and nothing else, but she couldn't help the way her body reacted when he was around, and she couldn't forget the way he looked at her before he shut himself down.

It was equal parts frustrating and exciting.

And she wanted more of it.

"Come on," Penny said, drawing her mind back to the present. "Let's finish up and go before Dom has us running Einsteins in stilettos."

Deuce was already packed with people when they arrived. The tables were gone and a small band played in the corner, leaving the large room open for mingling and dancing. Jack immediately stalked off to the bar, but Indy scanned the crowd, recognizing some of the best young athletes from around the world, their coaches at their sides. She'd been there for five seconds and this was easily the best party she'd ever been to.

Jasmine Randazzo was at the opposite end of the dance floor with her parents. She wore a bright pink strapless dress cinched in at the waist and flowing down to just above her knees. Harold Hodges chatted with Mr. Randazzo while his daughter, looking incredibly bored, crossed her arms over her chest. A few feet away, Alex Russell was surrounded by a crowd of girls. Looking closer, Indy saw Caroline beside him, hand resting on his arm, dominating the conversation. The other girls looked happy enough to simply stand near him, ignoring Dom's edict to stay away while he was at OBX. Then her coach made a beeline for the group and several of the girls scattered, including Caroline, who sidestepped him lightly and disappeared into the crowd.

Indy laughed and looked to Penny, hoping she'd seen it as well. Her eyes were still trained in that direction, but they were wide and her hand shot out and gripped Indy's wrist tightly. "Do not leave me."

Indy looked back and saw Alex stalking across the dance floor straight for them, a tumbler of amber liquid in his hand.

"Ladies," he said, but he never even looked at Indiana. He wore a black suit that hung perfectly on his tall frame, probably made for him, but no tie, and the top button of his sky-blue dress shirt was undone. His ever-present five-o'clock shadow was gone in favor of a close shave.

After Penny stared at him in silence, he finally glanced at Indy. "That's a beautiful dress, darling," he said, smiling at her, though it didn't quite reach his eyes. "I think I've seen it before. It has a tricky little clasp at the back, if I recall."

Finally, Penny let go of Indy's arm, though her nails had

left half-moon-shaped marks in her skin. "Alex, don't do this, okay?"

His eyes softened at her voice and he swayed in place, the glass in his hand clearly not his first. "You sure about that?" he said, taking a large sip and swallowing it cleanly.

Penny narrowed her eyes, taking a step closer and inhaling softly. She wrinkled her nose. "Positive."

"Shame," he said with a casual shrug of his shoulders, but one look into his eyes and Indy knew that the rejection stung.

Penny shook her head and turned to Indy. "Let's go."

"So when you said you wore this dress in Australia, you meant the night you two..." Indy whispered as they walked away. She glanced back over her shoulder, but Alex was gone. It didn't take a genius to figure out that the only way he'd know about the hidden clasp at the top of the dress's zipper was if he'd undone it himself, but Indy wasn't going to push, not with the way the color had drained out of Penny's face.

"I'm sorry. I shouldn't have let you wear it. Just trust me. It wasn't about you, okay? You look great."

"Okay," Indy said, wanting to say more but having no idea where to even start.

"Indiana!" a voice said over the crowd. Across the room she spotted Caroline, who, now that she was no longer talking to Alex, was with an older man in a finely tailored suit. The agent, wearing a pale pink sheath dress fixed at the waist with a large black patent-leather belt, waved her over with a flick of her fingers.

"I'm being summoned," Indy said, rolling her eyes at

Penny, who smiled. "Even though she's not actually my agent." In fact, Indy thought she'd made it pretty clear to Caroline that she wasn't interested after ignoring every call and text she'd sent over the last few days.

Penny snorted. "Looks like she thinks she is."

Indy turned and saw Caroline stalking toward them, the man matching her stride. She groaned.

"Indiana." Caroline air-kissed her cheeks when they arrived, totally ignoring Penny, then gestured to the man. "I'd like you to meet Mr. Edward Franklin. He's from Solaris Beachwear."

"I'll leave you guys to it, then," Penny said, nodding to Mr. Franklin. She looked straight past Caroline and then grinned a farewell to Indy.

"It's very nice to meet you," Indy said. "Call me Indy."

Mr. Franklin drew his eyes away from Penny's retreating back and shook Indy's hand. "I'm really looking forward to watching you play this week."

"Thank you."

"Caroline was telling me about the feature *Athlete Weekly* is doing on you."

Indy felt her face flush a little. "Well, it is on a few of us..."

"Modest, too. Here's my card." The man passed it over to her. "Good luck in the tournament, Indiana. Caroline, I look forward to hearing from you."

He excused himself and Indy turned to Caroline with an eyebrow raised. "Solaris Beachwear?"

"It's not Nike, but you haven't actually won anything yet. Then again, neither has Penelope Harrison—a big tournament, yes, but certainly not a major. They'll come calling eventually, but for now..."

"You think Nike is going to want me?"

"I speak as I find. You win something, Indiana, like this tournament, and Solaris Beachwear won't be the only one knocking on our door."

"We'll see," Indy said. "And anyway, you're still not my agent."

Caroline's smile grew wide like she knew something Indy didn't. There was meaning in that smile that didn't sit quite right with her.

As Caroline started to speak again, Indy saw Teddy Harrison pushing through the crowd in her direction. Jacket and tie nowhere in sight, the sleeves of his burgundy dress shirt were already rolled up to his elbows.

"Sorry, Caroline, gotta go," she said, and met him halfway. "Dance with me?"

"Do you really want to dance or did you just want to get away from her?" Teddy asked, laughing, as they moved through the dancing couples, the band playing a slow jazz tune.

"Sorry," she said, shrugging. "I know I need an agent, but there's something about her. She's..."

"She's a shark, at least that's what Jack says, and he's usually right."

"Is he?" Indy said, the memory of Jack's touch still at the center of her back, but Teddy didn't answer as she wrapped her arm around his neck and looked out over his shoulder. In the corner of the room, Jasmine, Lara, and Addison were twittering away and staring at them, not even pretending they weren't.

"We have an audience," Indy whispered.

Teddy's shoulders tensed under her hands. "Do you mind if I…" He nodded in that direction.

Indy glanced back at the girls, and the daggers flying out of Jasmine's eyes could've shredded her to ribbons. "Go," she said, and Teddy offered her a tight smile before leaving her on the dance floor and walking over to Jasmine.

Indy watched as he stuffed his hands in his pockets and rocked back on his feet. He nodded out to the dance floor, but Jasmine simply marched away, the others trailing behind her.

She made sure to stay clear of their path as she made her way to the bar. She had enough enemies at OBX, mostly because of things totally out of her control. She didn't need to earn any more by going after Jasmine's best friend.

"Seltzer and lime, please," she asked the bartender, leaning back against the bar to observe the party while she waited.

"Jack and Coke," a voice next to her ordered, and she glanced sideways to see Jack Harrison. Earlier, she'd been so focused on the feel of his hands against her skin, there hadn't been enough time to admire how well he filled out his navy-blue suit.

The bartender placed her drink on the bar, which was the perfect distraction from staring at Jack just a little too long.

"You haven't seen my sister anywhere, have you?" he asked her by way of greeting.

"Oh, um, she's…" She nodded to the other end of the bar, where Penny's eyes were glued to the television mounted high on the wall: A replay of a match in Rome was airing.

Zina Lutrova was soundly beating the world's number three player, Jin Jun Huang.

"Great, torturing herself."

"I don't know. If I were an agent, I'd be thrilled if my client wanted to win as much as she does."

"As an agent, I am thrilled. As a brother, sometimes I wish she could relax a little bit. I wasn't like that when I played."

"No? What were you like?" she asked, relieved he was as willing as she was to push past any lingering awkwardness from that moment in Penny's room.

Jack huffed out a short laugh. "Relaxed. Tennis was something I did for fun."

"At Harvard, right?" He tilted his head, leaving the question unasked. "The day we met you were wearing a Harvard tennis shirt," she explained, leaving out the part that she googled him and found an old Harvard roster from four years before with his name on it.

"Right, well yeah, four years at Harvard, before law school."

"Law school? Impressive."

He laughed again, his eyes crinkling as he did. "What? Not, 'Why didn't you go pro, Jack?' "

Indy smiled and shrugged. "I assume you weren't good enough."

Jaw dropping, but the smile not leaving his eyes, he nodded. "You're right. I wasn't." Then slowly his laughter faded, and with it so did the ease surrounding them. His shoulders straightened and his entire body stiffened as he looked past her. Indy turned, but all she saw behind her was Teddy and a few other OBX guys. When she faced him again, he said, "I . . . I better go. Good luck tomorrow. I know you're going to do well."

"Thank you," she whispered, off-balance again at his sudden but now predictable shutdown.

He finished his drink and placed the glass back down on the bar. Then he leaned down and brushed a kiss against her cheek. "Good night."

He was so confusing, and if she knew what was good for her, she'd just move on. She reached up to touch where his lips had brushed against her cheek, still warm and tingling, and her heart skipped a beat at the mere thought of it.

Yeah, no chance of that.

Sitting in the locker room the next day, Indy twirled her racket. A twist of her wrist had it spinning around fully before coming to rest in her palm again. This was it, her first match at the Classic. Indy's leg bounced up and down, her toes curling and uncurling in her sneakers.

"How's that?" the trainer asked, tapping Indy's wrapped wrist, drawing her from her thoughts. "Range of motion good?"

She flexed her wrist back and forth, the wrap there for some extra support, preventive against the power of her serve being too much for it. "Perfect."

"Have a good match," the trainer said as she left the room.

Once she was alone, her stomach clenched and her throat

tightened. There were the nerves. It was actually comforting to feel them. It had been two years since she'd been out on a court for a real elite-level match. Plus, this was the first time she'd be out on the court without her mom in the stands. Anyone would be a little jittery. Indy checked her racket, bouncing the heel of her hand against the crisscrossed strings. The tension was perfect, not too tight and not too loose, allowing both power and control.

Taking a slow, steady breath, she packed her racket into her bag and mentally ran through the match. Lara Cronin, the one who tried to bully her off a practice court and most likely the evil bitch who stole her dress for the reception, had a solid overall game. They'd played against each other a little bit during training. Good backhand, better forehand, could move well, but not well enough. The plan was to stick to the power game. Lara definitely wouldn't be able to handle her serve. Indy was prepared. Now all she had to do was execute.

"You ready to go?" a deep Southern drawl asked from outside the doorway.

Slinging her bag onto her shoulder, Indy nodded to Roy. "I'm ready."

They walked down the long corridor, past the Title Wall, and through another hallway that led to the OBX main court. The door was braced open. She could hear the buzz of the crowd and the hard-rock music blasting through the speakers. Lara was already standing at the door, waiting. Indy was the higher seed and thus had the honor of entering the court last.

The radio clipped to Roy's belt crackled. "Two minutes."

"Hang on right here, ladies," Roy said, pausing at the door.

Indy bounced on the balls of her feet to stay warm and burn off the extra energy flowing through her veins. She'd never felt anything quite like this before, a buzzing through her entire body, almost making her vibrate.

To her right, held in a glass case, was the Classic trophy. It was an old-school brass cup, about the same height as a desk lamp, with two large handles. The tournament was in its fifth year but only had two winners. The names of the previous champions were engraved on the cup.

AMY FITZPATRICK

PENELOPE HARRISON

PENELOPE HARRISON

PENELOPE HARRISON

By the end of the week, her name could be cut into the brass below Penny's; by the end of the week, she could be the Outer Banks Classic Champion.

The radio crackled again. "Okay, we're a go."

Lara entered the court first, the crowd applauding for her. Roy held his hand up, holding Indy back, and her eyes grew wide. It was really loud out there, definitely the loudest she'd ever heard a crowd for one of her matches.

"Good luck," he said, his hand squeezing her shoulder before he waved her through.

Empty, the OBX main court didn't seem that big. Compared to the huge stadiums at the Grand Slams, it was actually very small, but as she stood on the court with every seat taken, music blaring in the background, and the din of people chattering in their seats, to Indy it might as well have been Centre Court at Wimbledon.

All of these people were here to watch her play, to watch her win or lose.

Indy's heart pounded, mimicking the harsh bass echoing through the speakers. The music was meant to pump up everyone in the stands, but it was sending her pulse rate through the roof.

Glancing into the crowd, Indy noticed that Caroline was courtside, next to the rep from Solaris. A few rows back, Penny, long past the need to play in a tournament for up-and-comers, sat with Dom and Jack. Indy was pretty sure she caught Jack looking away from her once her gaze landed on their group. Infuriating man. Teddy was behind them next to Jasmine. Her match had been earlier that morning. She'd won easily.

Indy looked elsewhere. She had to take it one match at a time. There wouldn't be a chance to face down Jasmine unless she won this one and two after it.

She sat down in her chair and pulled the laces of her sneakers tight. She took several deep breaths, trying to block out the noise, but it was almost impossible.

"Players to the center of the court," the chair umpire said, standing next to the net. A coin flip would decide who served first.

"Heads," Lara said.

"The call is heads," the umpire said, and flipped it onto the court. The coin bounced once, spun, and then rattled flat onto the ground. "It is tails. Miss Gaffney?"

“I’ll serve.”

Lara’s face went pale and Indy’s nerves faded.

Her opponent was afraid, and there was nothing more devastating for an athlete than fear.

As they warmed up, Indy made sure to unleash her serve at maximum velocity, paying little attention to where it went. She wanted to nurture the fear, not give Lara the chance to overcome it.

Finally, the chair umpire said, “Play.”

The tennis balls were brand-new. They would fly hard and fast.

Across the net Lara was lined up far behind the baseline, shifting her weight back and forth, waiting. Indy didn’t make her wait any longer.

The serve was perfect, down the center of the court, skidding off the white painted line and past Lara, who flinched but had no chance to return it. Indy smiled, the tension releasing from her body, the rush of adrenaline settling into a comfortable ease.

The match was over before it started.

Chapter 10

"GAME, SET, AND MATCH, GAFFNEY."

Penny stood, applauding Indy's win, her third in three days. It was a decisive victory and she could remember what that felt like; a few years ago, she was down on that court, winning her first Classic semifinal. Long before there were sponsorships and British bad boys, there was tennis and her simple love for the sport. She still loved it, of course, but everything was so complicated now.

Indy and her opponent met at the net and shook hands to end the match, and Penny turned to leave. She had a training session with Dom and Alex in fifteen minutes. Coming down the stairs out of the OBX stadium with the rest of the crowd, Penny felt him before she saw him. It was like that in Australia, too. She'd felt his eyes on her long before he'd approached her. She tried to disappear into the throng of people, but he was head and shoulders above nearly everyone. If he wanted to find her, he would.

"Penny," Alex said, suddenly beside her. The people around them shifted, and she was forced closer to him. "Come on. We need to talk." His hand reached for her and then stopped, hovering and dropping away instead, flexing and then relaxing. "Please, love."

"What do you want, Alex?" she asked, acutely aware of the eyes that followed them as they started down the path leading away from the stadium.

"I want to talk to you."

He drew to a halt near their practice court.

"I don't have anything to say to you."

"Yeah, see, I don't believe you."

She shrugged. "Believe what you like."

"I get it. You're hacked off at me. You've been hacked off at me for months, since that night at the Aussie."

Penny blinked at him in disbelief. "Seriously? You really think now is the time to talk about this?"

"I meant to the day I arrived, but you radiate a sort of force field, so I put it off, and then the other night I worked up some courage."

"You mean you drank until you weren't scared of me anymore."

"Right, that. But you shot me down."

"You were drunk and you didn't *just* want to talk."

She arched an eyebrow at him and he shrugged unapologetically.

"I'm not drunk now, and while I'd much rather *not talk*, I think maybe we should."

"We can't. We have a training session. Dom'll be here in..." Her phone buzzed in her pocket, cutting her off. Alex's phone buzzed as well.

Only one person would be texting them at the same time.

"Dom's not coming," he said, reading off his screen. "He's got press to do with Jasmine and Indiana for the final tomorrow."

"Of course he does. I'm out of here."

In two strides he leapt out in front of her, blocking her path. "Oy, where are you going? We've got to train."

Penny looked up at the sky, a dusky blue color, as a few dark, wispy clouds gathered high in the heavens. Maybe if she were really lucky, lightning would strike and put her out of her misery. "First you want to talk, and now you want to train?"

"We can't do both?"

"Train first," she said, "then talk." Of course she had no intention of sticking around once they finished their session. He'd have to get over it.

They stretched out on their practice court in silence, like they had every day since he arrived, but even without words, the connection between them was practically tangible. Every time he shifted, her body wanted to mimic the motion. She fought it, trying desperately to focus on her own stretching regime.

What was it about him? Aside from the mind-blowing sex, of course. It was getting harder and harder to brush aside the memories. Every night he invaded her dreams and every day he was there, waiting on the court, their training sessions almost as arousing as her memories. She'd never experienced anything like it. Their bodies were made for each other, and though her mind was set against him, her body refused to let her forget. And as for her heart...she tried not to think about that.

"Okay?" he asked, pulling her from her thoughts, but not enough to make her forget the last time he'd asked that question, leaning over her, one hand gripping her thigh, the other holding himself up against the mattress, his body cradled by her hips, slick with sweat, straining with the effort of holding back, waiting for her permission.

"Penny?" She pushed herself out of the fog of the past and stood, brushing the clay from her shorts.

"Let's just do a short warm-up," she suggested, hoping he'd agree.

"Yeah," he said, a wicked grin blooming across his face. "Then let's play."

A few practice serves, forehands, backhands, and some net work later and they were both geared up for a set.

"Go on, then," Alex said, "let's see what you got." He chucked a ball at her from across the net and she plucked it neatly out of the air.

After bouncing it a few times at her feet, Penny let her weight fall back and then explode forward through the ball, sending a flat BB down the center of the court. He blocked it back, but she raced forward, putting away a short volley totally out of his reach.

"Fifteen–love."

And so, on and on it went, trading point after point, breaking serve, breaking back, forcing deuce, and losing at love, their level of play rising with every stroke of the racket for nearly an hour. They stopped keeping score early in, recognizing the need to just *play.*

"Next point wins," Alex called out finally as they caught their breath between points.

"Tired?" she challenged.

"Nah, I've got somewhere to be and you owe me a bit of a chat."

"Fine, next point."

It was his serve. He stood tall, then coiled his body down, his back bending as he lifted the ball up into the heavens. Then, like lightning, he sprung, the ball a missile, but she was ready, pouncing on it, returning it deep into his side of the court.

"Out!"

"Bullshit," she called back at him, jogging around the net. It was a clay court; there would be a mark where the ball landed. He met her there, pointing to the skid past the white line with his racket head.

"Out," he repeated. "Shame you refuse to take me at my word."

Penny's head snapped up. "And why should I trust you?"

"Have I ever given you reason not to?"

It was a fair question, she admitted to herself, not that she'd ever tell him that, so she shrugged. It's not like it mattered. Whether she could trust him or not wasn't the issue. She couldn't trust herself to keep her focus if she was with him. If it happened in Australia, it could happen again, and Penny wasn't willing to take that risk.

"I think I know what the problem is. You don't know me."

"I know you as well as I ever want to." She made for

the edge of the court, slid her racket back into its bag, and zipped up.

He waved away her response and kept talking. "I mean it. I like training here. I like working with Dom, and God help me, I actually like training with you, but if we don't figure out some of the shit between us, it's not going to work, not long-term."

"Yeah, you not around to torture me, that would be tragic."

He ignored the sarcasm and nodded. "Indeed, it would, so come here and lie down on the court with me."

She squinted at him, the request coming out of nowhere. "What? No."

"This will help your game."

Unconvinced, she lifted her bag over her shoulder, ready to leave.

"Jesus, do you fight everyone like this or is it just me?"

It was just him. No one had ever made her feel the way he did. "I'm not lying down."

"Do you want to win the bloody French Open or not?"

Did she want to win the French Open? Of course she did. So she put her bag down. "Sounds too good to be true," she said, and watched him as he reclined onto the court. "Was this what you were doing on your first day here?"

"Yes. It was something I hadn't done for a long time, but if you'll trust me for half a second, I promise it'll work. Now get down here."

She kneeled, the clay shifting beneath her and sticking to her sweaty knees. Then she rolled over onto her back, careful to keep a body width of distance between them. "Okay, now what?"

"Now close your eyes and let your mind go blank."

"That's not possible. I'll just be thinking about not thinking."

"Penny," he said, reaching out, his fingers wrapping lightly around her wrist. She wanted to pull away, but something about the way he said her name, a desperate note in his voice she hadn't heard before, kept her still. "Close your eyes and breathe."

He inhaled deeply and she followed him, matching his breathing pattern. A soft pressure on the inside of her wrist kept time for them, back and forth, his calloused thumb stroking against the sensitive skin.

"Do you really hate me?"

The question startled her so much, she actually answered. "No." She didn't have to open her eyes to know he was smiling. "I don't hate you."

"Then why did you leave?"

"What?"

"That morning, I woke up and you were gone."

It was so much easier to talk with her eyes closed, when she couldn't see him. It was almost like no one could see her—it was so easy, she decided not to be pissed off at him for tricking her into talking. "I was embarrassed."

"Of me?"

Penny shook her head, the clay beneath her caking into her hair. "No, not you, of me. I don't do things like that, one-night stands."

"Oh," he said simply.

"And then you grabbed the nearest supermodel, got drunk, and crashed your bike," she said, the dots finally connecting in her head. Had he gone out and gotten himself drunk because she left? Had he wanted her to stay?

"Something like that," he admitted.

"So it's my fault."

"No," he said. The soft feel of his thumb disappeared, replaced quickly by her entire hand being wrapped up in the warmth of his. "That was all me. I was spiraling."

"You've been doing really well here."

He had been different since he arrived, still a little wild, a little reckless, but his focus was on his game, on getting back to the top, that much was clear in how he trained. Back in Australia, he'd been like a tornado, taking out everything in his path. Even her.

"Like I said, you don't really know me."

Penny laughed softly. "Sure I do. The youngest man to ever win Wimbledon, the first English man to do it since 1936, youngest man to ever win the career Grand Slam..."

"All that's missing is the Olympic gold," Alex filled in for her.

"Well, the Olympics are only two years away."

"Yeah, in Los Angeles. Great city. They know how to party."

"Is that really all you think about?"

"No," he said, "I think about you a lot."

"Alex," she warned, but it didn't stop him.

"First time I saw you, it was in Australia."

"Yeah, and look how that turned out."

"Not this year. Two years ago, your first time down under, I think."

"Oh."

"I thought you were the most incredible-looking girl I'd ever clapped eyes on, and Christ, you could play, too. You reminded me so much of me, of who I used to be, focused, driven, not letting anything or anyone stand in my way."

"You can still be like that. You've been like that since you got here, mostly," she said, growing more and more uncomfortable with each sweet word that spilled from his lips. It was like a confession, one she shouldn't be privy to, even though he was talking about her.

"We'll see, but we're not here to talk about me. This is about you."

"I hate when things are about me."

His fingers laced between hers and he squeezed. "You put on a good show, then."

"I guess I'm used to it, but it doesn't mean I have to like it."

Alex grunted. "Speaking of not liking things and getting back to my original question, you may not hate me, but what exactly don't you like about me?"

"You're . . ." She hesitated.

"Say it."

He was probably the last person in the world she would choose to say these words to, but maybe he was the only person in the world who would truly understand.

"You said I remind you of yourself. I guess I know what you mean, and the truth is, you're what I'm afraid of becoming. I almost . . . I wanted to be with you that night. I wasn't thinking. I didn't want to think, at all, for once in my life. I could've been on that motorcycle with you and then maybe everything I'd ever worked for would have been gone in an instant, and you made me feel..."

"Like what?"

Terrified.

"Forget it," she said, ready to jump up and leave if he pushed her to say it. That she'd never felt so alive as she had when she was in his arms, not even on a tennis court. "It's not important. I was acting like an irresponsible idiot. I lost control for one night and it cost me, but not as much as it could have. It won't happen again."

That had practically become her mantra over the last few months.

"You can't be in control all the time. It's okay to let go sometimes."

"No it's not," she said, pulling her hand free from his and scrambling to her feet. She was halfway to the gate when he called her name.

"I'm sorry."

She froze but didn't respond.

"I'm sorry for making you feel"—he hesitated for a moment—"that way. I'm sorry I can't change that." His voice was soft but firm, just like his touch when he took her hand, and something in her heart cracked open.

"I..." Her voice failed her. "I've got to go."

"So that's it?"

"Yes, that's it."

She didn't owe him an explanation. She didn't owe him anything at all.

"You're a terrible liar."

It was the truth and she didn't bother to contradict him. What would be the point? Another ten rounds of verbal sparring that went absolutely nowhere and all the while her resolve weakening little by little. She should leave, get out of here before she lost control again. She should just leave before he—

"I want you." Her breath caught on a gasp as he continued. "You know I do and that scares you, but the only thing that scares you more is that you want me, too," Alex said, his voice deep and husky.

Penny's pulse thrummed in her throat and she closed her eyes, trying to keep herself steady. She could hear his sneakers moving against the clay, and when she opened her eyes again, he was right in front of her. He stepped closer, cupping her cheek, tilting her face up to his. He leaned in, his nose brushing against hers before following the path of his fingertips.

"Alex," Penny said, her eyes drifting closed as she leaned into the touch. "Wait." She pressed her hands against his chest, though she didn't push him away. "I'm sorry."

"Penny..." He bent, resting his forehead against hers, his hands dropping to her waist, tugging her closer.

"This isn't who I am," she said, twisting her fingers into the cotton of his shirt. "I can't...I can't do this."

"Can't or won't?"

"Won't," Penny whispered, hating herself for it.

Alex stumbled backward like he'd been sucker punched. "Fine. If that's what you want, fine."

"Alex? Are you finished? We have a reservation."

Penny looked up and saw Caroline Morneau at the gate.

The agent's timing was as impeccable as she looked. Her blond hair was elegantly arranged in a twist at the back of her neck; a sharp suit jacket and pencil skirt gave her an air of sophistication and grace that made Penny feel like an under-dressed little kid, especially since she had clay sticking to the backs of her legs and rubbed into her hair and clothes. Then she remembered, he had somewhere to be, and apparently wherever that was, Caroline Morneau was going with him.

"I've gotta go," she mumbled, nodding to Caroline as she passed her, careful not to get any dirt on the woman's designer clothes.

As soon as Penny stepped through the door of her house, she caught sight of Jack pacing back and forth in the living room, his cell phone glued to his ear.

"Who is that?" she mouthed, but he shook his head. She moved into the living room and plopped down on the couch, waiting for him to finish up.

"Thank you, Frank. I'll be in touch tomorrow and her schedule will be in your inbox as soon as we hang up. All right, have a good night," Jack said, and ended the call.

"Who's getting my schedule?"

"Frank Granholm from Nike Tennis." He nodded at a stack of papers at the center of the coffee table, brightly colored tabs protruding out of the pile. "They sent over your contract."

It was the perfect distraction: dozens of pages to sift through that would take her mind off Alex and everything that had happened while they lay side by side on her practice court.

They had almost kissed.

She wanted him to kiss her and she felt like a ridiculous child, especially in those last few seconds while Caroline Morneau bugged him about their date or whatever it was.

It wasn't jealousy. There was nothing to be jealous about. Maybe they were having a business meeting; maybe Alex was looking to sign with Caroline, or maybe he just wanted to screw her. It didn't matter. Despite what he'd said, about how beautiful he thought she was, he'd probably thought that Aussie supermodel was beautiful, too, and Caroline was undeniably gorgeous. Besides, Alex could go out with anyone he liked, why should it make any difference to her?

The contract required her signature in several places and there were three copies—one for Jack, one for herself, and one to send back to Nike. Each time she signed it, the small sparks of everything she'd felt for Alex since that night in Australia were pushed aside, and eventually, she hoped, they'd be gone for good.

Chapter 11

FOR AS LONG AS JASMINE COULD REMEMBER, HER DAD would give her a last-minute pep talk before each match, and the final of the Classic was no exception. It was hard for him, after so many years of playing, to sit in the stands and watch with very little control over the outcome. So he would create a strategy for every match. Most of the time it was helpful, especially if she didn't know much about her opponent's strengths and weaknesses.

At most tournaments she was too busy playing to scout out the competition, but she'd watched Indy every day at training and all week during the lead-up to the final. She knew what she had to do. Of course, that didn't stop her dad from giving his traditional pep talk in the locker room just minutes before she had to be out on the court.

"Keep your feet moving and don't give an inch on her

serve," John Randazzo said as Jasmine packed her racket bag. "On change-over have a banana, and then after the first set, an electrolyte chew." He handed her a plastic bag with the items already packed.

"Thanks."

"If she plays a baseline game, make her move and force an error. She's got power, but she's sloppy. Be patient like always and you shouldn't have any problems."

"I know, Dad," she said, trying to hide her exasperation. It was everything she'd observed about Indiana all week, and yet Dom was still gaga over the girl. Jasmine planned to put a stop to that today.

Her mom saw through her right away. "Okay, John. That's enough, let's go get our seats."

"What?" her dad asked, looking at his wife and then back to Jasmine. "Okay. Good luck, Jas. You'll do great. Just stick to the game plan."

"Thanks, Dad."

Jasmine sent a silent thank-you to her mom as she led her dad from the locker room.

She let out a sigh of relief and checked the clock. Her ankle was wrapped up tight. She'd sprained it last year and the wrap was a precaution, plus it gave her a little bit of extra stability. Her rackets were ready and her bags were packed. Fifteen more minutes until it was time to step onto the court and win her first Classic trophy. A thrill shot through her body at the thought.

Shaking out her arms and then her legs, she tried to stay warm, but it was impossible. The air-conditioning was pumping at full throttle as the temperature outside climbed into the mid-nineties, high for May in the Outer Banks. Jasmine was counting on that as well. She was in better physical condition than Indy and the heat would expose it. She planned to make her run, blocking back her shots, tiring her out. That would help weaken her serve and whatever advantage she had.

She checked the clock again: ten more minutes. A run in the hallway wouldn't hurt, just a light jog to keep loose. The hall was empty and she could hear the crowd echoing down from the main court through the door at the end of the tunnel. The steady thrum of her heartbeat spiked, the pre-match adrenaline starting to flow. She jogged in the opposite direction, swinging her arms around, trying to keep her body warm and her nerves under control.

"Hey, Randazzo."

She turned to see Teddy striding down the hallway from the door to Indy's changing room. Of course he'd go talk to *her* first, another girl on Teddy's list of potential conquests. She knew it was mean, but it would make beating Indy that much sweeter.

"Hey," she said, avoiding his eye and moving back toward the locker room to grab her bag.

"You don't call. You don't write," Teddy quipped. "Did you get any of my messages?"

Jasmine bit her lip, a small bubble of guilt building in her stomach. She got his messages, all ten of them, and ignored every single one. It was too hard to pretend to be his friend when she wanted so much more.

"I wanted to wish you good luck," he said, hovering in the doorway as she slung her bag over her shoulder.

Jasmine's heart clenched in frustration. He was smiling like nothing was wrong, like he hadn't just come from wishing Indy good luck and like he hadn't crushed her heart into a million pieces. "Right," she said, trying to push down the hurt. "Thanks."

"What's the matter?"

She used to find his obliviousness charming. Now it grated on her nerves. The hurt wrapped around her frustration, creating a knot of anger.

"You really have no idea, do you?"

"No," he said, shrugging. "Want to fill me in?"

"You know what I'm talking about, Teddy. You like Indy."

He gaped at her, his mouth opening and closing, before finding his voice. "I barely know her, but even if I did, why do you care?"

"I *don't* care," Jasmine scoffed, her anger skyrocketing. "I know you don't give a shit about it, but do you get how big of a deal this tournament is for me? Whoever wins is a shoo-in for major wild cards. If I win I'll be in the main draw in Paris. Indiana is standing in my way."

"I was being nice."

"Right, *nice*, and if she weren't gorgeous and blond, would you still have been nice?"

He rocked back on his heels and she saw the flash of guilt in his eyes. They'd been friends for too long for him to hide it, but then it was gone, replaced with annoyance.

"She was having a hard time. Most of the girls in this place have been acting like real bitches to her. Nice of you to step in and stop that, by the way."

Jasmine pursed her lips, glaring at him. "I don't control what those girls do."

"Please, one word from you and they would've stopped. What did you think? If you let them bully her, it would improve your chances to win this thing?"

The truth was she hadn't even thought about it, but she was too angry to defend herself.

"Screw you. You're supposed to be my friend. That's what we said, that we're better as friends."

His cheeks flushed red and his jaw muscles clenched as he crossed his arms over his chest. There was no sign of his easy smile now. "We are—"

"Some friend, trying to hook up with my competition," she said, not wanting to let the bitterness seep into her voice. She was unsuccessful.

He opened his mouth to speak and then closed it again as Roy appeared in the doorway, walkie-talkie crackling at his hip. Jasmine's shoulders sagged as the argument came to an abrupt end. She didn't want to know what he would've said next.

"Jasmine?" Roy glared at Teddy, who shrunk back against the wall. She didn't know how much the old man had heard, but it made Jasmine feel a little better to know he was on her side. "You ready to go?"

"I'm all set."

Five minutes ago, she was ready, mentally prepared and focused. Now, she was a mess of anger and frustration, her heart racing and her blood at a boil. She had to get herself under control. She pushed past Teddy, leaving him in the locker room as she followed Roy down the hallway. Indy was already waiting at the door to her changing room, fists clenched against the straps of her racket bag, knuckles white.

Though it felt like hours ago, her father's advice popped into her head. *Indy's got power, but she's sloppy. Be patient like always and you shouldn't have any problems.* If Indy was nervous then she'd be even more careless than usual. The more controlled and conservative Jasmine played, the more likely Indy would be to overplay and make an error.

Jasmine inhaled through her nose, feeling the anger flow out of her body as her game plan took hold. Then she let the air spill out from her lungs, and her nerves with it. She didn't have time for nerves right now; she could worry about everything later, after her victory party.

The radio crackled again as Dom's voice came through. "Let's get this show on the road."

"All right, ladies, if y'all are ready, let's get goin'."

The hum of the crowd swirled around them like a tornado building to a roar. The stands were full, coaches and players, sponsors and the media, all parties eager to catch a glimpse of the future of tennis. There were cameras surrounding the court from every angle. The match was being streamed live over OBX's website.

Jasmine's eyes flew over the stands, finding Harold Hodges sitting beside her father, notebook at the ready. The tournament would be a huge part of the *Athlete Weekly* feature. She found her dad and he gave her a thumbs-up.

A few rows away, Teddy walked down an aisle toward his brother. His face was drawn and serious. Jack said something to him; Teddy shrugged, then threw himself into his seat, arms crossed over his chest.

Since she'd known him, Teddy was always on her side. He was always a voice in the crowd cheering her on, supporting her. Now their friendship was torn to pieces and she wasn't sure if they could repair it or if she even wanted to. Was it worth it? Would she be able to stand watching him go back to his old ways, jumping from girl to girl or, worse, committing to someone else?

"Welcome, everyone, to the final of the Outer Banks Classic." Dom's voice, enhanced by the microphone he held in the center of the court, broke through her thoughts. "Today's final features two athletes from right here at OBX, Indiana Gaffney and Jasmine Randazzo. Ladies, please approach the net for the coin toss."

Jasmine tore her eyes from the crowd and pushed all thoughts of Teddy Harrison out of her mind. She glanced over at Indy, and if it was possible, the blond looked even more nervous than she had in the tunnel. There was no way to predict how a player would respond to the pressure of an important match. Some players, like Penny, were immune to it. Others battled with the nerves until they learned how to deal with them, and some players, no matter how talented, never overcame the fear of the big moment.

It was time to prove to the world—and Dom—what kind of player she was and, while she was at it, show Indiana Gaffney she was in way over her head.

"Out!" the line judge called, arm shooting out, indicating wide.

"Game, Randazzo," the chair umpire said.

Across the court, Indy stood, hands on her hips, staring at the ground beneath her feet. Her shoulders rose and fell with every breath, coming hard and heavy as they neared the end of the first set in the best-of-three-set match.

Jasmine had spent the days leading up to this match shortening her reaction time and prepping her return game in anticipation of facing Indy's killer serve. So far, all that preparation was proving unnecessary. She was playing well, but her 5–1 lead in the first set was due more to Indy's self-destructing than anything Jasmine was doing. Indy's serve was all over the place, and the rest of her game was inconsistent—she sprayed forehands and backhands with plenty of power but no accuracy and planted herself behind the baseline, leaving the front court wide open.

Indy was playing right into her hands as Jasmine forced her to scramble all over the court. The weather was cooperating, too. The sun was beating down on them, and slowly but surely, the velocity of Indy's serve was dropping, giving Jasmine an even larger advantage.

She checked the clock in the corner of the court. The match was only twenty minutes old. Jasmine was serving, and after she won this game, she would take the first set.

"Quiet, please," the chair umpire said, admonishing the crowd, most of whom had lost interest in the one-sided match and started conversations.

Jasmine approached the baseline and waited for Indy to do the same. She had the mental edge in the match and she wasn't about to relinquish it. Solid shots, nothing too crazy, allowing Indy to make the mistakes, and the first set would belong to her.

Finally, Indy stepped up to the baseline, bending at the waist, racket held out in front of her as she shifted her weight left to right.

Jasmine tossed the ball into the air, then, instead of hammering through the back of the ball, she hit through the side. It was a subtle adjustment, no more than a millimeter or two, creating a slice spin on her serve and forcing Indy to lunge out wide.

Indy got there, blocking the ball back. Jasmine charged the net, taking a swing on the run and smacking the weak return into the opposite corner, giving Indy no chance to retrieve it.

"Fifteen–love," the umpire said.

The crowd applauded politely.

Jasmine pulled a ball from the hidden pocket under her tennis skirt and compared it to the offering from the ball girl. She returned the fluffier one and looked to Indy, once again bent at the middle, physically ready to receive the serve but, from the look on her face, mentally all over the place.

This time Jasmine stuck to her flat serve. She didn't have a ton of power, but what she lacked in velocity, she made up for in control. The serve drew Indy to the center of the court, allowing her to return it but opening up the corners. Jasmine shifted her feet, angling her body as she hit a forehand. Then, as Indy's momentum carried her across the court, she moved up again, taking the next shot off Indy's racket and burying it deep into the opposite corner.

"Thirty–love."

Jasmine couldn't hold in her smile as Indy chucked her racket against the ground in frustration. Tennis, at the highest levels, was more a mental game than anything else. If a player couldn't keep her head, she didn't have a chance against one who could.

She served again, a measured, solid serve right down the middle of the court. It was even slower than her last. Indy's body buckled as she misjudged the velocity. She stepped into the forehand, a harsh grunt forcing its way out of her lungs as she sent the ball sailing long and deep across the court.

Jasmine stepped out of the way, letting the ball fly by her.

"Out," the line judge shouted.

"Forty–love."

She had three set points, three chances to close this one out and be halfway to the championship.

Across the court, Indy stood flat-footed, racket ready, but her shoulders slumped and her back was stiff. She looked beaten. Jasmine fired a serve as hard as she could down the middle of the court, but Indy didn't even react. She simply turned and moved back to her chair at the side of the court.

Jasmine pumped her fist. Looking up into the crowd, she found her dad, applauding like a madman, a large, silly grin spread across his face. One more set. All she had to do was keep steady for one more set. Defense, patience, and a cool head, that's all it would take.

"Game," the chair umpire said. "Randazzo leads, one set to love."

Chapter 12

PATHETIC, TOTALLY PATHETIC.

Indy fell into her chair and took her towel from the ball girl. She buried her face into it, muffling a scream, before tossing it over her head, trying to create some shelter from the blistering sun; the heat and humidity were teaming up to torture her.

She rubbed at her eyes, trying to clear her head, before sitting up and letting the towel fall around her shoulders. Reaching into her bag, she pulled out a sports drink. She needed to replenish the electrolytes she'd lost in the last—she glanced at the match clock in the corner of the court—twenty-three minutes. Twenty-three pathetic minutes and she was already down a set. It was the nerves; she couldn't shake them.

It began in the locker room. Teddy stopped by and wished her luck as she got her wrist taped. After he left, followed by the trainer, the pre-match jitters showed up, butterflies in her stomach—anticipation, not anxiety.

Then she heard the voices carrying down the tunnel from the locker room across the hall—Teddy's and Jasmine's voices. They were fighting about their friendship and a hookup and *her*. Everything suddenly made sense; Jasmine was in love with Teddy.

Indy refused to blame herself. She wasn't interested and it wasn't her problem that Jasmine liked him. Yet, she couldn't help feeling a little guilty, and that jangled her nerves more. Then Roy was at the door and they were walking onto the court, louder than earlier in the week, the heavy bass of the music pounding out from the speakers, pulsing through her chest, and the crowd buzzing with excitement. This match wasn't about beating Jasmine Randazzo or winning the Classic; it was about proving to herself that she belonged here. She caught sight of Caroline and Mr. Franklin from Solaris Beachwear in the stands. When Dom called her and Jasmine to the center of the court for the coin toss, her hands had started to shake.

They were still sitting together now, but Solaris Beachwear wouldn't want anything to do with her after this display. Maybe Caroline wouldn't either, and that would be the only positive thing about her performance so far.

Nothing was working.

Her serve was a mess and her rally strokes were out of control. Also, there was no denying it. Jasmine Randazzo was flat-out awesome. She could track down almost any shot, her quick feet eating up the court like a roadrunner. She also had the uncanny ability to force mistakes. Indy didn't know how she did it. The point would be rolling along and then, out of nowhere, her ball would find the net or spin wide.

Indy's grip on her racket tightened, the urge to slam it into the ground again rushing through her as she sat, leg bouncing, waiting for the second set to begin. She held in the frustration and closed her eyes.

She had to stop it. Dom wouldn't have brought her to OBX if he didn't think she could hack it. He wouldn't have ranked her fourth if he didn't think she could win. And up until the day she died, her mother had believed in her. If she couldn't conjure up any faith in herself, she could at least believe in *their* belief. Her leg stopped shaking and the tightness in her neck and shoulders ebbed away.

Forcing her eyes open, she stared at the scoreboard. The match was best of three. She still had time to fix this. She would serve to start the second set. Goal one, win that first game. The question was, how?

She had to change it up. Like Coach D'Amato taught her on her first day with her Einsteins, doing the same thing over and over and expecting a different result wasn't going to work. It was time to try something new.

Maybe serve and volley. She'd been focusing on her footwork since she got to OBX, but despite that, she still wasn't totally comfortable up at the net, where footwork was the most important thing. The idea did have one major advantage, though. It would shock the hell out of her opponent. What was the worst that could happen? She was already losing, halfway to a crushing defeat. Anything was better than what she'd suffered through in the first set.

"Time," the chair ump said through his microphone.

She glanced over at Jasmine, who was digging through her bag, probably confident she'd already won the match, maybe thinking about the party her parents would throw to celebrate the victory.

Indy leapt to her feet. This set would be better than the first, and that started with better body language. Sometimes standing up tall and lifting your chin could help make a long, uphill battle seem a little easier.

Jasmine took her time, examining her racket as she walked to her side of the court. Indy was ready and waiting at the baseline.

Finally, the other girl was ready to receive, twirling her racket in her hands, bent at the waist, a few steps into the backcourt.

Indy slammed a serve, and as it left her racket, she raced forward, careful not to get too close to the net. Jasmine blocked it back easily, but Indy was right there waiting. The ball touched the strings at the perfect angle, and with a quick flick of her wrist she hit a short volley winner while Jasmine stood stunned behind the baseline.

"Fifteen–love."

Indy turned to the ball girl, signaling for her towel. The heat was still crushing the court. Wiping her face and her arms, she didn't look back. She didn't need to see Jasmine's face. She could imagine the expression, mouth agape, holding her racket down at her knees, one hand propped on her hip, wondering where the hell that came from.

A murmur spread through the crowd. Indy had their

attention. Now she had to get them on her side. She just had to show them she had a chance.

She'd confused Jasmine with the last point. Tennis was a game of adjustments, but it was tough to adjust on the fly. If she piggybacked that serve and volley with another, Jasmine probably wouldn't be ready for it.

Indy fired a bullet up the T again, Jasmine returned it the same way, and again Indy raced up the court to meet it, slicing another volley beyond Jasmine's reach.

"Yes," she said, her voice echoing through the court, as the crowd was still quiet, respectful of the silence necessary to play the game.

"Thirty–love."

Their eyes met and she almost smiled at the hard expression on Jasmine's face.

Now it was time to switch it up. Jasmine would think she knew what was coming. She'd be ready to attack Indy's serve and volley, the same way she'd attacked her power game in the first set. Indy fired a serve and Jasmine returned it, but this time she stayed back at the baseline as Jasmine took a few hesitant steps in, anticipating a volley. Instead, Indy wound up and shot a forehand past her, skimming it off the white line for a clean winner.

"Forty–love."

The crowd cheered the point—not indifferent and polite applause, but loud voices engaging in the match. They were rooting for her, acknowledging her trying after such an awful showing in the first set. Tennis fans were all alike, and what they wanted was very simple: more tennis. If Indy won this set, the match would go to a deciding third, and that's what they wanted to see.

"Quiet, please," the umpire said. The crowd noise faded to a soft hum, but the buzz was there, like electricity flowing through the air. As Indy ran her towel over her forehead, she let that energy wash over her, drawing it into her. She looked back over the net. Jasmine was ready, but the confusion was written across her face; she was clearly wondering how this had all gone so wrong. Indy had her. Now all she had to do was execute.

Confidence flowed through Indy's veins. Her serve felt good for the first time all match, and she was ready to unleash it. She rocked forward and then back, her body coiling powerfully as her racket swung down and then up, whistling through the air, and she launched the ball as hard as she could. A split second later, the ball ricocheted off the wall behind Jasmine.

"Come on!" Indy shouted, pumping her fist and then looking up into the crowd. They responded, the noise growing to a roar. Her adrenaline spiked and she drew energy off them, despite the heat and the mountain she still had to climb. She was almost there.

"Game, Gaffney."

Tied. They were tied. Indy had never played a match this tough in her life. Jasmine was the best player she'd ever faced: poised, polished, and an absolute defensive demon, all-out effort all the time. But once Indy'd gotten over her nerves, they matched up pretty well. So well that she managed to eke out a one-game victory in the second set, and now... now they were even, two sets all and locked together in a third-set tiebreak, five points each, both of them two points from the championship.

One way or another, it was almost over.

And thank God, because she was fucking exhausted.

The crowd rose to their feet, giving them a standing ovation, showing their appreciation for such a hard-fought match, regardless of who won or lost.

Indy moved to the other side of the court. She checked the match clock in the corner: 2 hr 45 min. Definitely not pathetic; more than respectable, bordering on epic. There were no announcers, no TV crew in a box high above the court analyzing the match, but she could hear their voices in her head talking about how her power serve was a major advantage in a tiebreak, but that Jasmine's better conditioning might cancel it out.

Blissfully, cloud cover and a soft breeze swept in off the water. The cooler air was a relief against her skin after nearly three hours baking under the sun. Indy looked at the sky. A few more minutes, she pleaded with the clouds. She needed a few more minutes of shade. She couldn't last much longer; it was time to take a risk, go for a line and hope it landed in.

Jasmine was preparing to serve. It was the weakest part of her game, and the longer the match went on, the weaker it got. Indy was ready to expose that weakness one more time.

Jasmine leaned back, then pushed up and out, the ball hitting her racket with a soft *thwack*.

The serve was slow and flat, bouncing up at the perfect height for Indy's forehand. She stepped into the shot and rifled a winner up the line.

The crowd erupted, people leaping to their feet, screaming and cheering, applauding like crazy, but they weren't done yet.

"Gaffney leads the tiebreaker six points to five. Championship point."

Indy tried to ignore the wall of sound crashing down onto the court; it was almost as oppressive as the heat.

Match point.

"Thank you, players are ready," the chair umpire said. "Thank you." The crowd quieted, though not entirely, the energy still reverberating through the court, waiting to ignite again.

In a tiebreak, the players alternate serves, and it was Indy's turn. She had enough energy in her tank for one more. It was time to end this. She took her time, making sure her rhythm was perfect. Her muscles bunched and then she snapped up and through the air, sending a low-lying missile across the court. Then, with a final burst of energy, she sprinted forward, meeting Jasmine's return with a sharp-swinging volley. The ball hit the blue hard court just inside the line. Jasmine's sneakers squeaked against the ground as she raced forward to get to the ball, but before she could reach it, it bounced again.

"Game, set, and match, Gaffney."

She did it. She won, and that was her last coherent thought

before she collapsed to the ground in exhausted, victorious sobs.

Indy sat on the trainer's table in the center of the room, trying to slow everything down, but her head was still spinning. Showered and dressed, she was ready for the party at Deuce about to be held in her honor. She had brought a dress with her just in case, along with a pair of sweats and a T-shirt she would have worn back to the dorms had she lost.

It was all a blur after that last point. She remembered shaking hands with Jasmine and the chair umpire, then moving back onto the court and applauding the crowd, clapping her racket against the heel of her hand, thanking them for their support. Dom brought the trophy out to her, congratulating her on the win, and he hadn't seemed all that surprised at the result. Then she floated back to the locker room holding the trophy tightly to her chest.

She won. It was one thing to wish it or to imagine it, but it was totally different to have done it. She beat Jasmine Randazzo and a handful of the best young players in the world. That made her one of the best, right? No, that made her *the* best. This was everything she and her mom had dreamed about, and now it was real. A prickling of tears edged out of the corners of her eyes, and for the first time in a long time, she let them fall.

"You're going to freak everyone out if you show up at the party still hysterical crying," Penny said from the doorway.

Indy wiped at her eyes quickly. "Sorry, it's a lot to take in."

Penny pulled a tissue from the container on the trainer's table and held it out for her. "Don't try. You might hurt yourself. After all, you are pretty thickheaded. It took you an entire set before you figured out you had to go serve and volley."

Indy took the tissue, dabbing under her eyes, and laughed. "You coming to the party?"

"Uh, no, sorry. Tonight's about you."

"It's okay. I get it," Indy said, standing up and smoothing down the skirt of her dress. If Penny went to the party, she'd be a distraction to the sponsors and media.

"Anyway, I just wanted to be the first to congratulate you," she said, opening her arms, and Indy fell into the hug gratefully. "You should get up to Deuce. Everyone's waiting for you." She stepped away and turned to leave but paused at the door. "Oh and, Indy? Good luck."

"What do you mean?"

"You'll see. Welcome to the club."

Penny's meaning was crystal clear as soon as Indy stepped through the doors at Deuce.

A group of fellow OBX players rushed her, pulling her in for hugs and congratulating her.

"You were awesome, Indy," Addison said, hugging her tightly.

"Beyond amazing," a girl whose name she didn't know said, grasping her hand and squeezing it. She even saw Lara standing at the edge of the crowd, though she wasn't quite brave enough to join in. Could they be any more superficial? She was suddenly grateful for the way they acted when she first arrived. There wouldn't be a struggle to weed out the genuine people from the fakes.

"Thanks, guys," she said, pulling away from them, only to be intercepted by Dom. Her coach's arm came around her shoulders as he led her to a group of gentlemen, the rep from Solaris Beachwear among them. Jack was there, chatting with a man she didn't recognize, and a step or two away, Caroline was all smiles next to Harold Hodges, chatting with her hands flying around her as the reporter nodded along with whatever she was rambling about.

After more handshakes than she could count and hearing more names than she'd ever be able to remember, Indy was practically swaying on her feet. She had no idea where Dom had vanished to, but she was caught in a sea of well-wishers, all of whom seemed desperate to congratulate her.

"Indy, what a win," yet another man in a suit said. She had no idea who he was, but that was par for the course. She had to get used to people she didn't know knowing who she was. "I'd love to talk to you about representation." Apparently he was an agent. He held out a business card. Indy took it, but before she could even glance at the name, a hand snatched it from her grip.

"Now, now, Mark, you know better than that," Jack Harrison said, shoving the card back at the man, whose mouth turned down into a scowl, but then he nodded sharply and walked away.

Indy looked up at Jack, brow furrowed, but before she could speak, his hand cupped her elbow, and with the gentlest of pressure, he steered her away from the group.

"Sorry about that," he said when they reached an empty corner of the room. He stood in front of her, blocking her from view. "Mark D'Angelis is the worst kind of agent. He runs his clients into the ground, sucking every dollar from them, and then drops them as soon as their play suffers. Signing with Caroline Morneau is one thing. She's a shark, but she wants what's best for her clients. D'Angelis is a snake."

"Oh," she said, the tension that had been building in her shoulders since she arrived at the party suddenly loosening when she realized no one could see her. "Thanks for getting me out of there. I was . . . This is so . . ."

"Overwhelming? You looked like you were about to keel over," Jack said. "All this can be difficult at first."

She laughed a little. "Yeah, I think Penny tried to warn me, but I wasn't expecting . . . I don't—I guess I wasn't expecting anyone to care."

"Of course they care. You won. Congratulations, by the way."

Shrugging, she said, "It doesn't seem real. I can't believe it yet."

Jack laughed, his green eyes hypnotizing in their intensity. "I can." The soft tone of his voice sent her back to the night before the tournament. Just thinking about the kiss he gave her on the cheek made her toes curl. It was so innocent. But it still made her mind reel. If his lips against her cheek felt like that, what would it feel like to really kiss him? His mouth on hers or maybe her neck, and his hands, his hands at her hips and her thighs and then between them, forever making her own hands feel incredibly inadequate at the task.

"What are you doing here, anyway?" she asked, trying to banish those unhelpful thoughts and keep him talking, hoping he wouldn't shut down on her again.

"There were a couple of sponsors I had to firm things up with before they left town, *and* I wanted to congratulate you."

"Indiana!" Caroline's voice carried into their corner.

She groaned, not thinking, and leaned forward, her forehead landing against Jack's shoulder. He stiffened for a moment before his large, warm hand came up to rest against her back, not quite an embrace, but close enough for Indy to pretend. She let herself relish the closeness for a second and then she stood, straightening her shoulders.

"Ah, there you are," Caroline said, reaching out to drag her away again, but Indy pulled back.

"Just a second," Indy said, and Caroline stepped back a few feet, keeping her eyes locked on her.

Jack cleared his throat. "I should get going." He hesitated for a moment before he stepped closer, pressing his lips against her cheek. Indy tried to fight the instinct to tilt her head a fraction of an inch and end this torturous game he insisted on playing. It was a losing battle for them both. She turned, and so did he, their lips brushing softly, chastely, but it was enough to send instantaneous electricity snapping through her veins at the ghost of the touch, her entire body swaying forward into his. At the contact, he pulled back and stared at her wide-eyed, mouth opening and closing, breath ragged, but not uttering a word. Then, after a few silent, tense moments, he nodded a farewell, turned, and left.

Indy watched him go, pressing her fingers against her still-tingling lips.

"He is very handsome," Caroline said.

"Yes, he is," Indy agreed.

"He is Penny Harrison's brother and agent as well, no?" Her tone was casual, too casual to truly be so. Caroline was a shark. Jack was right. Of course he was right. He was brilliant and she'd kissed him—kind of.

"Indiana?" Caroline said, looking at her expectantly.

"Sorry, were you saying something?"

"Yes, I was congratulating you again on a wonderful performance out on the court today. Simply fantastique."

"Thank you."

"I have been speaking to several sponsors tonight. I do not have to tell you that you are very interesting to them. Your looks and the potential they see, it is an excellent combination. I will be speaking to Dominic. This win, it will mean wild cards, Indiana, and wild cards will put you on the biggest stage in the world. These companies will be willing to pay to see their brands showcased on that stage, but my hands are tied until you make your decision."

Caroline gestured out into the party, where men and women in business attire were working the room. Tennis was a high-end sport, and its sponsors leaned toward the ritzy side of the market. Which companies were interested in her? Rolex? Longines? Nike? Lacoste?

She bit her lip, suddenly feeling guilty. Caroline had been working on her behalf without any guarantee that Indy would actually sign with her. She was a shark, but maybe in a world where people treated you like bait, maybe she needed a shark.

"Okay."

Caroline tilted her head. "Okay?"

"Okay, I'm in. Where do I sign?"

The agent's smile was as wide as her stiletto heels were tall. She pulled a file folder from her large clutch purse and then offered Indy a pen.

"Your signature here."

She signed her name quickly.

"Magnifique," Caroline said, adding her own signature. "You will not regret this decision, Indiana. You are talented, very talented, more so than you even realize, I think."

"I think I'm starting to understand."

Chapter 13

RIVULETS OF SWEAT DRIPPED FROM HER FOREHEAD AS PENNY attacked the ball. Air pushed through her lungs; she grunted with the effort of playing the ricochets off the wall. She counted in her head: ninety-eight, ninety-nine, one hundred backhands. She let the ball fly by her after the last stroke, her eyes slipping closed as she tried to regain her breath. It was a good workout, but it hadn't solved the problem.

Her hands fell to her hips. "Damn it."

With the rhythm of each solid shot against the wall, she could hear Alex calling her "love," his voice in that half-sarcastic lilt, the smallest touch setting her entire body on fire, then that other way he spoke sometimes, the earnest, deep tones telling her she was the most incredible-looking girl he'd ever seen. They hadn't even spoken since their almost kiss, not even during training. She wasn't sure if he was avoiding her or the other way around, maybe both. Pushing herself to near exhaustion wasn't working. No matter how hard she went at it, it was impossible to clear her mind. It was like Australia all over again and she couldn't let that happen. Not when Paris was in five days.

She tossed her racket against the fence surrounding the small half-court used for groundstroke drills, grabbed a towel from her bag, and wiped the sweat from her forehead, down her arms, and across her midriff. Her sports bra and shorts were soaked through.

Her breath came back to her and she took a small swig of water before picking up her racket again—one hundred forehands and then she'd call it a day.

Penny wandered to the locker room, muscles aching pleasantly after her long workout, but she hesitated at the door. She didn't want to go home. She turned around and walked down the path, away from the locker rooms and toward the beach. Glancing up at the sky, she noticed that the sun was beginning to set. She could get in a quick run on the sand before it got too dark. And then she could pass out on her bed exhausted enough that maybe, just maybe, she wouldn't dream of him.

Her thoughts turned into a complete mess as her feet pushed through the sand. She stayed close to the water where the ground was firmer, but her calves still burned with the effort. Her focus needed to be completely on tennis and not on Alex Russell or his stupid meditation exercises or their almost kiss or why he was almost kissing her if he was going to dinner with Caroline Morneau or how four months after their night together, she could still feel a thrill surge through her body at the mere thought of those moments in his arms.

Up ahead, she saw a dark lump sitting in the sand, the setting sun reflecting off something next to it.

As she jogged closer, the lump took human shape: a man hunched over, knees up, and a glass bottle wedged into the sand beside him. Alex. He caught sight of her as she drew near and he held the bottle aloft, saluting her, before taking a long draft from it.

"What are you doing here?" she asked, stopping a few feet away.

"I live here," he said, jerking his thumb back to the house a few yards up the beach. "What are you doing here? Come back for that kiss, did you?"

She ignored the biting tone in his voice. "Trying to clear my head."

"Well, we wouldn't want that head of yours foggy, would we? You might do something stupid like give me the time of day."

"You're drunk."

"A little," he admitted, standing up and dusting off his jeans. "This is how I clear my head, love. You know, when the meditation doesn't quite do the job."

"There are better ways," she said, though she was vastly tempted to throw herself onto the sand, steal the bottle, and drown her problems in alcohol.

"You run until you're so tired you pass out. I drink until I pass out. Don't see there's much of a difference."

The conversation was going nowhere fast. "Fine. Enjoy your bottle." She wanted to turn around and keep running, but there was this inexplicable need inside of her to be near him. When he wasn't around, it was a tiny ache, a constant reminder that something was missing. Now that he was there, standing inches away, close enough to reach out and touch, it was so much worse.

"Penny?"

"Yeah?"

"You're still here."

"Yeah, um," she said, her mind racing to come up with an excuse.

He reached out a hand and she stared at it for a split second, hesitating as if it might burn her. She pressed her hand into his and shivered as the calloused tips of his fingers slid across her skin. Looking up, she saw he'd moved closer, close enough to bend his head to hers, if he wanted, close enough to—

"Penny," he murmured nearly against her lips before he touched them with his. He slanted his mouth over hers, deepening the kiss immediately. She could taste the alcohol on his tongue, but it barely registered as she pushed up onto her toes, winding an arm over his shoulders, hooking a finger into the belt loop of his jeans, anchoring herself to him. His stubble scratched against her cheeks and his hands fell to her hips, pulling her body into his, their hips colliding, before one hand slid up to her neck and the other down over her backside. A jolt surged through her as a low moan escaped from the back of her throat.

He broke away then and trailed his hot, open mouth across her jawline and over her neck. Penny shivered in his arms as his lips hovered over her pulse point.

"Stay with me," he mumbled, his teeth scraping lightly against her skin.

"What?" she asked, trying to force herself to focus on his words and not the feeling of his fingertips slipping beneath the hem of her running jacket, brushing against the skin of her waist.

"The house I'm letting, it's right there. Stay with me tonight," he whispered, cupping her cheek and pressing a soft kiss to her lips again. His eyes softened. "Penny," he started again, but she stepped away from him, cutting him off. He was drunk. She shouldn't be doing this. Who knew if he would even remember this in the morning?

"I'm sorry."

And she sprinted down the beach knowing her dreams would be full of him, no matter how fast she ran.

Awkward. That was the only way Penny could describe the heavy silence that hung over the office the next morning as she and Alex waited for Dom to arrive. There were only inches separating the two chairs in front of the desk, and that meant she was sitting only inches away from Alex after a text from their coach had summoned them both there instead of where they should be, out on the training court.

What the hell was taking Dom so long? It was seven o'clock in the morning. Nothing else was going on at OBX except breakfast, and so help her, if she was sitting in the most painfully awkward situation of her life while he was enjoying his morning coffee, coach or not, she was going to let him have it. She started tapping her fingers against the wooden arm of the chair.

Granted, she'd still have to be near Alex, but at least they'd have something else to do, a distraction from how good it had felt to give in, to finally close the space between them. Penny had never been kissed like that, not even by him, like she was the only thing holding him together, like he needed her.

She glanced to her right and had to suppress a sigh. He looked like hell—dark purple circles under his eyes, drawn expression, shoulders slumped. He looked as bad as she felt.

Suddenly, a large hand landed on top of hers, ceasing the tapping. "Please stop," Alex rasped. She stiffened and nodded. Their eyes met for the first time since she'd walked into the room to find him sitting there, head hanging back, legs extended out in front of him, crossed at the ankles.

"Ah, good, you're both here," Dom said, jogging up the last few steps into his office. They turned toward him together and Alex's hand shot away from hers, but not before Dom saw it and raised his eyebrows. He pushed on, however. "Sorry about the wait," he said, but didn't offer an explanation. He stepped behind his desk and sat down, picking up a thick envelope and fiddling with the flap.

"So," he said, looking back and forth between them, "do you want the good news or the bad news?"

"Bad," Alex muttered.

"Good," Penny said right over him.

Dom snorted and shook his head. "The draw is out for Paris."

Penny sat up straight, but Alex didn't move.

"Funny enough, you're ranked the same, twenty-five."

"Lovely," Alex said through a grunt.

"Damn it," Penny said. She knew her ranking might drop after not playing in Rome, but she'd hoped to stay in the top twenty. "When would I get Lutrova?"

"Third round," Dom said, winking at her. "So, the end of week one."

"Gotta win two matches first, love," Alex quipped, his posture unchanged.

Penny rolled her eyes and then turned to Dom. "Wait, was that the good news or the bad news?"

Dom grimaced, opening the envelope. "That was the good news." He stood, pulling out two packets of paper and handing one to each of them. It was a printout of the *Athlete Weekly* website, and there, front and center, was a collage of pictures from the past week, and every single one was of her and Alex. The photo in the center was from their photo shoot, but it was surrounded by candid shots. The first was from the Classic Reception, Alex towering over her, a tumbler in his hand, while she glared up at him. The next was of them arguing over a point on the practice court; another was of them on that same court, lying down, hands entwined; and the last was from that same night, him leaning in, his mouth hovering above hers, her fingers curled around the cotton of his T-shirt.

"Now, look," Dom said, "what either of you does off the court is none of my business, but—"

"You're right," Alex cut him off. "This is none of your damn business."

Dom raised his hands up in surrender. "Easy there, Al. I'm not the enemy here. I was on the phone with Hodges already this morning, but he claims he didn't take these pictures. He says they were sent in anonymously and when his editor saw them, he was forced to run them."

"Dom, this isn't what it looks like," Penny said, scanning through the article quickly. From what she could tell, they were creating their own narrative, starting with Australia—she and Alex leaving the Nike party together, then the motorcycle accident with another woman, filling in the blanks with whatever garbage they thought would sell the most magazines and whatever Hodges observed while he was at OBX. Apparently, she and Alex Russell had a rocky on-again, off-again relationship, which she didn't want to commit to because he was bad for her public image, and with that, Penny stopped reading and crumpled up the papers. "None of this is true."

"I don't know," Alex said, finally sitting up, as he read through the article. "Some of it they nailed right on the head."

Penny turned, ready to blast him, but Dom said, "Look, like I said, this is none of my business, but what do you want me to say once the phone calls start pouring in?"

"No comment," they said together.

Penny laughed, though there was absolutely no humor in it. At least that was one thing they could agree on.

Chapter 14

JASMINE BURIED HER FACE INTO HER PILLOW. SHE WASN'T ready to face the day. She could still hear it in her mind, like a song on infinite repeat for the last two days. The chair umpire's voice amplified by the microphone—*Game, set, and match, Gaffney*—as the crowd roared.

Sleep was impossible. She tossed and turned late into the night, body exhausted, but replaying the match over and over again. Then the expression on her father's face when he saw her afterward would swim behind her eyes, part disappointment and part disbelief. She'd let him down and that hurt even more than the loss itself.

"Jasmine!" Her mother's voice carried up the stairs, followed by the pounding of footsteps. "Jasmine, wake up!" Her mom, bracelets jangling, burst through her door and grabbed her duvet cover, yanking it away.

"Mom," she grumbled. "Go away."

She'd been staying at her parents' house in her childhood bedroom since the Classic, not wanting to face anyone on campus. Her dad's disappointment was one thing; the poorly disguised glee of the people she thought were her friends was another.

"You have to get up, mija. You gave yourself a couple of days to wallow. You lost. It happens from time to time, but today you must go back to training. The OBX Classic is over and the French Open begins. Simple as cake."

"Pie. Simple as pie or piece of cake." Even after nearly twenty years in the States, her mom tended to mix up her idioms.

"Cake, pie, I love both. Now, get up." She felt a soft tap against her backside and then her curtains and windows were thrown wide open, the morning air blowing in and the sunlight blinding her.

Jasmine rolled over, sitting up, and her stomach lurched. She couldn't go in and face everyone, not after that loss, and not after what the *Athlete Weekly* article wrote about her.

Dom probably went nuts on Hodges for focusing his article on Penny and Alex's off-the-court relationship in what was supposed to be a serious sports publication, but it wasn't the tabloid crap that worried Jasmine. It was a separate section entirely, one that focused on the results of the Classic.

> *Mental toughness is a necessary quality in any champion. Both John Randazzo and Lisa Vega had it in spades, along with superior athleticism and instinct, but the same can't be said for their daughter, who folded under the pressure in the*

tournament's final after coasting through a relatively weak field...

There, in black and white, was an analysis of what had happened during the final match that hit far too close to home. Athleticism, instinct, mental toughness, things necessary to succeed as a top athlete in any sport, qualities Harold Hodges, a tennis expert, didn't think she possessed.

That was why the loss was eating away at her. She'd lost big matches before and they were always disappointing, but this one was different. It was a match she should've been able to win. The competition at the Classic was good, but at the end of the day, it was only the up-and-coming talent that played in it, and up-and-coming didn't necessarily translate to a career on tour. Indiana was very good, but she had a week of elite-level coaching under her belt after a two-year hiatus and managed to beat her. It shouldn't have happened, and yet it did.

"What if he's right? What if I'm not good enough?"

"Mija, he is one man." Her mom sat down beside her on the bed and wrapped her arm around her shoulders. "He is one man who watched you play for one week. He is not God. He is not the final word."

"He's one of the best tennis reporters in the world." She slipped out from under the embrace and stood, crossing her arms over her chest.

"It's his opinion. He doesn't know you and the article is trash."

It didn't make her feel any better, but she knew her mom wouldn't stop, so she plastered a grin on her face and nodded.

"Fine, you're right. He's one man and he doesn't know me."

"Good, get dressed. I'll make you breakfast before training." Sometimes her mom saw what she wanted to see and not what was right in front of her.

Jasmine eyed the crumpled printout of the article sitting on her nightstand next to her phone, which had finally stopped beeping at her after she ignored Teddy's tenth message. Harold Hodges was one man, a man who didn't know her game beyond what he saw last week. Her parents were great, but they couldn't be objective. And Teddy, he was the last person she wanted to talk to about anything. There was only one person she knew who would be brutally honest.

The atrium was empty when she arrived at OBX, aside from Roy, his nose buried in his newspaper as usual. Jasmine made a beeline for Dom's office, knowing he usually set aside mornings for paperwork. As she climbed the stairs, she had to move aside for Penny, who nodded at her quickly, and Alex Russell, trailing behind, his eyes boring into the back of Penny's head.

"Jasmine," Dom said from behind his desk as she entered his office. He motioned for her to take a seat. "What can I do for you?"

She ignored him. "You know why I'm here."

Dom pinched the bridge of his nose. "That damn article. I wish I'd never agreed to it."

She nodded, but Dom's regrets were the least of her worries.

"Was he right?" she asked.

He leaned forward, rubbing his face with both hands, before looking at her again. "Jasmine, you've got to understand, Hodges wasn't writing about how you performed in the tournament, at least not entirely. You did a great job against your competition, and that final match, well no one saw that coming."

"Then what was he writing about?"

Dom paused, pulling his lips into a thin line.

Jasmine felt her knees shake and she let herself sink into a chair across from him. "You agree with him."

"No." There was no hesitation, and Jasmine felt a little better, but he still hadn't given her a straight answer. "I think his analysis was shortsighted at best."

"Then what? Either I have what it takes or I don't."

"It's not that simple. The tennis world isn't black and white. You've worked so hard all these years to try and measure up to your parents." She started to protest, but Dom kept talking. "Don't deny it. I've known you since you were seven years old. I know you want to prove to the world that you're every bit the tennis player the daughter of Lisa Vega and John Randazzo should be."

"But I'm not," she finished for him. "Is that what you're saying? That I'm not as good as my parents?"

"I'm saying that not everyone is top ten material, Jasmine. Not everyone is going to win Grand Slams and Olympic medals."

"Not me, you mean."

"*Not yet.* You're only twenty years old. You have to give

yourself some time. You can still have a very good career. You've got a great head for the game and you're a hard worker."

His words didn't have much meaning in that moment. The whole world expected greatness from her. Good, in the face of those expectations, wasn't good enough.

"Thanks," she said, leaping up from her seat and striding to the stairs.

"Jasmine," Dom called, but she didn't turn back. She didn't need Dom to see her cry. It would be one more thing to add to the list of her faults as a player: emotional basket case.

She raced down the stairs and flew through the atrium toward the women's locker room. There was a maintenance man standing at the end of the hallway, a small power drill pressed into the wall. The shrill whirring of the drill bit securing Indy's victory plaque into the Title Wall was worse than nails on a chalkboard, setting her teeth on edge. She swiped under her eyes, forcing the tears back. After stalking past him into the locker room, she changed into her training clothes and marched out to the practice courts. OBX was in full swing, courts packed with players and coaches.

"Bene, Indiana, keep your feet moving. No hesitation. Bene," Coach D'Amato said as Jasmine stepped onto the court where Indiana Gaffney and the others were on an agility course meant to increase stamina and improve footwork. Jasmine felt her stomach clench. The OBX Champion was getting better, doing what she needed to do to win again.

“Nice job, Indy,” Lara called from the line of girls at the baseline.

Indy skidded to a halt as she finished her agility run, then turned and nodded, but didn’t say anything as she went to the back of the line.

“Ah, Jasmine. Eccellente. Join us.” Coach D’Amato greeted her with a sharp nod. “I will be right back and then you girls will play a set.”

Jasmine blinked in total confusion as her coach left. She was late, but D’Amato hadn’t said anything about Einsteins. Did they really think she was that much of a lost cause? No sense in making her run, because it wouldn’t make her any better. She turned to Indy, whose mouth twisted into a pout, but obviously Indy couldn’t come up with anything to say, so she just shrugged.

Jasmine tried to ignore it, how easy it was for Indy to shrug and dismiss it, just like it had been easy for her to show up and win the tournament Jasmine had been working toward for years. Just like it was easy for her to make Teddy…

Fuck it. She couldn’t think about that. She was here to train.

She took her spot at the front of the line and ran through the agility course, as familiar to her as breathing after years training with Coach D’Amato, her shuffling feet controlled and smooth as she completed the short circuit. She finished up and then made her way to the back of the line, but as she did, her foot tangled with someone else’s.

She stutter-stepped, catching herself just before wiping out entirely, and then she whirled around to see who’d tripped her.

It was Indy's foot. Of course it was.

Jasmine saw red, something inside of her snapping, as blood roared in her ears.

"Really?" she barked, getting right up into Indy's face and looking her dead in the eye, rage fueling every word. "You didn't take enough from me this week, you need to finish the job?"

"It was an accident, I'm—" Indy began, taking a step back.

Jasmine cut off the fake-ass apology. "This was supposed to be my year. And then you came out of nowhere and stole it."

"That's not—" Indy tried again.

"Come on, Jasmine," Lara said, trying to step between the two.

"Stay the hell out of this, you little hypocrite," she snapped, and then whirled to Indiana again. "And don't pretend like you don't know what I'm talking about. You waltzed in here like you owned the damn place. You've been here two seconds. I've been training my whole life, and in one week, you took it all from me."

People were wandering over to the court—the guys' group from the adjacent court; Jack Harrison, who'd been working with them; and dozens of others drawn by Jasmine's raised voice—but the rage boiling through her veins couldn't be cooled, not even by embarrassment. She had to get away before she did something really stupid, like burst into tears in front of everyone. She turned and started to run off the court, but her retreat was interrupted.

"No," Indy yelled at her back.

"No?" Jasmine repeated, wheeling around so fast her

ponytail whipped Indy in the face. "What the hell do you mean, *no*?"

Indy stalked forward, coming straight at her, her hands clenched into fists. "No, you're not going to dump all your shit on me and then run away. I beat you. It's that simple. I beat you. You want to blame someone? Take a look in the mirror. Maybe next time you won't fold under the pressure."

With that parting shot, she spun away. Her long blond braid, a clear attempt to copy Penny Harrison, whipped out behind her as she did and smacked Jasmine straight across the face.

The sting of it combined with the *exact* words Hodges used in the article spilling from the lips of her biggest rival was too much for her.

"You don't know shit about me," Jasmine screeched, and she launched herself forward, grabbing that fucking braid and yanking hard.

Indy wheeled around in time for Jasmine's free hand to strike, open palm to the side of her face.

She lurched backward, her hair slipping from Jasmine's grip, and clutched her cheek, thrown off-balance from the blow. But Jasmine, ready to spring forward and tackle the bitch, wasn't done. Her forward momentum stopped, however, as an arm snaked around her waist and lifted her up and away.

"Easy there." Jack Harrison's voice rumbled through his chest and into her back. She struggled against him for a moment, but his grip was like iron. He took her weight easily enough and carried her off the court. She thought about kicking him in the shins, but once they were outside the gate, he let her down. She pushed her way out of his arms and whirled around to run away but was suddenly face-to-face with Coach D'Amato.

Jasmine felt herself deflate, the reality of what happened, what she'd just done, sinking in. She'd found a new rock bottom, maybe one there was no coming back from, and it was all her own fault.

Chapter 15

INDY SLUMPED IN THE CHAIR ACROSS FROM DOM'S DESK AND propped her elbow on the armrest. Her cheek was still stinging, and she winced as she leaned against an ice pack. Jasmine sat rigid in her seat, staring out of the floor-to-ceiling windows in Dom's office, looking over the grounds and the beach in the distance. Indy's day had started off great—a really tough training session with Coach D'Amato where she pushed herself through agility workouts that a couple of weeks ago would've been impossible for her.

Then Jasmine showed up.

If Indy's face didn't hurt so damn much, she would chuck the ice pack at her and finish off the fight Jack had interrupted. She had been clutching her face, still in shock, when she saw the eldest Harrison emerge from the crowd that gathered, spring over the fence, and pull Jasmine away from her. She almost wished he hadn't gotten there in time. Then her face would still hurt, but she would at least have gotten in a shot or two.

Heavy footsteps on the stairs drew her attention and she lifted her head gingerly as Dom stomped into his office, glaring at them. Indy glared right back. Jasmine could spin the story however she wanted. Indy knew it wasn't her fault.

"As if this day weren't already a shit show, now I have to deal with the two of you," Dom snapped as he moved in front of them. "Do you have anything to say for yourselves?"

"Yeah, I'd really like to know why I'm sitting here," Indy fired back. "I was minding my own business at practice when she storms up, freaks out, and then, when I defended myself, she attacked me."

"I was told exactly what happened, Indiana," Dom said, frowning down at her, "including what you said."

Jasmine made a soft noise in the back of her throat, but it was enough to draw Dom's attention. "As I said, I know *exactly* what happened. Violence is unacceptable, Jasmine. You're done training for the rest of the day."

"What? You can't."

"I can," Dom said.

Indy rolled her eyes. Some punishment. The day off after she already took two to lick her wounds. What a fucking slap on the wrist. She'd bet every dime she had that if the roles were reversed, that punishment would be the tip of the iceberg. No wonder Jasmine couldn't handle losing—consequences were a totally foreign concept.

"Can I go?" Indy asked, starting to stand.

"No. Sit down," Dom barked. She fell back into the chair and winced when her elbow bounced off the armrest, jarring her body and making the entire side of her face ache. "What happened today is my fault. I didn't realize the rivalry between you two had progressed to this level, but that stops today. From now on, you two will train together as a doubles team."

"Absolutely not. I can't train with—"

"You've got to be kidding me. There's—"

"Shut up, the both of you. This is how it's going to be. If you don't like it, you're free to seek out a different coaching situation." His jaw was set, his brow furrowed, and his shoulders held high, body language Indy recognized even after such a short time at OBX. He was dead serious. Silence reigned in the office as Dom looked at Jasmine, then back to her. He pursed his lips and then his posture relaxed, just slightly. "I've been in contact with the tournament officials in Paris. There's a spot in the women's doubles draw opening up. If you two can prove to me that you can work as a team, it's yours."

Indy felt Jasmine's eyes on her, but she wasn't going to look back. "Fine," Indy said, her patience wearing thin. "Now can I go?"

"Go."

She stood, careful not to press the ice pack too hard against her cheek. Not that it mattered much; the side of her face was almost numb and the ice was melting. Frowning, she tossed the damp bag wrapped in a towel to Dom, who caught it. "I'll see you tomorrow."

Jasmine stood, too, but Dom waved her back. "You, sit. We're not done yet."

Indy bolted out of his office and down the stairs, but not

before she heard Dom's sharp "What were you thinking?" Though she didn't hear Jasmine's reply.

The atrium, usually empty during morning practice sessions, was buzzing with players and even a couple of coaches. Most were at least pretending like they had a reason to be there, chatting with Roy or digging through their racket bags, but some were staring up at the windows to Dom's office, obviously trying to figure out what was happening behind the glass. The room held the unnatural silence of too many people trying not to make a sound, and when she emerged from the stairwell, every eye focused on her.

"What?" she shouted, and a visible jolt went through the crowd, sending them scattering.

As the large room emptied out, Indy caught sight of Caroline stepping through the atrium's front doors and then checking in with Roy.

"Indiana," she called out, striding toward her quickly. "I just heard what happened, are you okay?"

"I'm fine," Indy said. "Wait. How did you find out what happened?"

"Dom called me."

Indy scoffed. She didn't need Caroline for something like this.

"It's already taken care of."

Caroline's eyes narrowed. "How has it been taken care of?"

"We have to train together now. He wants us to play women's doubles at the French Open, which would be amazing, if we don't kill each other first."

The agent snorted and tossed her head like an agitated racehorse. "That is unacceptable."

"What's unacceptable?" Indy asked, but Caroline was already gone, the *click-clack* of her heels echoing through the atrium as she marched toward the stairs to Dom's office. "Caroline, what the hell?"

"He is allowing his ego to cloud his judgment, and I will not allow it," Caroline said as Indy caught up with her. "Dominic!"

"He's in there with Jasmine," Indy said just as Jasmine burst out of Dom's office and raced down the stairs. Without lifting her eyes from the floor, she took off for the locker room. "Or not." Caroline was halfway up the steps by the time Indy caught up again. "I really don't think this is a good idea," she managed to whisper before they reached the top.

"Ms. Morneau," Dom said from his desk, letting his head drop back so that he spoke to the ceiling instead. "To what do I owe this pleasure?"

"I heard you're punishing assault with a trip to Paris," Caroline said, stomping right up to the front of his desk.

Dom's head snapped back up to face them. "As always, I determine what goes on in my training facility."

"And that this player's father is the owner of said facility has nothing to do with your determination?"

"Dismissal for the day is standard practice in an altercation like what happened today, but besides that, I don't believe this is any of your business, Ms. Morneau."

Caroline pressed her hands flat against Dom's desk and leaned over it. "Indiana is my client and she is my business. That girl physically assaulted her, and you give her the chance to play doubles at the French Open."

"You'll note your client is included in that chance."

Caroline waved her hand in the air, dismissing his point. "Yes, but why doubles? Why not an entry to the French Open qualifying tournament? Or better than that, the women's singles? When Penny Harrison won the Classic, that is where she went next, no?"

"Penny had already qualified for that year's Australian Open and she'd have been given a spot in Paris either way, Caroline. You know that."

Caroline sniffed, clearly unimpressed. "Still, I wonder that you did not inquire?"

Dom stood up, resting his hands against his desk for support, his face close to Caroline's. "Of course I inquired, but I think the doubles will be a better experience for her, more worthwhile than the qualifying tournament. A little less pressure and a chance to acclimate herself to the tour." He shook his head. "I don't even know why I'm explaining this to you. *I'm* her coach."

Caroline's nostrils flared. "And *I* am her agent. It is my job to look out for her best interest, and I wonder what is your motivation for these decisions?"

Dom threw up his hands. "Here we go. You ever need a good conspiracy theory, Indiana, go straight to your agent. She's spectacular at making mountains out of molehills."

"Do not make this about me," Caroline said. "This is not about the girls. This is about *you*."

"Yeah, how do you figure?" Dom shot back.

"What are you even talking about?" Indy chimed in.

"Do you not understand, Indiana? Dom coaches a great men's player and perhaps the best women's player if Penny wins in Paris. Now he wishes to create a great doubles team. This experiment with you and the Randazzo girl, it is all about his reputation as a coach. He wishes to dominate all parts of the game."

Dom groaned, throwing himself back into his chair. "You're insane, do you know that? Totally insane. I knew it was a bad idea to let you in here. I should've kicked you out the day you showed up, just like I did five years ago."

"You have a broken memory. You did not kick me out. I kicked you out."

Indy exhaled in disbelief. Suddenly this entire argument made sense. It wasn't even about her. It was about them. "Oh my God, you two used to be a thing?"

They both stopped yelling and faced her, gaping like they'd forgotten she was there.

Dom sighed. "It was a long time ago."

"A very long time ago," Caroline added, crossing her arms.

"So, since this thing," she said, waving her hands at them, "clearly isn't about me, how about we settle it like this: Dom's my coach, so he makes the tennis decisions. Caroline, you work with whatever Dom sets up."

"Sounds like how things are supposed to go," Dom said, a smug grin spreading across his face as he looked back at Caroline.

"Right, okay, I'm going now," Indy said, spinning around and racing out of the office. Her mind was still reeling. Her coach and her agent. She tried to think back and she remembered things being a little tense between Dom and Caroline, but she never would've guessed they'd been a couple.

She went back to the practice court, but morning sessions were over. She could grab lunch at Deuce, but that would mean seeing everyone who'd watched her get bitch slapped by Jasmine Randazzo, and she wasn't quite up for that yet, so she turned and headed back to her dorm. With every step, what happened that morning started to hit home. She'd gotten into a fight, her coach yelled at her, her agent yelled at her coach, and apparently, they had a long history that had absolutely nothing to do with her, but none of that really mattered, because in the middle of all that, she'd also been invited to the French Open.

For half a second, as she unlocked her door and tossed her bag inside, she thought about calling her dad, but as soon as the thought fully registered, she dismissed it. She'd probably get his voicemail, and then in a few hours, his secretary would email her—or worse, Caroline would stop by, since it seemed she was his new go-between.

Indy sat down on her bed and kicked off her sneakers before lying back and staring up at the ceiling. She was going to a Grand Slam, the first of many if she had her way. A surge of energy flowed through her body. She punched her hands into the air and kicked her legs out, letting a small shriek escape her throat. Popping up onto her feet, she bounced on her mattress for a moment before throwing herself back down, laughter bubbling up into her throat. Holy shit. She was going to the French Open.

Chapter 16

ONE OF THE GREAT THINGS ABOUT BEING A PROFESSIONAL athlete in the twenty-first century was that even when practice was done for the day, there were hundreds of other ways to train. For Penny, that often meant sitting in the cool, dark analysis room studying video of herself and her potential opponents, breaking down strengths and weaknesses. Usually her attention was fully focused, pulling her into a zone not unlike what happened when she was actually in the middle of a match.

However, as she stared at the screen, trying to establish a pattern in Zina Lutrova's shot selection, her mind drifted. Rolling her eyes at herself, she paused the video, pulled her phone from her pocket, and thumbed through the pictures *Athlete Weekly* had used in its article.

A pictorial review of the biggest mistake she'd ever made and the constant distraction Alex had proved to be since then. His physical presence every single day was the sweetest torture, like nothing she'd ever felt before. So, what was stopping her?

Then someone flipped the light switch, blinding her for a second.

"What are you still doing here?" Dom frowned at her from the doorway.

"Just some video."

"Yeah, I can see that." He nodded at the paused screen that she obviously hadn't even been looking at, let alone analyzing. "Go home, get some rest. We've got a long road ahead of us once we get to Paris, and an even longer season after that."

"Right," Penny said, putting her phone back in her pocket and standing.

"Don't let this press bother you, okay? None of it means anything."

Smiling tightly at her coach, she nodded. "You know me, Dom. Nothing to worry about."

Before he could respond, she hustled out of the room, down the hallway, and into the atrium. It was empty at this time of night. She took a step toward the front entrance, then stopped. She didn't want to go home, where she'd have to face her family and talk about that article and Alex and everything. She needed some peace.

She didn't even realize where her feet were taking her until she found herself standing in a familiar spot. She stepped out onto the empty practice court and inhaled deeply. A breeze swirled up from the water and the salty air invaded her senses, but her shoulders were still tense, her mind still full of everything that had happened that day—hell, everything that had happened since she found Alex in this exact spot.

Maybe he was onto something. She lay down and closed her eyes. She was close enough to the water to hear the waves rumbling against the shore, a sound that was overshadowed during the day by voices and match noise and the general OBX buzz. A deep breath in and a slow exhale out, and then another, but it wasn't having the calming effect he promised her.

"This wasn't a good idea," she mumbled to herself, sitting up.

"It was. You're just doing it wrong."

Her back teeth clenched at the distinct British accent that rang out over the soft roar of the ocean. He stood just outside the court, leaning on the fence.

"Didn't ask you, did I?" she shot back, standing up and dusting off her shorts.

Alex raised an eyebrow at her, a smug smirk tugging at his mouth. "Then what are you doing here?"

"I don't know. I... Fine. Tell me what I'm doing wrong," she said, hoping that if he got in whatever shot he wanted to take, she could escape with at least some of her pride intact.

He hopped the fence, the chain link jangling against the frame, and approached her slowly. "You're thinking too much. That's your problem, Penny. You think too bloody much."

She refused to meet his eye as he drew closer. "So, I should be like you? No thinking, no worries, do whatever I want, to hell with the consequences."

Alex bit out a laugh. "Consequences? What consequences? A silly article that everyone will forget about in a week?"

"Never mind. Obviously none of it matters to you."

Turning, she started to walk away.

"That's right," he called out, "run away, like always."

She stopped, her feet rooted to the spot, determined to contradict him. His footsteps were soft but clear against the clay court, coming closer until he was right behind her, his breath warm and sweet against her temple. She wanted to lean back into him, collapse against his chest, and let him hold her, give in to what she'd craved since the moment they met.

Instead, she whirled around and said, "You don't know what you're talking about."

His eyes narrowed, his gaze moving from hers down to her mouth and back again. "You sure about that?"

"Yes," she said, not giving an inch as he moved closer.

"Still a terrible liar," he murmured, before lowering his mouth to hers.

The kiss was soft at first, despite his accusation, and there was a question in the gentle brush of his lips, at the way his hands hovered over her hips before resting there, simply a place for them to land rather than pulling her closer or holding her tight.

"Penny," he breathed as she lifted her hands, one palm against the rough stubble of his cheek, the other sliding around to the back of his neck, her fingers sifting through the ends of his hair.

He leaned into her touch, and then, with a twist of her fingers and a less-than-gentle tug of his hair, a deep groan tore from his throat, his hands suddenly gripping at her hips, pressing into the skin, while she drew his mouth back down to hers, nipping at his lower lip. Then a hand to her neck, his thumb at the line of her jaw, and the tilt of their heads as he deepened the kiss, an arm snaking around her entire body, drawing her to his chest.

No battle of tongues or teeth, like back in Australia, not the electric intensity of their recent battles on and off the court, but something deliberate and reverential and terrifying in its honesty.

She wanted that. Wanted him. Wanted the way he made her feel, beautiful and powerful and like she was more than a tennis robot cobbled together into something vaguely person-shaped. He wanted *her*, not her forehand or backhand or serve. And she wanted him even more because of it.

And why shouldn't she have what she wanted?

When they parted, gasping for breath, Penny brushed soft kisses along his jawline, pushing up onto her toes before whispering, "Take me home with you."

He blinked, his eyes unfocused and dazed, as he tried to understand her. "Yeah?" he asked, just as quietly, like if either was too loud, they'd break whatever spell had finally gotten them here.

"I haven't stopped thinking about you since that night in Australia. I *never* stopped wanting you, and you were right the other night. I am scared, I'm petrified that if I give in to this, I'll lose myself in it, in you, but..." She trailed off as his hand reached up to brush a lock of her hair away from her face.

"But..." he asked.

"But I don't let fear stop me from going after the things I want," she let out in one long breath before meeting his eyes and holding his gaze. "And I want you."

"Holy shit," he cursed, but her words were enough to break the hold he had on himself.

His mouth on hers, hot and open and all-consuming, her entire weight taken in his arms, a hand around her thigh, the other across her hips as she wound her arms around his neck, his shoulders broad and strong as he carried her to the back of the court, pressing her into the fence and then letting out a sound of protest when it proved to be too unstable for his intended purpose.

Penny laughed, sliding out of his grasp, and when her feet touched the ground, she grinned up at him, eyes wild. "Race you."

Then, slipping out from under his arms, she took off at full speed across the court, through the gate, and straight for the stairs down to the beach, his pounding footsteps echoing behind her.

The wind whipped against her face as she ran, and she knew he could catch her easily if he chose. Instead, he was a step or two in her wake and followed her up the long, sandy path to his house; lights illuminated their way every few feet until the path led up to a back porch overlooking the water. When she reached the back door, she stopped and whirled around as he took one final stride and stood in front of her, his breath as ragged and uneven as hers.

"I..." he started, staring down at her in wonder. "I...are you sure?" he finally managed to ask, the open vulnerability clearly uncomfortable for him. "I don't think...I don't think I could take it if I woke up tomorrow and you were gone, so if you..."

Penny shook her head, her heart clenching at the thought

of hurting him again, knowing he didn't show this side of himself to just anyone. She wasn't the only one who was scared, and that made everything so much easier, knowing they were in this thing together.

She stepped closer, reaching for him, taking his hand in hers and lifting it to her lips, pressing a kiss to his palm. "I'm not going anywhere," she promised, bringing their joined hands to her cheek and leaning into his touch as his fingers slipped into her hair, cradling the back of her head.

The insecurity was gone from his gaze and replaced by that fire she'd come to know so well, and she reveled in it. She'd always marveled at his talent, but his ability to lift her into his arms while sucking a bruising kiss into the sensitive skin just beneath her ear *and* get the door behind them open—and then closed again—as he carried her inside was beyond impressive.

Her sneakers fell to the floor and her socks, too, and she felt the shift of his weight as he toed his own shoes off—she'd compliment him on his multitasking the next day.

She wrapped her legs around his hips and let out a shuddering gasp when his hands palmed her ass, grinding her into him, pulling matching gasps from him as he stumbled the last few feet into his bedroom, an uneven "Fuck me" breathed against her skin when she nipped at the sharp edge of the jawline that had tempted her for weeks.

"Yes, please," she answered, giggling at the sardonic grin he shot her before he dropped her down to the bed.

He lifted a brow at her and her laughter died as he pulled his shirt up over his head and tossed it away, exposing his long, lean frame, the sharp cut of muscles in his chest, and his stomach lightly lined with hair, shorts slung low at his hips. Her breath caught in her throat. He was gorgeous in the golden light that poured in from the wall of windows that framed the ocean in the distance.

Never one to back down, she crawled toward the edge of the bed, rising to her knees when she was close enough to feel the warmth of his body radiating onto her skin. She lifted her shirt up, his hands joining hers, and then her grasp falling away as he finished the job. He gazed down at her as he let the shirt fall to the floor.

"Still the most incredible-looking thing I've ever seen. Fuck, Penny, do you know what you do to me?"

Running her hands over the plains of his chest, grinning at the light hiss he expelled when her blunt nails scraped against his skin, she said, "Why don't you show me?"

Challenge lit in his eyes as he pressed forward, his mouth capturing hers, trapping her hands between them as his body lined up with hers. He bumped her backward toward the mattress and lowered her to the sheets as his hands and mouth danced over her skin, trails of open-mouthed kisses at the lace edges of her bra. Goose bumps rose along the path of calloused fingertips at the waistband of her shorts, then under the elastic and around to the rise of her ass. As he lifted her up and into him, the overwhelming sensations prevented her from doing anything other than writhe into the contact, nails digging little half-moons into his shoulders.

"Alex," she managed as his tongue traced the contour of her abdomen toward her belly button, and he stopped to look up at her, chin resting on the rise of her hip, a clear question written across his face.

He hooked a finger into her shorts, and the small secret smile she sent his way was all the permission he needed. The scrape of that stubble against the inside of her thighs was almost enough to do the job, but his clever mouth was just as adept at driving her wild.

When she finally came back to herself, his head was pillowed on her thigh, lips gleaming and swollen, hair a wreck from what her hands had done to it. He looked as smugly satisfied with himself as she had to admit he deserved.

He was truly the most ridiculously gorgeous man she'd ever seen.

He brought himself back up her body and pressed a kiss to her lips. Before he could pull away, she deepened it, wrapping her arms fully around him, and then hooked her leg around his hip and rolled them over. He stared up at her, his hands falling to her hips when she reached back to unfasten her bra. She let it fall between them before tossing it away and settling against him fully.

"Like this?" she asked as he reached one hand up to cup her breast, the rough pad of his thumb sending shock waves over her skin.

"However you want me, Pen," he said as she slid down his powerful thighs, pulling his shorts with her, and then allowing herself a little giggle at the socks still on his feet. She rid him of those as well and waited as he rolled to his side to dig through the drawer of his nightstand for a condom.

She took it from him and then let him watch, eyes heavy-lidded with passion, as she deftly had it on him in seconds. He settled back against the pillows and reached for her hand, twining their fingers together as she straddled him again, taking him in, slowly letting the stretch wash over her, familiar and foreign at the same time.

A roll of her hips at the perfect angle sent a swell of heat through her and pulled a soft "Yes" from her throat.

They rocked together, his fingertips running up and down the line of her back, her mouth at the cords of his neck, until she was shaking in his arms, losing herself as he let her ride out wave after wave of it. Opening her eyes finally, she let out a shaky breath and marveled at the feeling of him still inside her. His grip flexed against her hips; he was clearly holding himself back, waiting for her.

"Incredible," he murmured as her hands slid up into his hair. She lightly scratched her nails against his scalp, and then a short tug at the ends drew a deep rumbling groan from his throat. "I need—" His words cut off when she pulled just a little harder. "Fuck, Pen, please," he begged, but didn't he know? She would give him whatever he wanted.

"What do you need?" she asked, her grip tightening again. "Tell me exactly what you want, Alex."

A growl tore out of him and she felt his control snap as he wrapped his arms tightly around her, getting the leverage he needed to begin thrusting up into her again. "I want to fuck you until your voice is raw from screaming my name." With a hand at the center of her back, he laid her down against the mattress and kept up his rhythm. "I want to fall asleep inside you and wake up tomorrow morning with you still wrapped around me. I want that every single morning."

She loved it when his control broke.

He rose up on his hands, one on either side of her head, and she stared up at him in awe. God, she wanted that, too.

So much. But when he picked up his pace, dropping down to his elbows, finding that sweet friction again where they were joined, she could only answer with her body, arching up to meet him as he drew new levels of pleasure she hadn't known existed.

And then one word managed to fall from her lips, the only word he'd asked for tonight. "Alex," she called mindlessly, desperate for more, wanting everything he could give her. His name spurred him on, brought him to a new level.

"C'mon, love," he grunted through the mind-blowing press of their bodies. "One more, give me one more and take me with you. Can you do that for me, Pen?"

The honeyed gravel of his voice begging her was the last little push she needed before she let go entirely, his shaking oblivion only a fraction behind hers.

So good.

Too good.

Somehow better than she remembered, the rare moment where her memory had failed her.

She wanted him, just like this, forever.

And wasn't that the scariest part of it all?

Chapter 17

"HOW DO YOU FEEL?" ALEX'S VOICE RUMBLED IN HER EAR. SHE lay draped across his chest, their bodies entwined in the center of his bed. His fingertips traced patterns over her back, making her shiver despite the heat they generated together.

The sun rose behind the water in the distance, reflecting in through his bedroom windows, a spectacular sight to wake up to. She stretched against him and brushed a kiss to the sharp cut of his collarbone, trailing kisses up over his neck, his stubble scratching against her lips until her mouth hovered over his.

"Incredible," she said, letting her lips move against his. It felt so good to give in, to stop fighting against what her body had been pleading for since he'd arrived. The battle against her own will had been exhausting.

"Incredible sounds about right," he said as her mouth

moved down his jawline again. He drew her face to his and pressed his mouth to hers in a short, sweet kiss. "Good morning."

"Is it?"

"Barely. It's only six. You fell asleep on me," he accused playfully, running his knuckles over the curve of her hip, then opening his hand and sliding it over her waist, pulling her even closer. "I was ready to go another round."

"It's been a long couple of days. I was tired," she said, tracing a line of freckles that dotted his chest with her fingertip. She watched, fascinated, as gooseflesh broke out over his skin.

"Hmm, sleepiness is weakness of character." His hand crept down her thigh and he lightly stroked the back of her knee, sending a shiver through her entire body.

Laughing, she snuggled closer. "You stole that."

"Doesn't make it any less true," he teased, sliding out from beneath her and letting her head fall onto his pillow. He reached for his nightstand, brushing aside the two empty condom wrappers, and picked up an orange plastic bottle. He shook two pills into the palm of his hand and swallowed them dry.

"What's that?" she asked, propping herself up on her elbows.

"Just some anti-inflammatories."

She raised an eyebrow. "Prescription strength. Your knee?"

Alex smirked, and before she could react, he was leaning over her, his lips brushing against hers as he said, "I carried you in here last night, love. Did it seem like my knee was hurt?"

She could still feel his broad chest as she rested against it, his arms easily taking her weight, and the feeling that she was going to burst out of her skin. "No, but—"

"No buts." He cut her off and the mattress shifted as he got out of bed. In seconds he had on a pair of basketball shorts and was digging around in his dresser for a shirt.

Feeling a little exposed, Penny pulled a sheet over her body.

He turned, mouth open, ready to say something, but he stopped himself. For a moment he stared, his eyes scorching her skin the way his hands and mouth had…

"What?" she asked, feeling heat rising in her cheeks. It seemed so natural to let him look at her during their frenzy in the night, but in the light of day, even the barely there red and orange beginnings of the sun rising through his windows, it was different, more personal.

He blinked and shook his head. "You feel like a run before we go to meet Dom? Unless I wore you out completely…"

Then, unbidden, a soft growl echoed up from her stomach.

Penny bit her lip. "Breakfast first?"

"As the lady wishes," he said, his gaze raking over her again, before turning abruptly and leaving the room.

Penny slipped out from beneath the sheet and gathered her clothes. After stepping into her shorts and sliding her shirt over her head, she sat back down on the bed, trying to tame her hair into a ponytail as reality set in. She'd done exactly what she promised herself she wouldn't do, and now what? Had she woken up to a happily ever after or another walk of shame? It felt more like limbo, like their fate was entirely in their own hands, but that the slightest misstep could shatter everything.

She wandered out of the bedroom and down the hallway toward the kitchen. A small pang fluttered through her chest when she saw his luggage against the wall. They weren't leaving for another three days, and he didn't strike her as the type to pack way in advance.

"You're already packed for France?" she asked, propping herself against the archway that opened to the kitchen.

Alex was leaning against the island at the center of the room, facing away from her, flipping through a newspaper. "Nah, heading to London tomorrow to see my mum before the tournament."

"Does Dom know?" It stung a little that *she* hadn't known, but then again, why would he have told her?

"Yeah, had it planned for a while now."

"Oh," she said, moving to him. Her bare feet cold against the tile floor, she stepped up behind him, wrapping her arms around his torso and pressing her cheek against his warm back.

"I would have told you," he said, turning in her arms, "but—honestly, love—I didn't think you'd care."

She sighed. He was right, she wouldn't have cared or at least she would have pretended she didn't.

Blinking up at him, she shrugged. "It's okay. I'll have to recruit Jack to hit with me until we leave."

Narrowing his eyes, he leaned in close. He was about to kiss her, but her stomach growled again.

"I believe I promised you breakfast," he said, motioning to the counter behind him, where two tall pink smoothies were waiting. "Strawberry banana."

Her favorite. "Did you google me?"

Smirking, he shrugged. "Maybe. Drink up," he said, handing her a straw, "and then we run. Gotta keep our legs under us if we're going to kick ass in France."

They drank in a comfortable silence and when they finished, Penny took their glasses and washed them out in the sink.

"Let me grab my trainers and we'll go."

"No," she said, drying her hands. She grasped his hand and led him toward the glass doors that opened to the beach. "Barefoot."

"Barefoot in the sand?"

"Barefoot," she confirmed as she released him and took off across the beach, sand kicking up around her legs. He caught up easily enough and they ran together, their strides matching remarkably well for two people separated by almost a foot in height.

The rhythm of their steps set a beat behind her thoughts as she ran to the end of the inlet. Past the jetty, she could see the edge of her neighborhood bathed in the early-morning light. She was just a few blocks from home, could run there if she wanted. Her parents' faces swam in her head and for a second she entertained the idea of bringing him home with her and introducing him to her mom and dad. And just as fast, she dismissed it. She still hadn't figured out what this was for herself yet. Bringing her parents into things would be way too much, way too fast.

Penny stopped, and it took a few strides for Alex to realize she was no longer beside him. He jogged back, his breathing harsh.

"What's wrong?"

She didn't know how to put it into words. How could she explain that she wanted him to be a part of her life, but she didn't know if it was possible?

"I..." she began, but stopped, shaking her head and looking up into the sky for answers.

"I swear to God, love, you're scaring me. Whatever it is, out with it."

"I don't know what this is, you and me," she said in one breath.

He brought a hand up and ran it through his hair. "Christ, is that all? I thought..."

"What did you think?" Her eyes met his.

"I thought you were..." He hesitated, searching for the right words. "I don't know, regretting it, like in Australia."

Shaking her head, she stepped closer. "Should I? Regret it, I mean?"

Alex stepped forward, his hands reaching for her, settling against her cheeks, his thumbs brushing gently over her skin. "Penny, I've never—I don't know how to describe how I feel about you, but I know I've never felt it before, and I've spent every moment since I got here scared shitless that you wouldn't want anything to do with me. For a while there, I thought I'd have to live with that, and trust me when I say, it wasn't pretty."

He was one of the most confident men she'd ever met. She couldn't imagine what he said was even possible, let alone how he actually felt.

"I don't believe you," she said with a laugh, pulling away—the seriousness in his voice was a little scary.

Alex reached for her hand. "Maybe we ought to have a

little more faith in each other. Can you do that? Can you have faith in me?"

Penny pushed up onto her tiptoes and pressed a kiss to his lips, hoping he wouldn't notice she didn't answer. The truth was, she wasn't sure if she could, at least not yet.

A few moments later, she pulled away breathlessly. "As much as I'd love to stay here all day, we better get going."

"Relax, love. It's early still."

"It's not that early. Dom'll be waiting for us. Come on."

Dom stood on their practice court, arms crossed, clearly unimpressed that they'd arrived ten minutes after seven, the time he'd asked them to be there: an early start time to help them acclimate to the time change once they arrived in Paris. He raised an eyebrow, clearly expecting an explanation, but Alex beat Penny to it.

"My fault," he said. "I asked her to wait for me."

Their coach's mouth twisted into a frown. "All right. You know the drill. Ten minutes, ten Einsteins. Stretch out and then get going."

Alex groaned beside her, but Penny laughed. "I told you so," she said as they ran through their stretching regime, starting with the toes and working their way up the body. Then they ran side by side, sprinting from line to line, pushing each other with every stride. They ran through the last line after their tenth circuit, and as they pulled up, his shoulder bumped hers. She caught herself easily and brushed against him as she turned back toward the court.

"All right, enough messing around," Dom barked, pushing off the fence where he'd been watching them run. "I'm not going to have another fight on my hands, am I?"

Penny glanced up at Alex, who'd sidled up to her, leaning over her shoulder. A day ago, she would have pulled away, but now she reveled in having him close. If she was truly going to surrender to this, to stop fighting, she had to go all in and try to maintain a balance between those feelings and what she wanted to accomplish on the court.

"Good," Dom said. "I want the both of you at the top of your game in Paris."

He tossed Alex a ball. "You serve first."

They fell into the routine they'd established over the last few weeks of training as they warmed up. The tension from their previous sessions was gone, replaced by a comfortable rhythm, controlled and precise.

When they were both ready, Alex tossed a ball high in the air and fired a laser beam down the centerline, a perfect ace, impossible for anyone to return.

"Wow," Penny called out across the court, but her eyes narrowed when she saw a flash of pain flit across his face. She wasn't the only one who noticed.

"Al, you okay?" Dom asked, rising from his seat on the sidelines and ignoring the wave of dismissal from the younger man.

"I'm fine," Alex protested when Penny jogged to the other side of the court.

"You're not fine," Dom said. "It's your knee, right?"

"Left, actually, and it's fine, only a twinge."

"But you took meds this morning—you shouldn't have

any pain at all," Penny said, but as the words flew from her mouth, she knew they were the wrong ones. Dom's eyes widened.

"You're on pain medication?" he asked. "You told me that knee was fine."

"It is fine," Alex snapped. "I wouldn't even call it pain, like I said, just a twinge now and again."

"Bullshit. Go get it looked at in the trainers' room and we're going to get an MRI done before you leave for London."

"If I say I'm fine, I'm fine, Dom," Alex said. "I'm not one of your students. I don't jump when you snap your fingers."

"Alex, maybe you should get it looked at," Penny said, her brow furrowing as she studied his knee, like she could see what was wrong with it from the outside.

"Don't be bullheaded about this, Al. We're just asking you to have it checked," Dom said, his tone softening.

Alex wasn't having any of it. "And I'm asking you to trust me, but apparently there isn't a lot of that around here."

He said the words to Dom, but Penny felt them deep in her chest, and as she watched him walk off the court, his stride confident and steady—no hint of a limp at all—she knew they were meant for her.

Chapter 18

JASMINE TIPTOED DOWN THE STAIRS, GLIDED ACROSS THE tiled kitchen floor, then slid through the French doors at the back of the house. She held her breath as she braced the door against her palm, letting it shut with a soft *click*. Sighing in relief, she sprinted across the patio and down the wooden walkway that led to the beach. She felt like a criminal escaping after a heist, her heart pounding as she started down the beach toward OBX.

Her parents had found out about the fight. It was easier when she was a kid—they would have punished her. Now, she felt the suffocating weight of their clear disappointment in her, not as a tennis player, but as a person. She could barely look either of them in the eye and couldn't wait to get back to training.

The fastest way to get to OBX in the morning was to cross the private beaches that sat between the house and the training center. She could avoid the crush of cars in the parking lot, the dozens of younger athletes who would want her attention—oh, who was she kidding? She snuck out of the house to avoid her parents and was sneaking into OBX to avoid the stares and gossip.

Nowhere was safe anymore.

The usually bustling locker room was empty, no voices echoing off the tiled floor and walls. The fluorescent lights that lined the ceiling flickered to life as she made her way to her locker, hoping to dress and grab her equipment long before anyone else arrived. As she pulled her hair into a ponytail and clipped back her bangs, her luck ran out.

"I wonder if she'll even show her face." Lara Cronin's voice echoed through the room, dripping with ill-concealed glee.

A laugh, high-pitched, bordering on the edge of a screech, responded. That was Addison. "I know. I mean, *everyone* saw what happened."

The girls giggled together.

"Really, though, how pathetic can you get?"

"Please, she's so overrated. The only reason Dom lets her train here is because of her parents."

Jasmine slammed her locker shut and stepped into the main walkway. The same girls who'd made Indy's life miserable when she first arrived stared in shock, then small, cruel smiles slipped over their features. Spinning on her heel, Jasmine didn't give them the satisfaction of eye contact even as she heard one of them say, "Oh my God" before they dissolved into uncontrolled cackles.

That was what Indy had felt like those first days, with

everyone against her. It must have been awful, and Jasmine could have put a stop to it, but she didn't, just like Teddy said. A knot of regret twisted in her stomach. Exhaling a harsh breath, she adjusted her bag over her shoulder and marched toward the courts. Those girls didn't matter, and she could only hope that the people who did would forgive her.

First, she had to talk to Dom. She had to set things right with him. He was her coach, but while she lay in bed the day before, avoiding her parents, she realized something else. He was right about her game. He knew her strengths and weaknesses better than anyone. And if she wanted to have the career she'd always dreamed of, he was the person who could get her there. She needed to suck it up, be an adult, and apologize, then prove to everyone that she was more than just a nepo baby who got by on her parents' rep and the access to elite training their money paid for.

Jasmine mumbled to herself. "Dom, I'm so sorry. What I did was awful and I'm grateful you're giving me a second chance." That sounded about right. She nodded and pushed through the gate, catching sight of her coach setting up the ball machine.

"Dom," she began, but her voice caught when she saw Indy dumping a basket of balls into the machine's feeder. Their first private doubles practice was scheduled for eight and it was still a quarter to the hour. Why was she here already?

"Jasmine," Dom said, waving her in, "welcome back."

His words said one thing, but his eyes, trained on her like a hawk, said another. He only meant "welcome back" if what had happened over the weekend would never happen again. She tried to assure him it wouldn't, but he cut her off.

"Warm up, then we can get started."

She nodded and began her stretching routine. She would apologize the first chance she got, probably after he got whatever training torture he had in mind out of his system.

She and Indy stretched together. Jasmine kept her eyes glued to the fence at the end of the court but felt Indy watching her. Her stomach twisted again, like in the locker room, only worse. She still couldn't stand the bitch, but a sharp sliver of empathy cut against her conscience.

"Ladies, are you ready?" Dom called, striding toward them. They stood and Jasmine glanced quickly at Indy, but she was looking at their coach now. "Today we're going to start with some light conditioning." There was something in his voice that drew Jasmine's attention. She turned to him and saw a sadistic glint in his eyes. He nodded at the doubles line. "Einsteins."

"How many?" Jasmine asked.

"Until I tell you to stop."

The trick with Einsteins was to not think about how awful you felt, to clear your mind of the burn in your legs and the shortness of breath, and to try to focus on something else. Dom was leaning against the fence, watching them to make sure they ran to each line and not short of it. Jasmine didn't count as their feet pounded down upon the hard court; she focused on Dom and ran her apology over and over again in her mind like a penance for her sins. *Sorry, grateful, second chance, sorry, grateful, second chance*; the words were like a mantra to the thuds of her sneakers. *Sorry, grateful, second chance, sorry, grateful, second chance.*

"Okay, grab some water," Dom called, and they skidded to a stop. Jasmine glanced at Indy. She wasn't huffing and puffing, not like she did on her first day. Still, her breath came hard and quick, while Jasmine wasn't all that winded. At least that was one thing she had over her new partner. No, that wasn't actually a good thing. Indy's weaknesses were her own weaknesses now.

They both grabbed their water bottles and sipped slowly.

"What's he doing here?" Indy said eventually. Jasmine turned to see Alex Russell striding up to the court and waving Dom over. The two men spoke for a few moments, keeping their voices low, then Alex shook Dom's hand and left.

"All right, ladies, footwork, on the service line, no rackets," their coach said, ignoring the curious looks they were both shooting him.

The drill was pretty straightforward. They stood where the service boxes met, halfway between the net and the baseline, with Dom opposite them, a ball in his hand. He moved his arm left and right, and they would mirror the action with their footwork until he released the ball. Without a racket, they were expected to catch it before the ball could bounce twice. Jasmine loved this drill. It played to her strengths: quick feet and quicker reactions.

She felt Indy's eyes on her and she met her gaze for the first time all morning. Jasmine motioned out to the court and said, "After you."

Dom kept Indy's feet moving—short, quick steps against the clay court—before he tossed her the ball and she lunged to her left and caught it with the tips of her fingers. Indy tossed the ball back to Dom.

"Beat that," she muttered.

"Game on," Jasmine mumbled back as they switched places.

"What was that?" Dom asked.

"Nothing," Jasmine said, setting her feet shoulder width apart and waiting for Dom's first cue.

Twenty minutes later, they were both dripping with sweat, but neither had dropped a single ball.

"Okay, take ten."

"No," Indy protested, dragging her wrist across her forehead, then over her knee, which she'd scraped when she laid out for a ball.

"Not yet," Jasmine agreed, hands on her hips, bent slightly at the waist to try to regain her breath.

Dom laughed at them outright, clearly satisfied with their performance. "Take ten and rehydrate."

He began to walk away and Jasmine saw her opportunity. "Dom, hang on a second," she said, jogging to catch up with him. "I wanted to—"

"I know what you want to say, Jasmine, but I don't want to hear you're sorry. I want you to *show* me you're sorry."

The laughter and smile from seconds before were gone, replaced by a stern glare and a set jaw.

"I will," she said. "I promise."

"Good. Now try not to start another fight while I'm gone."

After Dom walked away, Jasmine made eye contact with Indy for a second, but Indy looked away, bent and dug through her racket bag, pulling her phone out and shooting off a rapid text.

"Dom's been pretty tough so far, huh?" Jasmine said, swallowing back her pride.

It was bland as hell, sure, but it was the best she could do, and at least she was trying.

Indy looked up from her phone, disbelief written across her face. "Yeah, I guess." The phone *binged* and drew her attention.

Jasmine watched as Indy wandered to the opposite end of the court, tapping away at her phone screen. "Or we could just not talk."

"Hey, Randazzo."

Her shoulders stiffened as an involuntary shiver slid pleasantly through her body. It was so annoying that Teddy could still do that to her, even when she was pissed as hell at him. He was standing just outside the fence, smiling at her. A sense of déjà vu niggled at the back of her mind; they'd been here before, after they kissed.

"Isn't it a little early for you?" She glanced over her shoulder at Indy, who was still focused on her phone.

Teddy shrugged. "We need to talk and I knew you'd be here."

"I don't want to talk to you."

She thought she'd made that pretty clear right before the Classic final, and if that hadn't done it, she'd ignored every single text and voicemail he'd sent since. When was he going to get the point? Why couldn't he accept that things would never be the same between them? And why, despite everything, did what she just said feel like a lie? Because she did want to talk to him, she *always* wanted to talk to him, and that was the problem.

"You don't have to talk. You can just listen." His eyes crinkled at the corners, the damned dimple appearing alongside his easy smile, and then he hopped the fence. Her heart pulsed and then fluttered into a faster beat. Seriously, screw those dimples. "Or you can stand there and pretend like you're not listening while I talk."

"You're such a stubborn ass, you know that?" Jasmine avoided his eyes. If she looked into his eyes, she'd be lost. She'd smile, and his would widen, and she'd give in, and that would be that.

"So, how's it going?" he asked, a hand gesturing across the court.

Her patience was already gone. "Seriously, that's what you're leading with? 'How's it going?' Did you actually want to talk to me or are you just wasting my time?"

"Not well, then, huh?"

"Teddy—"

"Fine, look, I wanted to talk to you because..." he began, but immediately lost his momentum. Jasmine had had enough of his hesitation and stepped forward, pushing past him, but he caught her arm. "Because I feel terrible about what I said to you. You were right. I was being a shitty friend."

"Come on," Jasmine said, shooting a glance toward Indy, who was still focused on her phone. The last thing she needed was for Indiana Gaffney to know what a fool she made out of herself with Teddy. She led him through the gate and around the corner back behind the courts where they would have some privacy.

"You wanted to talk, so talk." She crossed her arms and waited.

"Don't look at me like that, Jas. We both said some crappy things to each other. And look, you were right about Indy. I wasn't helping her just to be nice. I—"

"You always did have a thing for blonds." She cut him off, pushing the hurt down as best she could. "If you like her, you should go for it. Ask her out, I mean."

Nah," he said, shrugging. "I don't think she's into me."

Jasmine looked away, studying the twisted chain-link fence intently and avoiding his gaze. "I shouldn't have let those girls be horrible to her. I could've put a stop to it and I didn't."

Teddy sighed. "We shouldn't have done a lot of things, huh?"

Like getting drunk and kissing and nearly destroying their friendship. "You got that right."

They lapsed into a comfortable silence for a moment, and then Teddy looked down before shooting her a boyish grin, that dimple reappearing, making it impossible for her not to smile back, just like she knew it would. He probably knew it, too. Though maybe he didn't, and that somehow made it worse.

"So, how is it going, really? Penny told me Dom paired you guys up as a doubles team."

"We haven't done much yet."

"I think you two would make great partners."

"You would," Jasmine drawled.

"Not like that. Your games, they're complementary. It's like pairing up Federer and Nadal: power and precision with speed and hustle. Her weaknesses are your strengths, and vice versa. A perfect match, and Dom's a genius for thinking of it."

"Yeah, he's a real Einstein." The muscles in her calves twitched at the mere mention of the word. "Besides, that's not the worst of it."

He was silent, waiting for her to continue, but the words caught in her throat. The girls she thought were her friends clearly weren't, and she definitely couldn't tell her parents. She didn't have anyone else to talk to, and Teddy used to be the person she'd trust with anything, but she couldn't anymore. She couldn't tell him about how Dom agreed with Hodges about her game and how he didn't think she had it in her to be in the top ten. That she wouldn't win Grand Slams or Olympic medals or live up to her parents' legacy and that everything she'd worked for all these years was nothing but a dream, one that they all let her believe in for way too long.

So instead, she let the dam inside her break, a lump in her throat choking her as the tears burned her eyes and fell in streams down her cheeks.

Somehow, even after all the crap they'd been through, he knew exactly what she needed. She needed him to be there. Teddy didn't love her, not the way she wanted him to, but in that moment, as his arms tightened around her and he hushed her lightly and she fought back the rushing of her blood and the tingling warmth that settled in her lower belly, Jasmine knew she would never find a better friend, and maybe one day that would be enough.

Chapter 19

YOU KNOW STARING AT YOUR PHONE ISN'T GOING TO MAKE a text magically appear, right?" Indy gazed into her dorm closet, positive nothing inside of it was appropriate for Paris. "And you're supposed to be helping me pack."

It was another surreal thing about her life in the last few weeks: Penny Harrison was, somehow, becoming...not just a friend, but a close friend. The kind of friend who waited for her after training and had no problem helping her find something to wear to the Roland-Garros Players Gala.

The dress had to be elegant and sexy and strike Jack Harrison speechless. Not that it would be much of an accomplishment. He hadn't uttered so much as a word to her since the day she won the Classic. Even when he'd jumped in to stop Jasmine from tackling her on their practice court, he'd barely spared her a glance.

Indy couldn't figure out what his deal was. He was attracted to her for sure and he definitely felt the connection that she did. He seemed determined to stay away, though, and she wasn't going to chase him. She didn't play games like that.

Penny sat on Indy's bed, laying her phone down beside her. "I'm sorry. Things were so weird before Alex left for London. We barely had a night together and then he was so mad when I spilled about that medication. It's...it's making it almost impossible to focus on training. And Jack's an okay hitting partner, but he's not even close to the same level of play."

Another completely unhinged thing, her new friend hooking up with...in a relationship with...was definitely *something* with Alex Russell.

Indy sighed, sitting next to her. At least Penny had someone who wanted her or would admit that he wanted her. "He's busy. He's probably got a lot on his plate, and besides that, he's got to train."

"I know," Penny said, flopping back on the bed. "I know you're right, but everything happened so fast."

"Please, like you two haven't been circling this thing for months," she said, leaning over Penny with a wicked smile.

Penny grabbed a small pillow and smacked her in the head with it. "I know, but I barely had time to catch my breath after we hooked up this time, and now it feels like none of it happened, like it was some dream."

"You could always check out what the gossip accounts are saying about you if you need proof." Penny chucked the pillow at her this time, but Indy caught it before it could hit her. "You're leaving for Paris tomorrow. You'll see him there, and after you kick Zina Lutrova's ass in the final, you two can figure things out."

"Third round," Penny corrected. "If we play, it'll be in the third round."

"Third round, then," Indy said, and as she did, Penny's phone vibrated against the bed. Indy grabbed it and held it out of Penny's reach. "You don't get to talk to him until you remember that you're Penny Fucking Harrison and he's lucky you've allowed him to breathe the same air as you, let alone everything else you let him do. As much as I appreciate the knowledge that you are in fact human and not a tennis bot put on this earth to destroy the rest of us, you gotta get it together."

"Fine, you're right," Penny admitted, but a little too quickly.

"Say it."

"You're kidding," Penny said, gazing longingly at the phone.

Indy just raised an expectant eyebrow.

"Fine, I'm Penny Fucking Harrison and he's lucky I allow him to breathe the same air as me, let alone everything else I let him do."

Nodding in satisfaction, Indy said, "And I still don't understand how he was able to do that thing with his hips. How—"

"Indy!" Penny cut in.

With a sigh, she handed the phone back to her desperate friend. "Fine. Here."

Penny's thumb raced over the screen and her shoulders

slumped as she read the text. "He says he'll see me in Paris. That's it, nothing else."

"You will see him in Paris *tomorrow*. Now, come on, you promised to help me find something to wear."

"You're right, and we've got to get back to training. Forget the dress. Jack's going to have some sent over to the hotel for me—you can wear one of those."

"Ah, you're the best!" Indy said, dumping her clothes back into her closet before following Penny outside.

"How's it going, by the way?" Penny asked as they walked. "It can't be easy training with Jasmine."

"It's awkward and uncomfortable and really hard, but when I'm locked in, I can kind of see why Dom thought it was a good idea."

"Your styles are incredibly different. It'll make it hard for your opponents to adjust mid-point."

"Exactly," Indy said.

"Well, try not to commit murder in my absence," Penny said as she veered right, toward her personal court.

"I'll do my best." Indy smiled, turning to the left. When she arrived at her court, she found Dom and Jasmine already there.

"Indy, glad you're back," Dom said as she approached, waving her over to where he and Jasmine stood just outside the court's gate. "I was about to tell Jasmine, your draw has been confirmed and it looks like you'll be playing Lutrova and Grishina in the first round."

"Wow, that's—" Jasmine started, but Indy cut her off.

"Scary as hell." Indy looked at her doubles partner and smiled, all thoughts of homicide gone. She could see Jasmine fight it for a moment, but then a bright smile spread over her face as well.

"Go big or go home, ladies. Now, let's get started," Dom said, grinning from ear to ear.

"Indiana, I am glad I have found you." Caroline's voice ricocheted through the locker room.

"Yep, this is usually where I am after practice," Indy said, tightening the towel around her. "Do you want to turn around? I have to get dressed."

Caroline waved off the request and Indy shrugged, dropping the towel and grabbing her underwear. If her agent didn't mind, then neither did she.

"I have fantastic news," Caroline said.

"You're a little late," Indy said, pulling her OBX T-shirt over her head and then buttoning her white jean shorts. "I know it's really exciting, Caroline, but we did already kind of know this was going to happen."

Caroline breathed a dismissive sound through her lips. "You are speaking of the doubles tournament?"

"Of course. What else would I be talking about?"

Her agent smiled. "An old friend of mine is the assistant tournament director."

"Old friend?" Indy asked, raising her eyebrows. "The same way Dom is an old friend?"

"No," Caroline said, examining the clear sheen painted on her nails, which made Indy believe she was right.

"Sure, okay, what about him?"

"He has managed to procure you an entry into Bari. Dom was unfortunately correct about your lack of experience hindering a spot in Paris, but this is most certainly the next best thing. I expect, after how you destroyed those other girls in the Classic, that you will have no problem winning that tournament as well. There are sponsors who will be very interested to see these results."

Indy pulled her hair into a ponytail and tried to keep her excitement down. The truth was, she was beyond ecstatic at this news. It was a solid next step, a lower-level tournament, but it was on the actual tour and it made so much more sense than playing doubles with a girl she could barely stand. Dom probably wouldn't see it that way, though, she realized with disappointment.

"Dom is supposed to be making all the tennis decisions."

"He will be thrilled, of course. This will bring more exposure for both you and this place," Caroline said, spinning away on her stilettos. Indy followed slowly, dreading the explosion Caroline was about to ignite.

"Absolutely not," Dom said, leaping up from the bench beside a practice court, making the tiny ten-year-old boy he was coaching literally jump in terror. "Didn't we just have this conversation, Caroline? It's not your place to go looking for tournaments for my athletes."

Caroline laughed off the reprimand. "Do not be ridiculous. Of course she will play."

"No, she won't. It's too much too soon."

"You are angry because you were unable to give her this yourself."

"How do you know that?" Dom asked, arms crossing over his chest.

"She is more than capable. You know this."

"She isn't ready."

"*She* is right here," Indy cut in, pretty fed up with them forgetting it was *her* career they were fighting over. "Or should I leave?"

Dom turned to her, his face apologetic, or at least as close as it ever got. "Indy, it isn't as simple as your agent would have you believe. Your game is up to scratch, and I have no doubt that you would do well, but your endurance level simply isn't where it needs to be for your first pro singles tournament, even if it is a lower-level tournament."

"C'est n'importe quoi!" Caroline said, moving closer and nearly bumping chests with him.

"It is not bullshit, Caroline, and you know it. You're so desperate to find the next big star, you're willing to put this girl's career on the line."

The volume of their argument grew with every insult, and Indy rolled her eyes. She hated when adults who were supposed to have their shit together acted like this, which was a lot more often than any of them would ever admit. "You two let me know when you've worked it out."

Her words went unacknowledged and she spun away from the court, practically running down the pathway to get away from the shouting. It was like she was seven years old again and her parents were screaming at each other over whatever crap they were always fighting about.

She made it into the atrium, leaned against the wall, and slid to the floor. Roy sent her an encouraging smile from his desk and Indy managed a grimace in return, despite how pissed off she was. This should have been one of the most exciting days of her career. She was going to Paris tomorrow. She'd be playing on the famous clay courts of Roland-Garros like so many legendary athletes before her. This wasn't how she imagined feeling. She should have been ecstatic and nervous and maybe even a little scared, but not annoyed. She let her head fall to her knees.

"Well, this can't be good."

Her head shot up at the sound of Jack's voice. He stood over her in a sweaty T-shirt and shorts, racket in hand.

"Hey," she said, feeling a flush creep up over her cheeks. The last time they'd spoken she'd thrown caution to the wind and kissed him, and even if it was just for a moment, he'd kissed her back.

"You okay?"

"Peachy."

"Want to talk about it?"

"No," she said, resting her head against her knees again, hoping he'd take the hint.

"Okay, then," Jack mumbled. She raised her head an inch to watch him go and saw his broad back as he moved to the far end of the atrium.

"Wait," she called out, leaping to her feet and racing to catch up to him. He was part agent, part coach, and regardless of what was—or wasn't—going on between them, he was probably the best person to ask about the argument most likely still raging out on the practice court.

He stopped without warning outside the door to the men's locker room and stepped to the side, a move Indy hadn't anticipated. It put him right in her path and she crashed into his back. He whirled around, probably to try to catch her before she fell, but as he did, his elbow collided with the side of her head.

Stars exploded in front of her eyes and a sharp pain began to radiate from the point of impact.

"Shit, Indiana, I'm sorry."

"I'm okay," she said, her eyes squeezed shut. She pressed her hand against her temple, only to pull away with a hiss when the ache increased with the pressure. Just what she needed, another blow to the head.

"Come on," he said, his hands cupping her face. "Open your eyes and look at me."

His tone was so authoritative that she obeyed without question, meeting his gaze. "Any blurriness?"

"No." She could see every fleck of green and gold in his eyes and small brown ring around his pupils that she'd never been close enough to truly appreciate before.

"Ringing in your ears? Are you dizzy?"

"Nope," she said, shaking her head. "I'm okay."

"Good," he said, and she could actually see his concern melt away and his mask of indifference fall back into place. She hated when he did that, when his personality shut down like he was afraid if he was nice to her for more than two seconds she'd try to rip his clothes off or something. Maybe that was why he always shut down, maybe he *didn't* want her and she'd been lying to herself the whole time. "Tell me what's got you so upset. I'd like to help, if I can."

Indy sighed in defeat, the adrenaline spike fading with his words, so instead of calling him out on it, she explained the power struggle going on between Dom and Caroline on the practice courts.

Jack looked thoughtful for a moment and then said, "That's an easy fix. Caroline must have Dom really tied up in knots if he didn't figure it out right away."

"Yeah?" she asked.

"You accept both invitations and you wait it out. Bari doesn't get started until the second week in Paris. You'd have to at least get to the third round of the women's doubles draw before you'd play your first-round match. If you have to drop one after that, so be it, but there's no reason to worry about that until it actually happens, if it actually happens. Once those two calm down enough to think clearly, they'll figure it out on their own. No sense in you worrying about it."

Indy smiled and all the stress of the last few minutes completely disappeared. "I should have hired you to be my agent."

Jack shrugged, his expression blank again. "I don't know about that."

Her smile dropped. "Well, thanks. I've gotta get going. I'm sure rumors are flying around here about me dropping doubles by now. I better talk to Jasmine before she has a total breakdown and decides to slap me again."

Finding Jasmine was a little more complicated than she expected, because she actually had no idea where her doubles partner lived. She was pretty positive Jasmine had been staying with her parents for a minute after the Classic, but she was equally sure she also had a dorm on OBX's campus... somewhere.

But Indy knew who to ask, and after a stop in the main atrium, Roy pointed her in the right direction.

It shouldn't have come as a surprise that Jasmine didn't live in the standard dorms that housed everyone from the junior players on up, but in one of the outer buildings that were mostly used as vacation rentals for distinguished guests. The apartment was on the top floor and had its own elevator with one button, PH written on it. Penthouse, obviously. Only the best for John Randazzo and Lisa Vega's little girl.

Before she could chicken out, Indy knocked. She heard the telltale sound of footsteps padding toward her and then something brushing against the door.

Then nothing, just silence.

She could picture Jasmine standing on the other side of the door, hesitating.

"I know you're in there," Indy called out. "Can we talk, please?"

Another moment and then the lock clicked and Jasmine opened the door—barely—and wedged herself into the space. She was wearing an old oversized US Open T-shirt and shorts, her feet bare and her damp hair in a bun at the top of her head. She was blocking Indy's view inside except for over her head, where there was a wall of windows that faced out over the water. Indy's own tiny dorm room definitely didn't have a view like that.

"What's up?" Jasmine asked.

"Can I come in? I have to talk to you about something important."

Jasmine rolled her eyes but stepped back and spun on her heel as Indy followed. The view was even more impressive now that she could completely take it in. For the first time since arriving at OBX she considered calling her dad. The least he could do after inflicting Caroline on her was upgrade her living situation.

"What's so important you couldn't tell me in a text?" Jasmine said, arms crossed, lips pursed unhappily, as she propped herself on the back of her couch. No offer to sit down or for something to drink.

Shit.

She already knew.

OBX was the smallest town in the world, and the news about her entry into Bari had clearly already gotten to Jasmine. It wasn't a huge leap from that information to the idea that Indy would be leaving her in the lurch in Paris.

Indy decided to just say it. "Look, I don't know what you heard—"

"I heard you're going to Bari. Congrats."

"Right, exactly, and I know there are rumors probably flying around right now that I'm dropping doubles, and I came here to tell you that's not true."

Jasmine raised a disbelieving eyebrow. "I might have gotten a text or two about it."

"Well, like I said, it's not true. I'm going to accept both invitations and then see what happens from there."

"See what happens?" Jasmine repeated, like she wasn't sure what it meant.

"Yeah, the way the schedule works, we might be okay." Indy left out the part about what Jack had said about eventually choosing which to drop if she had to. She didn't need to borrow trouble just yet.

"So, is that why you came all the way over here?"

"Yeah, and well, I wanted to, I guess apologize. All those things you said the day we fought, I'm sorry I made you feel that way. I didn't mean to."

Jasmine sat still for a second and then nodded. "I guess I knew that, at least now I do. I was looking for someone to blame for, well, for everything. This year isn't exactly going how I imagined, so I took it out on you."

"You're sorry for smacking me?" Indy asked.

"No, you deserved that," she said flatly, but a glinting mischief lit in her eyes.

Despite herself, Indy smiled. "Maybe I did, a little. Look, I think Dom's onto something here with this doubles thing."

Jasmine tilted her head. "I think so, too."

"If we can get our act together during your service games, I think we'll be fine," Indy said, hoping the joke didn't cross a line and ruin this extremely newfound peace.

Jasmine smirked, but there was obvious laughter in her eyes. "Excuse me? The problem isn't my serve. The problem is your net game."

"Right," Indy agreed, and then bantered back lightly,

"because I'm supposed to be able to cover the entire court when you serve up a meatball."

"I know it might be a foreign concept to you with that serve," Jasmine laughed softly, "but sometimes you do have to hit more than one shot to win a point."

"Didn't have a problem doing that against you during the Classic, did I?" She saw the hurt flash in Jasmine's eyes and Indy cringed. That line she wasn't supposed to cross. It was behind her. "Shit, I'm sorry."

Jasmine shook her head, her eyes suddenly looking very tired. "Forget it. Are we still playing doubles or was this all a ploy to get me to drop out so you could focus on Bari without Dom having a shit fit?"

"What? Of course I'm playing doubles. I just told you that."

"Good, then if you don't mind, I have some packing to finish up before we leave."

Jasmine silently led her to the door. "I'll see you tomorrow," she said.

"Yeah, tomorrow," Indy said, but the door was already closed behind her.

Chapter 20

CHARLES DE GAULLE AIRPORT WAS A LARGE, BUSTLING international hub and yet its customs line was painfully slow. The entire tennis world was descending upon Paris for two weeks and apparently someone forgot to warn the French Passport Control. Penny could see fellow players, their coaches and families, along with dozens of tennis people—reporters, officials, and their ilk—all trapped and waiting their turn.

She looked over the faces, wondering if she'd find Alex in the crowd, but the familiar tall frame, broad shoulders, and sandy-blond hair were nowhere to be seen, which wasn't surprising. According to Dom he wasn't scheduled to get in until later tonight. She exhaled through her nose and felt her stomach tighten. She hated having things so unresolved between them. The French Open deserved her total focus, but she wanted Alex in her life, and that meant trying to strike a balance. It wouldn't be easy, but she was willing to try. It would be a lot easier if he would just talk to her instead of the near complete cutoff of the last few days.

At the front of the line a haggard-looking civil servant with a stern face asked, "Passeport?" rolling the *r* at the end of the word in that effortless way only a native French speaker could.

She slid her passport across the counter.

"D'où venez-vous?" the customs agent asked.

Penny couldn't speak French, but she'd done this enough to know what she was being asked. "North Carolina in the United States."

"Pourquoi êtes-vous en France?"

"Roland-Garros," she said simply.

The agent's eyes flew up and lit with recognition. A tennis fan. The corner of the agent's mouth lifted in what could almost be called a smile.

"Avez-vous quelque chose à déclarer?"

"No."

"Très bien. Bonne chance, Mademoiselle Harrison."

Her passport was passed back across the counter with a new stamp adorning its pages. "Merci."

Jack's interview was just as fast, and they soon found themselves dragging two weeks' worth of luggage and equipment toward the exit. They stepped out of the arrivals gate and into a rainy Paris morning. Raindrops dripping from the overhang assaulted them.

Penny let out a sigh of relief when she saw a man holding a sign with her name on it. Having a waiting car was a large improvement over standing on yet another taxi line and hoping the driver wasn't in the mood to take a creative route to their hotel like the last time they were here. Her brother slash agent was the absolute best for thinking of it.

"You rock."

"This wasn't me," Jack said, his eyes darting around as he shuffled her toward the car. "Things are different now, Pen. The tournament arranged for it. They want their stars getting to their hotels safe and sound."

"Mademoiselle," the driver said, drawing her eyes away from the rain as he held the door open for her.

"Merci," she whispered, and slid into the back seat.

The driver edged the car away from the curb and soon they were humming along the highway through the outskirts of Paris—mostly open grass fields, modern office buildings, and shopping centers—a view you'd find around almost every airport in every major city. Penny closed her eyes and rested her head against the seat. The vibrations of the car nearly lulled her to sleep.

"Don't conk out yet," Jack warned a few minutes later.

She opened her eyes. They were almost into the city itself, and Penny didn't want to miss it. This was likely all the sightseeing she'd get. At first the road was lined with buildings built in the last half of the twentieth century, brand names held aloft on their roofs by scaffolds. Then the car sped through an underpass, made a sharp right turn, and they were in the real Paris—at least the part of Paris that everyone imagined. The rain faded into a light mist, making the entire city glow.

The car pulled to a halt in front of their destination. During her last trip to the French Open, she'd stayed at this very same hotel, and since she'd won the qualifying tournament that year, Penny didn't see any reason to mess with good karma. La Metropolitan was a beautiful boutique hotel only a few minutes from Roland-Garros, making the commute to and from the courts no longer than her drive to OBX, plus the upper floors of the hotel had some of the best views in Paris.

The driver opened her door, and as soon as she stepped out of the car, camera flashes barraged her. Shit, paparazzi, lots of them. They were yelling—mostly in French—and she barely understood a word of it.

Then a voice rang out clear as day: "Penny, where's Alex?" The rest of the paparazzi took the cue, switching to English.

"Penny, do you know what Alex is doing in London?"

"How long have you two been together?"

"Did you cut the brakes on his motorcycle so he'd crash in Australia?"

Then, a bellhop launched himself out of the front entrance, dodging through the throng of frenzied reporters. "Allez," he said, waving them toward the door. "Je vais porter vos bagages. Allez."

Jack came around to her and she pressed into him as the crowd of reporters pushed forward. Stepping easily into the role of bodyguard, Jack snaked an arm around her shoulders and used his bulk to shove the camera-laden men aside, breaking a path into the hotel.

Her heart pounding, Penny stared at Jack in shock. "What the hell was that?"

"Like I said, things are different now, Pen," Jack said, shaking his head in apparent disbelief.

"Yeah, I'm getting that."

"Next time we'll call ahead, come in through the back or something."

She nodded, still trying to catch her breath. That was so intense, a claustrophobic thrill—scary and beyond exciting all at the same time.

They checked in and followed the bellhop who'd rescued them into the elevator, up to the sixth floor, and then down a long hallway to her suite.

"If you're with him, that crowd down there and the attention, it's only going to get worse," Jack said as soon as they were alone. "Are you sure this is what you want?"

Penny wandered toward the balcony and rolled her eyes.

"I can see your reflection in the window. Don't roll your eyes. Be honest with me."

"Don't worry about it," she said, brushing off the question. Of course she wanted to be with Alex. She'd been fighting it for months now, but whether what she wanted was good for her, she had no idea.

"Fine. I'm going down to my room. You need anything?"

Glancing around the luxurious suite, she grinned at her brother. A large sitting room, the furnishings new and clearly expensive, an attached bedroom with a king-sized bed, an en suite bathroom with a shower big enough for two, and a soaking tub. It was nearly as big as the entire second floor of her parents' home. "I think I'll be fine."

The door clicked shut behind him, and finally alone, Penny turned back to the balcony. Her suite was impressive, but the view—that was spectacular: the 16th arrondissement, spread out before her with the Eiffel Tower looming in the distance as the sun began to peek through the fading rain clouds. She sat on one of the chairs, a cushioned chaise lounge, and allowed her mind to go blank, letting the scenery wash over her—not fully awake, but not quite asleep either.

Her phone buzzed with a message from Indy: *We're here!* She wasn't sure how long she'd been sitting there, and a quick glance at her watch told her nearly an hour had passed by in a blink. She was typing a response when a shrill ring from the phone sitting on the desk just inside the balcony door interrupted her. "I'm so popular," she mumbled, stepping back into her room to answer, as she texted her room number to Indy.

"Hello?" she asked, balancing the receiver between her shoulder and her neck.

"Mademoiselle Harrison, there is a package for you at the desk," a woman with a French accent not unlike Caroline's responded. "Shall I have it sent up?"

A few minutes later, a knock sounded against her door. A bellman was on the other side holding a small square black velvet box wrapped with a cream-colored ribbon, a card tucked into the bow. Then a flash of blond hair appeared behind him. The bellman handed Penny the package, she slid him a tip, and with a nod, he was off down the hallway.

"Hey," Indy said, smiling. "What's that?"

Penny shrugged as they went back inside her suite. "I have no idea."

The card slipped free of the ribbon easily enough and she opened it, smiling as she read the note.

For luck—Alex

Slowly, she pulled the bow free, but she paused before opening it. It was definitely jewelry, probably a necklace, from the shape of the box. Why would he send her jewelry? Was he apologizing for his near-total silence for the last couple of days? No. She had to stop overanalyzing everything and open the gift.

"Wow," Indy said from over her shoulder. "So, I guess he doesn't hate you."

"It's perfect," Penny said, running a fingertip over the old British coin attached to the long chain. It was a 1936 penny, minted the same year Fred Perry won Wimbledon, the last English man to do so before Alex. It was exactly what she would have picked out for herself, except that she wouldn't have thought of it in a million years. The gift was beyond thoughtful. It wasn't some expensive, shiny object, but represented both of them. Still, having him with her was what she really wanted.

"You're going to wear it to the gala tonight, right?" Indy asked. "If you don't, I will."

"It's a *penny* necklace, Indy. I don't think people will get it if you wear it."

"Ha! The paparazzi would probably make up some story about me ripping it off your neck and stealing Alex away from you. Caroline would love that. Think of the buzz that would stir up." Indy looked back at the necklace. "God, it's the most perfect gift I have ever seen. You two are just—you kind of make me want to vomit."

"Love you, too," Penny said, checking her phone. No messages.

Where was he?

Should she text him?

Just to say thank you?

Or wait to do it in person?

In person. That was better and she needed to stop obsessing.

She'd see him later, at the gala.

"How was your flight?"

Indy tossed herself back onto the bed and let out a long-suffering sigh. "Jasmine didn't speak to me the entire trip here. How do you think it was?"

"You can't take all that negative energy out onto the court. You guys will get destroyed."

"Don't sugarcoat it or anything." Indy stretched her neck and groaned. "I'm working on it, promise."

"Good, but for now I think I have something that'll cheer you up," Penny said, grabbing her phone and texting Jack. "The dresses will be here in fifteen minutes."

Penny couldn't help but admire the dress she'd chosen for the players' gala. Strapless taupe silk embellished with beading at the waist and hem, it gave her a chicer look than her usual style. She bent her arm back, gave the zipper one last tug, and it slid into place.

"There," she said, turning and twisting in the mirror. Perfect.

A knock sounded and she moved to open the door. "Indy, hurry up," she called toward the bathroom. "We've only got like..."

When she opened the door, he was there. Penny bit her

lip, trying to stop her grin at the sight of him, hair still damp from the probable mad dash from the car into the hotel, his bags dropped at his feet, a hand supporting him against the doorframe, head ducked before he looked up at her, his eyes already burning into hers from beneath his furrowed brow.

It was a losing battle, and as soon as her mouth curved into a soft smile, he reached out with his free arm and pulled her in, bracing her back against the doorframe and bending his head to her.

The kiss was hot and deep and all-consuming, and his hands buried into her hair, totally ruining the silky curls she'd meticulously arranged. Penny didn't care as she curled her leg around his calf, pulling him even closer.

Ignoring the pointed throat clearing from behind them, likely Indy emerging from the bathroom, Penny pulled away, then kissed him lightly one more time as Indy's gagging noises faded back into the bathroom. They finally moved out of the hallway and let the hotel room door close behind them.

"You got the necklace." His hand came up to where the coin rested against her skin, just above the neckline of her dress, rising and falling with every breath she took. "Do you like it?"

"I love it."

"I've had it with me during every Grand Slam I've ever played in and I wanted you to have it." She leaned forward again to kiss him, but he rested his forehead against hers, stopping her. "I'm sorry about how I left things between us," he murmured against her lips. "I couldn't figure out a way to say that over the phone, so I thought this might do it for me."

If he kept this up, all of her lingering doubts would be long gone in no time. This was how it needed to be, them talking things out, not stressing over silly misunderstandings when their minds needed to be on the court. "You thought right. It's perfect. That doesn't mean I'm not going to worry about your knee, though, okay?"

He winced. "Yeah, about that. I saw my surgeon in London while I was there. I told him about the pain and he took a look. Knee's fine, I promise, but worry away if it'll make you feel better."

"Oh," Penny said, the flurry of information making her mind whirl as much as his arrival. "You could've said something."

Alex shrugged. "Might have been a little embarrassed about how I snapped."

"Next time talk to me, okay? Don't disappear."

"Promise," he said, pressing his lips against her forehead. She closed her eyes, reveling in the feel of the kiss, but her mind was still spinning; she was still unsure if she could let go enough to trust him completely.

"I stand by what I said, you two make me want to vomit," Indy called from the opposite end of the room, balancing against the dresser to put on her black heels, which were paired perfectly with an emerald-green halter dress with a metallic sheen that hugged her long, lean figure tightly. Penny couldn't help the soft snort of amusement against Alex's neck. He hushed her lightly.

"You look lovely tonight, Indy," Alex said, and Penny lifted her head in time to see her friend blush.

"Thanks. Are you guys actually going to the party, or should I finish up here and leave you to it?"

Penny rolled her eyes. "We're going. Do you want us to wait for you?"

Indy grabbed her makeup bag and waved them out of the room. "No, go ahead. I'm almost done."

They walked hand in hand toward the elevator bay, but once there, Penny couldn't resist. She stood on her toes, leaned against his chest, and kissed him lightly once, twice, then, slowly opening her mouth beneath his, she nudged her tongue against his bottom lip. They broke apart and came together over and over again, neither willing to stop until they both pulled away, gasping for air, shaky breaths matching the trembling in her body.

"Jesus," he breathed. "How do you do that?"

"Do what?" she asked as his hands fell to her waist, squeezing gently.

Alex shrugged. "I don't know. It doesn't matter. Do it again."

Laughing a little, she pressed her lips to his again. "Your flight got in early?"

"Took an earlier one," he said, reaching around her to push the elevator call button. "I wanted to get here in time for the gala."

"So you could go with me?" she asked, only half teasing him. "We can't even stay that long. I have my first-round match tomorrow."

"So I could see you in a dress like that, and I don't care

how long we stay. In fact, I'm all in favor of making an early night of it." He stepped back and let his eyes travel up from the floor over every inch of her body.

Penny laughed. "You're so smooth."

A deep chuckle echoed from his chest. "Apparently not that smooth."

"Smooth enough," she said, then grasped the front of his crisp white dress shirt and pulled him in for another kiss.

A ding from the elevator's arriving registered in her mind, but she didn't care.

"Damn it, could you two not do that in front of me, ever?"

Alex pulled away at the sound of her brother's voice. She fell back on her heels, turned, and glared at Jack.

"Can we hold hands or is that too much for your delicate sensibilities?"

"Jack, good to see you, mate," Alex said, extending his hand toward her brother.

Jack frowned but shook his hand. The handshake lasted longer than it probably should have. Penny watched as the knuckles of both men's hands turned red and then briefly white before they both released their grip.

"Are you done?" she asked Jack sharply.

He ignored her question. "Is Indiana ready, too? Dom's downstairs holding a car for all of us."

As if on cue, Indy appeared around the corner looking like someone who belonged on a runway rather than a tennis court, long blond hair in wild waves hanging down her back, smoky eyes, and gloss making her lips shine. Penny saw Jack suck in a breath and a sudden heaviness cut through the small space. She glanced between her brother and her friend, but as quickly as she felt the tension, it was gone again.

"All right, let's go," Jack said, calling the elevator again. The door opened immediately. They all stepped inside. As the door closed and the car started moving, Alex slipped his hand around Penny's and squeezed.

It was going to be a good night.

"Penny! Alex!"

"When's the wedding?"

"Look this way!"

"Give her a kiss!"

Alex stepped out of the car and then offered her his hand as the camera flashes assaulted them. Penny steadied her heels against the cobblestone street, feeling his arm slide around her waist. Indy, Jasmine, Jack, and Dom followed behind, but the reporters were in a frenzy for tennis's new golden couple. No more unsubstantiated rumors. They were clearly together. And as if to emphasize the point, Alex's hand slid a little lower. Penny bit her lip and glanced up at him through her lashes.

He winked at her and then nodded at the red carpet. The flashes were blinding and it was almost impossible to understand anything in the cacophony coming from the camera pool.

"You okay?" Alex muttered into her ear about halfway down the line.

"This is wild," she said through her teeth, keeping her

smile firmly in place, but moving closer to him, pressing her side into his.

He exhaled into her hair and then brushed a kiss against her temple, his neatly trimmed five-o'clock shadow scraping lightly against her skin. The paparazzi went wild. If it hadn't sunk in that her life had changed forever when she'd arrived at the hotel earlier to a sea of cameras, the point was hammered home now. She couldn't just be Penny Harrison, tennis player, anymore. She was a celebrity, whether she wanted to be or not.

Chapter 21

"WOW," JASMINE SAID AS SHE WATCHED PENNY AND ALEX finish their red carpet walk and head into the party. Next to her, Jack, Indy, and Dom were all gaping at the reporters going nuts for the couple ahead of them, but Jasmine started making her way down the line. That jump-started the rest of the group.

The reporters weren't quite as enthusiastic as before, but she and her new doubles partner got plenty of attention from the cameras.

"Stand together for some," Dom muttered to them as he passed behind them about halfway down the carpet. "Present a united front."

Their united front would probably last as long as their doubles run did.

Indy didn't look any more thrilled than Jasmine felt, but they smiled for the photographers' pool together. As if their personalities didn't clash enough, the tangerine sheath dress and funky purple belt Jasmine was wearing up against the green metallic fabric of Indy's dress didn't really make a pretty picture.

They finally made it to the end of the row and immediately stepped away from each other and followed Dom into the party. The music was loud, but the buzz from the crowd was louder as people mingled in the dimly lit room. Jasmine looked around for a familiar face and couldn't find one. Things had changed a lot since her dad retired. Back then she would've known half the party before stepping through the door. Now she was in a crush of strangers, people who were supposed to be her peers, but none of them knew who she was and never would unless someone pointed her out as John Randazzo and Lisa Vega's daughter.

"Screw this," she mumbled, and turned back to the entrance. She'd have one of the staff call her a car, go back to the hotel, and order some room service. She didn't need this party or these people. The only thing she needed was to get some rest and train well tomorrow. If she wanted to prove everyone wrong, she had to be at her best.

"Wait, where are you going?" Indy asked, grabbing her arm.

"Let go of me," she said, pulling free. "I'm going back to the hotel. This is such a waste of time."

"Don't be ridiculous. We're at the French Open. This is...You shouldn't miss this," Indy said, sweeping a hand at the party.

"Do you know how many of these I've been to?"

"Yeah, but how many of them because you were playing?"

Jasmine's shoulders dropped and she looked back out into the sea of partygoers. "But I don't know anyone."

Indy bit her lip. "We know each other."

"Yeah, me and you," Jasmine said, crossing her fingers and holding them up for Indy to see. "We're like that. Why don't you go find Penny, she's your new best friend. Or is she too busy for you tonight?"

"She is my friend," Indy said, "and she's obviously a little busy, but you're my doubles partner."

"Save it," Jasmine said, trying to push past the taller girl, but Indy stood her ground.

"No. Every time we take a step forward, we take like ten back. We have a couple of days of training to get past it before we have to go out in front of the whole world and compete together. We're both professionals. We should be able to put the personal stuff aside and be..." She waved a hand through the air.

"Professional?" Jasmine finished for her.

"Exactly. Look, I know you don't like me, but I mean, look around, we're at the French Open. How many people can say they've been here? We should soak this in. Who knows if it'll happen again? We should have fun and enjoy the whole thing."

She made a good point. Jasmine didn't know when she would be back at a tournament like this, especially if doubles didn't work out. If Hodges was right, she was probably headed to the Challenger circuit, the minor leagues of tennis, or maybe even to a college team. Maybe she could go to Duke with Teddy. They could rule the ACC together. That was what everyone expected of her now. They didn't think she should win just because her parents won all the time. Indy was right. There was no pressure . . . at all.

The constant weight of expectation she'd been carrying for years suddenly fell away. It didn't matter. None of it did. She had to live in the moment. She could worry about the future and other people's expectations later . . . or maybe never again.

"Jasmine?"

She looked back at Indy, and for the first time, she didn't see the girl Teddy thought was hot or the girl who beat her at the OBX Classic. She saw her doubles partner. "Maybe we can find a table or something."

"Great," Indy said, standing on her tiptoes in the five-inch heels that made her tower over most of the crowd even more than she already would have. "I see an empty one, come on."

Jasmine struggled to keep up with Indy's long strides, but they got to the table and slid into the small booth with a perfect view of the entire room. As soon as they were seated, Jasmine lifted her hand to call over one of the passing waiters. She was going to enjoy this party and that meant she wanted some champagne.

"Won't Dom mind?" Indy said as Jasmine took her own glass from the waiter's tray and then one for Indy as well.

"It's one glass of champagne and we're of age here," Jasmine said, and took a long sip.

"Yep," Indy agreed, but she still pushed her glass away as her eyes focused on the crowd, darting from group to group. Then her gaze locked and Jasmine followed her line of sight straight to where Jack Harrison was standing, talking and laughing with a few party guests, including several really gorgeous women. Despite that, he seemed to be constantly searching the room but unable to find whatever he was looking for.

"So, it's Jack, not Teddy, huh?"

"What?" Indy said, snapping her eyes away from the group and staring at Jasmine wide-eyed. "No."

"And yeah, that confirmed it." Jasmine leaned forward in her seat. "He doesn't know?"

"Oh, he knows, at least I think he does, but he's too... he's too Jack to do anything about it."

Jasmine giggled. "Too Jack?"

"It's what I've decided to call it, because he seems super into me one second and then just completely shuts down the next." Indy took another sip of her champagne, longer this time, nearly draining the glass.

"Maybe he sees it as a conflict. You're a player, he's an agent. You're friends with his sister. It could make things complicated."

Plus, his little brother made it clear he liked you when you first showed up, Jasmine added silently because, despite everything, that wasn't her secret to tell.

"Maybe, or maybe he's just a tease," Indy said, rolling her eyes.

"I'm just saying, it's not as simple as 'I like you, you like me, let's make out.'"

"Right," Indy said, "but it still sucks."

"I know," Jasmine said. "Believe me, I know."

They sat in silence, a much more comfortable one now, and watched the party swirl around them, people dancing and flirting and lots of fake smiles followed by eye rolls behind backs. They drank their champagne slowly but never let a waiter pass without grabbing another glass.

"So, what do you think?" Indy said, nodding at a short, extremely buff man in his forties with an orange tan and way too much hair gel. His arm was wrapped around the waist of a girl nearly a foot taller than him, but probably half his age. "Still lives with his mom, right?"

Jasmine nearly spit out her champagne, but then smiled wickedly. "No way, he has a huge penthouse apartment to compensate for his other deficiencies."

A man stopped in front of their table and Jasmine looked up, her smile fading. "Hi, Dom," she said, cringing at their table of champagne glasses, some still full, but most of them drained.

"Ladies, I see we're having a good time," their coach said, a massive crease between his brows as he frowned down at them.

"We were," Indy muttered, "but I'm guessing that's over now."

"Damn right," he said, shaking his head. "Let's go."

They followed him through the party and to a side door, where Dom had one of the tour officials call them a car.

"Straight back to the hotel," he told them before leaning in the window and telling the driver where to go.

"Feels like I just got sent to the principal's office," Indy muttered.

"We kind of did," Jasmine giggled, feeling the buzz starting to wear off just slightly, and then her laughter faded.

Disappointing Dom was not on her list of ways to make him take her seriously.

Driving through the streets of Paris was an experience all its own. The streetlights reflected against the windows of their car and each street looked like it was the set of an epic love story. Indy sighed from the seat next to her.

"It's beautiful, isn't it?" Jasmine asked.

"Almost too beautiful to be real. Have you been here before?"

"Yeah, with my parents."

"Right. Me too. My mom and I did the London and Paris thing when I was thirteen. I definitely didn't appreciate it at the time."

They pulled up to the front of the hotel and the driver got out to open the door for them. As they stepped out onto the sidewalk, the Eiffel Tower—lit up for the night—twinkled in the distance, the rest of the city's lights a mere stage for the famed landmark to stand upon.

"Why didn't your parents come?" Indy asked as they moved through the lobby toward the elevators.

Jasmine frowned. No one else had thought to ask that. Not even Dom, although it was possible he already knew why. "I asked them not to."

"Why?"

"I..." She hesitated as they got into the elevator car. "I wasn't sure how well we were going to do and I didn't want to, I don't know, disappoint them, I guess." Then, feeling a lot more exposed than she had in a long time, she shot back, "Why isn't your dad here?"

"I doubt he even knows I'm playing."

Jasmine raised an eyebrow in disbelief and the elevator dinged, signaling their arrival on the sixth floor.

Indy sighed and kept talking. "My dad loves his job. He loves his job more than he loved my mom, and he loves his job more than he loves me. When my mom died, he let me keep on living in the house I shared with my mom instead of asking me to live with him. He hired a housekeeper, paid for the maintenance, and kept my bank account full. I get a card from him on Christmas and a present on my birthday, but his secretary sends them."

"That sucks."

"Life's not fair and all that. I have it a lot better than most people."

"I guess we both do."

"Yeah, and look, I didn't mean what I said about your serve."

Jasmine snorted. "Yeah you did."

"Okay, maybe a little, but it's not terrible, and you were right, my net game could really use a lot of work."

"If you miss, I'll be behind you to get it."

"Good to know."

Jasmine smiled. She should leave this newfound peace alone, but she couldn't help herself. They were getting everything out in the open, so why not this? "So, if we get into the third round, which will it be?"

"What?" Indy asked.

"If it comes down to it, if you have to choose, doubles here or singles in Bari?"

"I... I don't..."

"Listen, I know how this works. If we get into week two

here, you're going to have to choose, and I won't hate you forever or anything if you choose singles. I get it."

"No, it'll be doubles," Indy said finally.

"Seriously?"

"Yeah, and not because you're standing here asking me. I honestly wasn't sure until right now, but really, it's the opportunity of a lifetime to play in a main draw at a Grand Slam tournament. I wouldn't be able to drop it, not even for a chance to win in Bari."

A sudden surge of gratitude swept through Jasmine like she'd never felt before. Why should she be grateful to a girl she didn't even like all that much for taking advantage of an opportunity to play at a Grand Slam? It didn't really make sense, and it was probably fueled more by the champagne than anything else, but before she could stop herself, she hugged Indy.

"Thanks," she said, pulling away before Indy had a chance to react.

Indy narrowed her eyes, like she didn't quite trust what just happened. "You're welcome," she said, her voice lingering on that last syllable, making it more of a question.

Jasmine ignored it and gave her a smile and a nod. "I'll see you tomorrow morning for training."

"Yeah, see you tomorrow." Indy turned and started down the hallway before she stopped and called back, "Wait!"

Jasmine stopped, tilting her head in question.

Indy rambled, "I know I said we didn't have to be friends, but you know, I think I might like being friends. If you want, if that's . . . cool with you."

"I would like that, actually."

And she was surprised to realize that was the truth.

"Good," Indy said. "So would I, so that's...that's good. Good night."

"Night!" Jasmine turned the idea over in her head as she stepped into her hotel room. She kicked off her heels and rummaged through her suitcase for some pajamas. It had been a long day, and curling up in her bed sounded like a pretty good way to end it. After scrubbing off her makeup and washing her face, she stared at her reflection. Maybe Indy was right. Maybe they could be friends. And maybe eventually it would stop feeling a little bit forced and turn into something real.

She switched off the bathroom light and climbed into bed. On her nightstand her phone lit up, vibrating, and Teddy's contact appeared on the screen. Her stomach flipped and her heart skipped, and she didn't have the energy to be annoyed at herself for it. She answered the call. "You'll never guess what happened."

"Good job, ladies!" Dom called from the sidelines as they finished up their workout with a set of Einstein sprints that made the other players on the practice courts stare in horror.

Jasmine slowed to a halt and held her hand up for Indy, who slapped it, hard. "Nice," she said, and meant it. Indy looked fabulous during their practice session, despite the champagne. Actually, they both had. Indy's conditioning level was finally catching up to Jasmine's, and they'd torn up the court for the two hours Dom had reserved it. Their sneakers and the lower halves of their legs were covered in red clay, but their faces were both lit up with smiles. Jasmine finally understood what Teddy meant about Dom being a genius. She felt it every time Indy served a bullet up the center of the court, or she got to a ball Indy couldn't quite reach. They had a real chance to open some eyes if what they brought at practice translated into their first-round match the next day.

"I've got to get to Penny's match," Dom finally said, checking the time on his phone. "Cool down, shower, and I'll see you later."

Jasmine was ready just before Indy, but once she was, Indy turned to her and said, "You wanna go to Penny's match? She invited me, and I know they have a few empty seats in the box."

"Sure," Jasmine said, feeling somehow like she'd gotten an invite to the inner circle, one she hadn't even realized existed but was also desperate to be a part of.

They made it to the player's box just in time for the coin toss. Jack's seat was on the aisle, with Dom next to him and Alex the farthest down the row. She and Indy settled into the seats behind them.

It was as big a mismatch as Jasmine had ever seen. Penny Harrison, who'd defeated the number one player in the world in her last tournament, against some poor random French qualifier. The first couple of rounds at a Grand Slam tended to be like that. The highest-ranked athletes usually drew players who came through the qualifying rounds or a wild card and who'd spent most of the tennis season on the Challenger circuit and not on the main tour.

Pulling her phone from her bag, Jasmine held it up to snap a picture of the court where Penny and her opponent were warming up. She added a quick caption—*Courtside at Roland-Garros for Penny's match!*—and sent it out into the void.

A minute later, her phone vibrated and a message popped up from Teddy:

Updates please!

Don't you have twin ESP? You tell me how it's going to go.

Maybe I just want to talk to you.

Talked to you last night.

Too long ago. Call me tonight?

The chair ump climbed up into his seat and said, "Play," and Jasmine put her phone away, Teddy's message unanswered.

"Here we go," Indy said.

Penny got off to a blazing start, and after fifteen minutes of dominating play, she was only a point away from winning the first set. Her opponent looked exhausted and beaten, sitting in her chair during a changeover and staring out into space.

Finally, during the break between sets, as everyone else stood to stretch their legs, Jasmine looked at her phone. Teddy had sent five messages, the last a picture of him sitting up against the fence at OBX, shirtless and sweaty, sticking his tongue out and crossing his eyes. God, he was so hot it actually hurt. Laughing, Jasmine sent a message back: *Nice face. Penny's up a set.*

"What's funny?" Indy asked, sitting down beside her.

"Nothing."

Indy narrowed her eyes and focused on her phone. "Who are you texting?"

"Did anyone ever tell you that you ask too many questions?"

"Did anyone ever tell you that you have the worst poker face ever? You're texting Teddy, aren't you?" Indy plucked the phone from her hand.

"So what?" Jasmine said, stealing it back.

"He's never going to appreciate you if you're always at his beck and call."

"*Beck and call*, what are you, eighty?" Jasmine shut the phone completely off and tossed it into her bag, then crossed her arms. "He's my friend. It's not like I'm never going to talk to him again."

"You shouldn't. Maybe if you cut him off it'll make him miss you."

"That's worked before."

"Wait, you've tried that?"

"Yeah and it worked. He missed me."

"But as what? His friend? You're never going to get over him if you guys stay friends. You should end it now and stop torturing yourself."

Jasmine's gaze flicked toward Jack, who was standing in the aisle and talking to a rep from one of Penny's sponsors—Nike, if the swoosh logo on his shirt was anything to go by.

She turned back to Indy, who was still staring at Jack, and it had Jasmine hoping that wasn't what *her* face looked like when she was around Teddy.

"Maybe you should take your own advice."

Indy's shoulders deflated a little. "Maybe I should."

Chapter 22

THE PLAYERS' LOUNGE WAS PACKED. INDY FIGURED THAT MADE sense since it was only the second day of the tournament and almost no one had been eliminated yet. She took in the players and their coaches discussing match strategy, some friends and family hovering in the background. Jasmine sat next to her, scrolling through her phone like she didn't have a care in the world, even though their first match was minutes away.

Sitting back, leg bouncing, Indy looked around the room. She was a nervous wreck and the crowd wasn't helping. She hated this. Just like at the Classic, she felt fine until right before a match, and then the jitters started. Except now there was no hope of stepping out onto the court against a weaker opponent. She was at the fucking French Open and they were playing Zina Lutrova and Ekaterina Grishina. Though the two Russians hadn't played together before, they were training for Olympic doubles and were using this tournament as a practice run.

Jasmine glared at her and then glanced down at her knee. Indy muttered an apology and stilled the constant, nauseating motion. But she squirmed in her seat, bringing her thumb to her mouth to chew on her fingernail instead.

"Ladies, good news," Dom said, throwing himself down in a chair across from them. "You two have a walkover."

"You're kidding," Jasmine said.

"Nope," he said, passing her an updated copy of the draw. "Lutrova withdrew from doubles. She wants to focus on singles. No match today."

"So, we won?" Indy asked.

"That's one way of looking at it, I guess. Next match is scheduled for the day after tomorrow. You've got a real opportunity here. Let's not let it go to waste. I reserved a few hours on a practice court so you can get some work in and stay fresh, but congrats, you're through to the second round." He stood and left, moving to the buffet.

"Wow, that was easy," Indy said, grinning, her nerves gone now that they didn't actually have to play.

"Not really. Did you see who our potential next-round match would be?"

"No, I didn't look at the draw."

"Why wouldn't you look at the draw?"

"I thought you weren't supposed to. You know, like whenever anyone in an interview is asked if they know who they're playing next, they always say they have no idea. I figured it was bad luck or something."

"They're lying when they say that. Everyone looks at the draw."

"So..." Indy trailed off.

"So what?"

"Who are we playing?"

"Oh right, sorry." Jasmine glanced down at the page Dom gave her and pointed out their likely opponents for their next match. "The Kapur sisters, Pallavi and Ananya."

"Shit."

"Exactly."

The Kapur twins were one of the top doubles teams in the world and the number one seed for this tournament. They'd both given up playing on the singles circuit a few years ago and since then had won dozens of tournaments, most notably the Australian Open. Facing them in their first match together would be like deciding to run a marathon after a couple of hours of jogging on the treadmill.

"We are so screwed," Indy said.

"We could go watch them play. They're scheduled for right now."

"Why not?" Not that knowing exactly how they were going to be dismantled in a couple of days would help her nerves, but at least she'd know what she was in for.

They made their way to one of the outer courts, where the Kapur sisters were scheduled to play a wild card team directly across from where their own match had been scheduled. The crowd was sparse and they found a spot along the chain-link fence surrounding the court. There were stands on the other side, but the view was better against the fence.

Indy was just settling in to watch when a voice interrupted her.

"Indiana."

Indy turned her head, and her jaw dropped. A few feet away was a tall man dressed in khaki pants and a crisp light blue Lacoste polo. His dark blond hair, beginning to gray at the temples, was cropped close. Caroline was beside him, hanging on his arm, her wide-brimmed hat and sunglasses hiding her identity from passersby. Not that it was working: Caroline was the kind of woman people noticed, disguise or not.

Indy knew who she was immediately. So did Jasmine, apparently.

"Who's that with Caroline?" Jasmine asked.

"That's my dad."

"Your dad? But I thought..."

"So did I." Indy pushed off the fence and crossed the pathway between them. "Hi," she said, making sure to put a question in her tone as they both hugged her.

"I called your father," Caroline said, kissing each of her cheeks.

"Obviously."

Her dad had the gall to smile. "I hadn't realized you had progressed this quickly."

"You should've asked me before you called him," Indy said, glaring at her agent.

"It is done," Caroline said with a dismissive shrug. "Now, why are you not preparing for your match?"

"Jasmine and I got a walkover into the second round."

"Ah," her dad said, looking at Caroline. "Well, if there's no match, I should go back to the hotel and call the office."

"Good," Indy said, trying to stifle the hurt. Of course he didn't want to spend any actual time with her, not that she wanted to either, but she would have liked the option of turning him down flat. "My next match is the day after tomorrow. Come if you want. I don't care."

She spun and walked away, catching Jasmine's eye as she passed her.

Anger bordering on rage coursed through her at his audacity and at herself, for not seeing it coming. Of course he showed up now. Of course he acted like everything was fine and that he hadn't ignored her entirely for most of her life and dipped completely after her mom died and pawned her off to Caroline when she dropped out of college on what he probably thought was a whim. But now that it had worked out, he'd swoop in, like he'd been there all along, a loving, supportive father who wanted to nurture her dreams.

Fuck. Him.

Angling her way through the teams of spectators exploring the outer courts, she circled back toward the players' exit and ran into Jack, her face almost colliding against the Nike swoosh logo on his black T-shirt.

"Indiana?" he said as she pushed past him. "Indiana, wait."

She whirled around and snapped, "What?"

His eyebrows shot up. "Are you okay?"

"I'm fine," she said, trying to step around him again. People around them in the busy hallway, athletes, coaches, and staff alike, were staring at them. Most of them probably had no idea who she was, but they definitely knew Jack.

"You're not fine," he said, leading her away from the

crowd and down a separate empty hallway. "What's the matter? Maybe I can help."

Indy ran a hand through her hair. "My dad is here."

Jack studied her carefully. She liked that about him. He always thought before he spoke. "And that's bad?"

"Of course it's bad. He's only here because... because..."

"He's your dad. He's here because he wants to support you."

She twisted her mouth into a pout. Jack didn't get it. She hadn't met his parents, but she knew the Harrisons were a happy family.

"He's here because I'm interesting now. I'm doing something worthy of his attention, so he showed up."

"Indiana..." he said, sighing heavily, his eyes softening... pitying.

Pity was the last thing she wanted him to feel for her. "Don't. My dad is an asshole. He's always been like that, but I don't need you to feel sorry for me, okay? I don't need your pity."

"I don't feel sorry for you."

"I..." She trailed off. "What?"

"I kind of want to go shake him for not realizing what an amazing daughter he has, but I don't feel sorry for you."

Her heart fluttered. "You think I'm amazing?"

Jack ran a shaky hand across the back of his neck. "You know I do."

He reached out and tucked a strand of hair behind her ear. His hand didn't fall away, but hovered over her cheek. He blinked down at her, hesitating for a moment before his hand descended, large and warm against her skin. Breathing in deeply, she leaned into the touch.

This wasn't the lightning bolt attraction she normally felt around him but a slow, burning ember, comforting and safe, and she wanted this, too, this wall around the world keeping all the bad shit away, helping her forget how hard all of this was simply by being there. She collapsed into him and he held her close, one hand cradling the back of her head, his thumb brushing soothing circles just below her ear, coaxing her breath back into a slow, even rhythm, her temper cooling, all the tension in her sliding away.

Finally, she pulled away and he let her go, but she didn't step back and neither did he.

"Thank you," she said softly, and when she looked into his eyes, all his work to calm her down went to hell in the best possible way. Her breath caught and she wet her lips, his gaze flicking down to follow the motion. She was close enough to hear his shaky exhale.

"Indiana, I..." He trailed off, finally bending his head to hers.

The electricity that accompanied their innocent kiss a few weeks ago was like a tiny little sparkler compared to the fireworks display exploding behind her eyes as his tongue gently nudged against her lips, deepening the kiss. He held her firmly at her hips, his fingers flexing with every stroke of his tongue, pulling her closer. Then she felt him tense, and in the next second he was gone, putting several feet between them, staring at her.

"I'm—"

"Jack, I swear to God, if you fucking apologize."

"I wasn't going to."

"Of course you were," she said, shaking her head, "because that's the kind of guy you are. Just like how you always show up whenever I need rescuing. I know you feel *something* for me, but I don't understand why you won't do anything about it."

"I . . . I'm sorry, I . . ."

He flinched, clearly knowing he'd said the wrong thing, and Indy felt all her anger and rage fly back to the surface and boil over as she leaned in closer. "If any other man were standing in front of me right now, he wouldn't be apologizing."

Jack pressed his lips into a thin line. "You don't understand. It's complicated."

"How? Explain it to me."

He hesitated, but then said, "I'm too old for you." His eyes darted away from her before he even finished his weak-ass excuse.

Indy snorted in disbelief. "Please, spare me."

"Six years is more than you realize. The shit I thought I knew when I was twenty . . ." He trailed off, but there was something in his eyes, something that told her that the age thing, even if it was part of why he was holding back, wasn't the only reason.

It just didn't add up.

"I think you're full of shit."

He snorted. "Don't you think I'd rather just take what I want and damn the consequences? But I can't do that. That's not the kind of man I am."

"That's not what I meant and you know it."

"Then what the hell do you want from me?" he snapped, throwing up his hands in the air.

"I want you to stop being a coward."

The words were liberating, like she'd been holding them in since the moment she first saw him, and now he knew the truth, even if he'd never act on it—at least not again. The seconds ticked away, and the longer he was silent, the clearer it was that he wasn't going to respond, but Indy wasn't finished. She was done pretending.

"If you don't feel the same way," she said, taking one step and then another toward him, until her body was nearly flush against his, "if you don't want me, that's okay. But if you want this as much as I do, well, you know where to find me."

With her last words, she pressed a soft kiss against his cheek, inflicting the same sweet torture he'd put her through back when they first met. Then she turned and walked away.

Chapter 23

THE SOUND OF RAIN AGAINST HER WINDOWS DREW PENNY from her sleep. The room was still dark, a product of the overcast skies outside. She let her eyes drift closed, and that was when she noticed it: a weight, heavy and warm against her stomach, an arm curving protectively around her body, two fingers tucked slightly into the waistband of her pajama shorts. She could hear his soft, even breathing on the pillow next to hers. She recognized the deep, slow rhythm. Alex was next to her and he was sound asleep.

She carefully rolled over. His arm remained around her, instinctively pulling her closer. He was practically radiating heat and she snuggled into it, pressing her lips to his shoulder. Penny closed her eyes again and let sleep slowly overtake her.

She woke later, sleepier than when she'd roused the first

time, the rain still pelting her windowpanes. Alex was awake now, still holding her close, his eyes focused on her.

"Hey," he whispered, nudging his nose against hers.

"Hi," she breathed, their lips brushing together softly. "This is nice."

He nodded in agreement. "Mm, more than nice. If I could wake up like this for the rest of my life, I'd die a happy man."

She tucked her head into the crook of his shoulder. "I think that can be arranged. I sleep better when you're here," she said, her fingers absently drawing patterns against the skin of his bicep.

She reveled in a few more moments of peaceful bliss before she remembered why she was here and what she had ahead of her—the toughest test of her career—and she wouldn't get any closer to it just lying here with him. "I have to get up."

He groaned. "No you don't. You have to stay right here."

"I have to get up," she said again. "Dom booked a practice court for ten. I have to take a shower." A wicked grin spread across his face at the idea. "By myself. I need to get my head in the right space for my match tonight."

"It's raining. They're going to cancel your match," he argued against her neck, his hands already finding purchase against her hips, pressing her down into the mattress. Alex had dispatched his first-round opponent in straight sets the night before, his knee not giving him any trouble at all, and his second-round match wasn't until the next day. He'd earned a morning of rest, but Penny definitely had work to do that day.

"It's drizzling, and regardless, I have to prepare like I'm

going to play," she said, despite wanting to agree with him in the worst way.

"Fine," he said, releasing her and burying his head beneath a pillow when she turned on a light.

"Drama queen," she muttered as she dug through her suitcase, pulling out the practice clothes Nike had sent for the tournament.

Stepping under the hot spray of water, she let it soak her hair, and her mind drifted to the tournament draw. Her opponent was Patricia Smyth, a veteran with a decent all-around game. They'd played once before in Miami: 6–3, 6–1, in an easy victory. There was nothing to be concerned about. What else did she know about Patricia? She was English, like Alex, which wasn't exactly information that would help her during the match.

She had to stop relating everything to him. She wouldn't become one of those girls whose life only revolved around a guy, no matter how good he made her feel, both in his bed and out of it.

The water grew cool and she countered by pushing the hot handle a little farther down. Every muscle in her body sang with relief as tension she hadn't realized was there slipped out through her pores. Letting her chin fall to her chest, she exhaled heavily. Her mind drifted, imagining Alex's broad chest pressing up against her back, his hands exploring her skin, his lips trailing down her neck, over her shoulder... Then she was jolted from her daydream by a flash of light through the shower's glass door.

Wiping at the shower door to clear the fog away, she squinted through the glass. Alex's phone was plugged into the wall, charging, its screen lit up with an incoming message. She turned off the water and stepped out of the shower, wrapping a towel around her body and tucking it closed between her breasts.

Leaning over, careful not to drip on the phone, she saw a message flashing over his locked screen—a picture message from Caroline Morneau with a caption: *Just one more. I couldn't help myself.* The picture was tiny, but Penny could make out the gist. It was Alex on the night of the gala. He had Penny pressed up against a wall, his mouth at her neck, his hand covered to the wrist by the skirt of her dress, disappearing between her thighs. Her head was thrown back, eyes closed, fingers digging into his shoulders. Penny swallowed back a wave of panic. They'd snuck away from the party briefly, not quite willing to wait until they got back to the hotel. Obviously, someone had followed them, snapped a picture, then sent it to Caroline. Or had Caroline taken the picture herself?

But the real question was, why the hell was Caroline messaging it to Alex?

Penny pulled the phone from its charger and swept out of the bathroom, tossing it onto the lump of covers she assumed Alex was buried under.

"Your phone was buzzing."

His head popped out from under the blankets and he picked up his phone, glancing at the screen before looking back up at her. "Did you see?"

"If you mean, did I see the screen and wonder why Caroline Morneau is sending you photos of us with your hand up my dress? Then yeah, I saw. What does she mean, she couldn't help herself?"

"Penny, listen," he said, sitting up, rubbing his hands over his face.

"I'm listening."

Alex let out a quick breath. "She's my agent."

"Your agent?"

"That night when we were on the court, when she interrupted us, I was meeting her to sign the papers."

"I don't understand," she said, looking back at him. "What does her being your agent have anything to do with a picture like that?"

"She probably wants to stir up some buzz off the court during the tournament."

A long breath escaped through her lips as it all clicked in her head. "Like she did before the tournament with the *Athlete Weekly* pictures."

"Penny..." He trailed off, but he didn't deny it or call her crazy or even have a moment of realization, like the idea had never occurred to him before.

"Did you know?" she asked, needing him to confirm it.

"Penny, love—"

"Did. You. Know?"

"Yes."

The word was so simple that it took a moment for the implications to hit her. She sat on the bed and felt the mattress shift as he crawled toward her, sitting beside her at the edge of the bed in only his boxer briefs, his thigh pressing against hers. He slid an arm around her waist, but she shook him off.

"Don't touch me."

He flinched and then moved away, giving her some space.

"Penny, I swear, I don't know why she took this one and I'd never let her use it."

"Is that supposed to make it okay? And why did you let her use the others?"

He hesitated and then said in a soft voice, "I thought you hated me. I was angry and hurt and confused. I told her I didn't care what she did. I should have told her to get rid of them and I'm so fucking sorry."

"You didn't care? You didn't care that these incredibly private moments would be out there for anyone to see? God, I trusted you and you just...yeah, that's the point, isn't it? This is my fault. I trusted you and that's on me."

"No it's not. I'm sorry. I'll fire her. I'll do it right now."

"I don't care that she leaked the pictures, Alex. I care that you didn't seem to care one way or the other. Were you ever going to tell me?" He looked away and that was all the answer she needed. "Of course not."

She had to go. She had a practice court reserved in a little less than a half hour, and Dom would be there any minute. Chucking off the towel, she dressed quickly, not even sparing Alex a glance.

Then her own phone, charging on the dresser, started vibrating, and message after message began popping up on the screen. Behind her, she heard Alex's phone doing the same, a steady stream of *blings* echoing in the large hotel suite.

"Fuck," Alex muttered, his eyes on his phone. Then he looked up at Penny, his shoulders slumped in defeat, and she knew.

It was too late. Caroline had leaked the photo.

She should have felt panic rising in her chest or her head

aching from the onslaught of bombshells in the last few minutes, but instead a calm washed over her, a stillness that she'd only ever felt before on the tennis court.

"I have training soon. I should get going."

Moving back across the room, she grabbed a band and pulled her hair up into a quick ponytail. Through the reflection in the mirror, she saw the eyes of the man she'd trusted with her body and nearly with her heart, focused on her, agonized bewilderment written clear on his face.

"Penny," Alex began as soon as she turned around, but she shook her head. Whatever he had to say, however he thought he could make this better, she didn't want to hear it.

"I knew something like this would happen. It was all too damn good to be true." She couldn't look at him. If she looked him in the eye, it would weaken her resolve, and she had to be strong.

"Penny, please," he tried again, but she ignored him.

She opened the hotel room door and then looked back at the man still sitting on her bed, head in his heads. "You shouldn't be here when I get back."

Neither Dom nor Jack asked her about what happened when she met them in the lobby, but by their tense silence, it was clear they knew about the picture. No one uttered a word as they walked down through the lobby and out of the hotel and hopped into the car waiting to take them to Roland-Garros. By the time they arrived, the rain had stopped and the sky was clearing to a bright blue.

Dom told her to warm up, so she did. Then they worked on a few footwork drills, followed by their usual pre-match routine, sticking to the basics, making sure her shots were strong going into her match that night. The workout got her heart rate up, and a fine sheen of sweat coated her skin by the time they were finished, but it didn't do anything for her mental state. The odd calm that had settled over her at the hotel had disappeared as soon as they got on the court, replaced by a cloudy mess of confusion, and by the way Dom was looking at her, he definitely noticed. Penny didn't need him to tell her she'd practiced like crap.

Her hands shook, vibrating with frustration as she packed up her gear and left the practice court. She wasn't sure who she was most angry at, but she quickly settled upon herself for letting herself give in. She was prepared for this tournament, thanks mostly to Alex. Playing with him every day had brought her game to a whole new level: Her reaction time was shorter, her feet were quicker, and no other player had ever tested her will, on and off the court, so thoroughly—but then it had all gone to hell so quickly. When had this become her life? Men and sex and drama instead of what she'd always wanted, to be the best tennis player in the world. Was it so wrong to want someone to share that with? A dull ache settled in around her heart, her chest tightening.

"Stop it. You have to snap out of it," she muttered to herself as she turned a corner nearing the street exit and nearly collided headlong with another young woman headed in the opposite direction. A long blond braid flashed past her face as the other girl tossed her head in annoyance.

Penny narrowed her eyes as she regained her footing. "Zina."

"Watch where you are going. Oh. It is you," her rival said with a small smile. She didn't sound all that surprised. "I did not expect to see you. I thought maybe you would withdraw."

"Why would I do that?" Penny cocked her head to the side, not letting Zina's slightly larger frame intimidate her. There were a few people loitering around and she recognized most of them as reporters. This had setup written all over it.

"You have no chance to win."

"You have a short memory."

She wasn't going to give Zina or the reporters what they wanted; she wouldn't be goaded into a fight. Not even while every fiber of her being was screaming at her to haul off and smack the smug, superior smirk off the Russian girl's face.

"My memory is good. You played your best tennis. I played my worst. I have won two tournaments since that defeat, and you have spent time since then not training, but fucking Alex Russell."

Her stomach lurched at the mention of his name, but she kept her reaction off her face. "We'll see, won't we?"

Penny walked away, feeling every set of eyes fixed upon her. In a few minutes the internet would probably explode with pictures and reports of her little tête-à-tête with Lutrova, but at least for the first time since she'd arrived in France, they'd be talking about tennis.

Chapter 24

JASMINE WAS READY TO STRANGLE HER DOUBLES PARTNER. IT wasn't the all-consuming envy from a few days ago, but she had no idea that being friends with Indiana Gaffney would be more torturous than being rivals. Indy had made it her mission to find Jasmine a replacement for Teddy.

"What about him?" Indy asked, and nodded to her left as a guy walked by them, studying the strings of his racket.

"Too short," Jasmine said, wrinkling her nose.

They were killing time in the players' lounge before Penny's match, which had been rescheduled from the day before because of the rain. She'd asked them to be her cheering section and they were more than happy to oblige. The entire tournament was buzzing about the picture that had been leaked to every major media outlet Caroline could find. Jasmine had barely glanced at it, but that was enough to tell it was a totally private moment that was put on display for the entire world.

"Okay," Indy said, scanning the men in the room. "Him, over there by the window, with the bright blue shirt."

"Gay," Jasmine said, dismissing him as a candidate.

Indy tilted her head. "Really?"

"Came out last year."

"Huh, okay. You're going to have to explain your type for me, then, because I've pointed out like a dozen perfectly hot guys and you've shot down every one."

"It's not my fault the last one was gay. Otherwise, he would've been an option."

Indy narrowed her eyes, leaning forward. "I call bullshit. I think you don't want to be attracted to anyone else, so you're not."

Scoffing, Jasmine examined her nails, picking at a broken cuticle. "Attraction is biology, Indy. You can't force yourself to ignore it or make it go away."

Indy shrugged. "Love makes you blind."

"Maybe." Her eye caught on a flash of brown hair across the room. The hair belonged to a young man working his way down the buffet table.

"Paolo Macchia," Indy said when she saw where Jasmine's eyes had focused. "I saw him play in New York a couple of years ago."

Jasmine grinned. Olive skin and a floppy mess of dark hair, tall but lean, and like pretty much every guy on tour, in incredible shape. "He's cute."

"Very cute, with an amazing Italian accent."

"Good to know."

Indy leapt to her feet and started in that direction.

"Where are you going?" Jasmine asked, following her.

"To say hi," Indy said over her shoulder, making a beeline for Paolo.

Jasmine grabbed her arm and tried to pull her to a stop. "You don't even know if he speaks English."

"He totally does," she said, stepping in front of Paolo as he started loading his plate with lettuce. "Hi."

He stopped and looked up, a wide smile spreading across his face as he looked back and forth between them. "Hello."

"I'm Indiana," she said, but leaned away, giving Jasmine a gentle shove forward. "And this is my friend Jasmine."

"It's very nice to meet you," Paolo said, his hazel eyes crinkling as his smile deepened. His Italian accent was soft and musical, his English very good.

Indy coughed. "And I've gotta go make a call. Be back in a second." She pulled her phone out and walked away before Jasmine could say a word.

Paolo cleared his throat softly.

"Sorry about that."

"Do not apologize," he insisted, like he really wasn't bothered at all. "Your name is Jasmine?"

"Yes, Jasmine Randazzo," she said, waiting for the immediate flash of recognition in his eyes, but it didn't come.

"I am Paolo Macchia."

"I know." She cringed inwardly. Shit. He probably thought she was some silly girl with a crush who hadn't been brave enough to approach him on her own. The last part might be true, but the first definitely wasn't. She still had feelings for Teddy, and there wasn't room in her heart for anyone else.

Jasmine forgot her embarrassment when an unnatural quiet

settled over the players' lounge. Alex Russell had entered the room. Wearing a gray sweatshirt, hood pulled up over his head, hands tucked into the front pocket, he ignored the stares and whispers that erupted as soon as they were sure it was him.

"People suck," Jasmine muttered.

"Yes, they do, very much," Paolo agreed. "Scusi, signorina, but he is my friend. I have to speak with him."

"Oh," she said, "of course."

Paolo left his tray of food and made his way across the room to Alex, who stopped and spoke to him for a moment before they walked together out the door at the opposite end of the lounge.

Indy appeared at her side from nowhere. "So, how'd it go?"

Jasmine whirled on her. "Don't ever do that to me again."

"Please, you were both all smiles before Alex dragged that black cloud in here. Look, Teddy Harrison isn't the only guy in the world. That's all I'm saying."

"Is this about Teddy and me or about the fact that it's been two days since you kissed his brother—"

Indy shushed her, cutting off the last word, her face suddenly peaked and drawn. "That is *not* public knowledge."

Jasmine shrugged her shoulders in defeat. "I'm sorry. Anyway, you were right, Paolo's accent is amazing."

Indy brightened, latching on to the change of subject. "Told you so. Come on, let's go down and watch the match. Penny could probably use some moral support right about now."

"Yeah, sure."

As they made their way down toward the court, Jasmine's

mind was whirling. Maybe she wasn't such a lost cause after all and maybe Indy wasn't either.

"Jeu, set et match, Harrison."

In the seats next to her, Dom, Jack, and Indy all let out a collective sigh of relief as Penny looked up at the sky, thanking whatever higher power had pushed her through the match. It was a close call, but she managed to squeak past her opponent, 7–5, 6–4.

"I'm going to talk to her," Dom said, standing and making a hasty exit from the player's box. "See you all back at the hotel."

They watched him go and Jasmine cringed. She could imagine the lecture Dom would give her if she ever played like that, and maybe for the first time ever, she didn't envy Penny at all.

Then she realized she had her opening, the moment she had been trying to engineer in her head since they sat down to watch the match. She and Indy were friends now, and while Indy's efforts to help with her love life had been a little heavy-handed, Jasmine appreciated the effort. And not only because she hadn't been able to get Paolo's soft smile and beautiful eyes out of her head. The least she could do was return the favor.

"Maybe you better go with him. She's probably going to need a friendly face after their *talk*," she whispered to Indy, who nodded and left, but not before glancing quickly at Jack, who was making a rather obvious show of not looking in Indy's direction. It made Jasmine's decision to go through with her plan even easier. They had to get out of their own way.

She and Jack sat in an awkward silence as the crowd around them started to disperse for the bathrooms and concession areas between matches. Jack made to stand, but Jasmine grabbed the cuff of his pullover jacket and tugged.

He squinted at her, obviously confused. She knew it was odd. In all the time they'd known each other, she couldn't recall ever having had a full conversation with him—just the two of them—without Penny or Teddy around. Jasmine pushed past the awkwardness.

"I need to talk to you."

"What's up?" he asked, sitting back down, giving her his full attention. When their eyes met she was startled by how much he and Teddy resembled each other. They were different in so many ways that it was easy to forget sometimes that they were brothers.

"You've met my dad, right?" she asked, wanting to approach this the right way. She didn't want to scare him off before she could make her point.

"Yeah, of course I have."

"Would you say he's a good guy?"

Confusion clouded his eyes, but he nodded. "Yeah, your dad's a great guy. Are you okay, Jasmine?"

"Me? I'm fine. At least, I think I'm fine. I know I'm a little spoiled and I tend to freak out sometimes, but I think my parents did a good job of raising me."

Jack's forehead wrinkled and he put a hand on top of hers. "Seriously, Jasmine, are you having some kind of issue with your parents? I don't think I'm the best person to talk to about something like that."

She rolled her eyes, pulling her hand free. "Jack, chill, I'm trying to make a point."

He studied her carefully but nodded. "Okay, I'll play, what's your point?"

"Do you know how old my mom was when she met my dad?"

"No, I don't."

"She was eighteen years old."

"Okay."

"Yep. She was eighteen years old and they've been together for almost twenty years now. Kind of nice, right? That they've been together so long?"

"I guess so."

"You know how old my dad was at the time?"

Jack narrowed his eyes at her, obviously finally figuring out her point. "I'm guessing not eighteen?"

"Nope. More like twenty-two."

"Did Indiana send you to talk to me?"

Jasmine snorted. "What? God no. She'd kill me if she knew, unless she died of embarrassment first. Then she'd probably haunt me for the rest of my life."

"Then I don't get it. I distinctly recall having to literally hold you back from beating her to a pulp. Why are you doing this?"

Jasmine shrugged.

"And this has nothing to do with my brother?"

"Teddy?" she asked, tilting her head. "What would he have to do with this?"

"If I were with Indiana, then my very easily distracted little brother would be less distracted."

Jasmine ignored the implication that literally *everyone*, even Jack, knew how she felt about Teddy and focused on the matter at hand.

Was that the actual problem? That made a lot more sense to Jasmine than the age thing. Jack was, above all else, a great brother and would sacrifice anything for his family, like a career in corporate law to manage his sister, so yeah, he might not go after a girl he liked because his brother saw her first.

Jasmine shook her head. "Teddy's my friend. If I thought he'd be hurt by you and Indy getting together, I wouldn't be here talking to you."

Jack raised a skeptical eyebrow, but Jasmine pressed on.

"And as far as the age thing goes, I think you're making excuses. Indy's twenty, not twelve. I'm not saying you guys have to get married or whatever, but seriously, for two people like you, a few years are not a big deal."

He didn't answer. She stood and walked away, leaving him to his thoughts. As she left the stadium, her phone buzzed. The screen lit up with Teddy's picture, but she ignored the call and kept walking.

Chapter 25

FOR INDY, THE DAY BETWEEN THEIR WALKOVER AND SECOND-round match flew by faster than one of her serves. She had a good practice session with Jasmine, watched Penny win, even if it was by the skin of her teeth, and then it was straight to dinner and bed, avoiding all contact with both Caroline and her dad.

They were staying at the same hotel, but whenever she'd seen them in the distance, she'd done a quick about-face and even once hid behind a column in the lobby until they passed. She hadn't had to avoid Jack, because it seemed he was avoiding her. She figured he was freaked out enough to stay away from her for good.

Now, she was back in the players' lounge, dressed in the match outfit she and Jasmine had picked out together, a traditional white pleated tennis skirt paired with a bright turquoise tank. The color looked good on both of them, a rare thing for two people whose features were so opposite.

If only the color of her outfit were her biggest worry. She wished Lutrova and Grishina hadn't dropped out. Then these nerves would already be gone and she wouldn't have to think about going out onto the court for the first time. Maybe the Kapur sisters would drop out, too. Maybe they would wake up with a mysterious virus and withdraw from the tournament.

Her throat tightened and her stomach lurched.

Why was this happening again? When had she become this player who wanted to throw up before a match or hoped her opponents forfeited? That wasn't who she wanted to be. She had to get over this and get over it now. She felt like she had before the final of the Classic, jittery and ready to burst out of her own skin. What had she done to calm down then?

Nothing. She hadn't done anything; she went out there a total wreck and fell behind in the match. She couldn't do that again. There was too much riding on it and their opponents were too good. If they fell behind, a comeback would be almost impossible.

"Hey," someone said from over her shoulder, and she jumped in her seat. "Whoa, sorry. Didn't mean to scare you." Penny stepped into view. "Dom was looking for you. He needs you down in the prep room in five."

"Oh, okay, I'll just... I'll just go, then." She stood, wiping her palms against the sides of her skirt.

"You okay?" Penny asked, tilting her head in concern.

"Hmm?" Indy stalled for a second. "Yeah, I'm fine. Amped up, you know?"

"Look, I...I'm not going to be there. I'm all over the place right now. I don't want to bring any negative energy to your box, so I'm going to watch from here, okay?"

Indy shrugged. "Sure, whatever."

"Okay, I'll see you after, then?"

"Definitely, see you after."

Indy started down the hallway that led to the locker rooms.

"Indy, hang on," Penny called out. "I almost forgot. Ana Kapur—her serve is tougher, so that's who you'll be facing. She tends to start off really powerful and then back off later in the match, opting for more consistency than velocity. If you wait her out, you should be able to handle her no problem."

"Right. Thanks." Dom had reminded her of the same thing earlier, but she'd forgotten about it as her nerves took over.

"You're going to do fine. Relax and let your training take over."

Indy nodded and made her way to the locker room. Jasmine was getting her ankles wrapped for some stability on the slippery clay courts, but she looked up with a smile as soon as Indy walked in.

"This is going to be so much fun," Jasmine said.

The last of Indy's nerves faded. She was about to play in the French Open against two of the best players in the world. A month ago, she was just another college student wondering what the hell she was going to do with her life.

There were six thousand miles separating her from that girl, but she may as well have been on Mars. Jasmine was right. The match, win or lose, would be the greatest moment of her life, and she was going to enjoy it.

"We're ready for you," a tournament official said from the doorway, headset in place, instructions coming from courtside.

Time was up.

They stepped out of the tunnel and onto the court. The Kapur twins were already stretching and getting warm. The stadium was at least twice the size of the OBX main court, with double the number of speakers pumping in music. There was a sizable crowd and she caught sight of Dom in the player's box. One row back, her dad and Caroline were both dressed to the nines and sitting with the bored disinterest that people who sat in expensive seats at any sporting event always seemed to exude. Indy looked away, focusing instead on the rest of the crowd, all of whom were there to watch her play. She wasn't going to let anything negative get in her head.

A tap against her arm drew her attention and she turned to Jasmine. "Let's go."

The chair umpire announced that warm-ups should begin and so they moved onto the court.

She had to keep her feet moving. That was the key. Keep her feet moving and use her serve. Get as many aces as possible so they could save all their energy for Jasmine's and their returns. And keep her feet moving.

The chair umpire signaled the end of warm-ups.

"You ready?" Jasmine whispered as they retreated to their chairs.

"Damn right I am."

Indy's legs were giving out. No match she ever played had taxed her like this. The Kapur sisters were legit. It was like they could read each other's minds. Hell, it was like they could read her and Jasmine's minds, too.

But Indy was proud of their effort so far, even if she couldn't feel much below her knees anymore. It was close. Very, very close, but most tennis matches were close, until they weren't, and as they neared the end of the third set, it had begun to slip away.

"Balle de match, Kapur et Kapur," the chair umpire called.

She and Jasmine walked toward the baseline together.

"Let's not make this easy for them," Indy said softly so only her partner could hear her.

"We fight," Jasmine agreed, and they knocked fists and took their positions on the baseline.

Pallavi was serving, the slightly weaker of the two, and Indy prepped to receive it, stepping inside the baseline. The serve was solid, but Indy was ready, and she fired her return down the line—but Ananya was there to receive it, and she fired it crosscourt to Jasmine, who charged and volleyed it back near the net.

And then it was on, back and forth, a long lob from Pallavi that sent Indy chasing it back to the baseline to return it with a backhand just to keep the ball in play, and then a screaming forehand from Ananya that Jasmine blocked back, sending Pallavi sprawling to get her racket underneath before it hit the ground.

She did a little drop shot that barely cleared the net.

Indy raced forward, her thighs screaming in protest, using every last bit of energy she had in the tank as she hit the ball in stride down the line.

The world ground to a halt, the ball clearing the net in slow motion, their opponents caught flat-footed, too far to reach it, and it landed . . . just beyond the white chalk line.

Out.

"Jeu, set et match, Kapur and Kapur."

Indy bowed her head and tried to catch her breath. It was over and she'd wanted to win. Of course she wanted to win, but she couldn't be upset with the result. They'd fought hard against the best team in the world. There was definitely a victory in this defeat.

"6–2, 4–6, 7–6," the chair umpire said as they shook hands with their opponents, congratulating them with a kiss on each cheek.

"We will see you again, I think," Pallavi said, grinning, before she released Indy's hand.

The crowd cheered their effort as she and Jasmine gathered their things and exited the court. Her eyes darted up to the player's box where Dom was on his feet and applauding for them. Caroline and her dad were nowhere in sight. She lifted her hand and waved a thank-you to him and the fans.

About a half hour later, Indy and Jasmine were both showered and changed into their street clothes, packing up their gear.

"That wasn't bad for a first time out," Jasmine said, and Indy turned to her.

"A couple of shots go differently and we might have won. We could really do some damage in our next tournament."

The door to their locker room slammed open and they turned to see Dom standing in the archway. "Ladies, that was amazing! Phenomenal. I am so proud of you both."

"Thanks," Indy said, her chest tightening.

She knew he'd see this loss for what it was, a first step on a really exciting path. And her mom, she would have loved every moment of this, even in defeat. But her dad? The man who was supposed to support her no matter what, win or lose? He didn't even stay to watch the end.

No. No, she wasn't going to let him ruin the moment. She wasn't going to let him ruin anything ever again.

"Thanks, Dom," Jasmine said. "And I really appreciate you giving me this chance, even after what happened."

"I take it you've worked out your differences." Looking between them, he grinned when they both nodded. "Good, because I have plans for the two of you."

Indy had plans, too. This was only the beginning for her and Jasmine, both on the court and off.

As soon as they arrived back at the hotel, Indy excused herself from the group, finding a chair in a quiet corner of the lobby. She just wanted to sit and think for a second. She and Jasmine had done really well, and her nerves hadn't been a problem at all. Now she could go into Bari and dominate, like she had at the Classic.

"Indiana." Her dad's voice pulled her from her thoughts.

"What do you want?" she asked, her eyes snapping up to his.

Why couldn't he leave her alone?

"I wanted to say goodbye," he said, shifting awkwardly from one foot to the other and then running his hand through the blond strands of his slightly receding hairline.

She should've been thrilled that he was leaving, but her heart sank. "Okay," she said, trying not to betray herself. It was beyond annoying that she could want him gone and then be totally gutted when he decided to leave.

"Caroline thought it was best. She thinks it's too much pressure having me here and—"

Indy shrugged, cutting him off. "Well, whatever Caroline thinks is best, and speak of the devil."

Caroline emerged from amid the mass of people milling around the lobby and exclaimed, "Indy! Très bien, chérie. What a wonderful performance to build upon for Bari."

"Thanks," she said, searching desperately for an escape route, but there was a wall behind her and she'd literally have to push them aside to get away.

"I was telling your father after the match that, despite the loss, with the way you played, the sponsors will most certainly come knocking. I have already been in contact with Nike, and they will submit an offer for outfitting by the end of the week."

Indy watched in horrified fascination as her father's hand

landed upon Caroline's shoulder. "She's doing a great job, isn't she?" He squeezed gently and the older woman's brown eyes filled with warmth when she looked back at him.

Indy's jaw dropped. "Oh my God. Are you two . . . are you two sleeping together?"

"Indiana!" her dad scolded, but he pulled his hand away like Caroline's skin burned him. That was all the confirmation Indy needed. She was a little annoyed that it hadn't occurred to her before. Thinking back, it seemed obvious, but to be fair her mind had been on other things and she tried to never think about her dad's love life, ever.

"Is that why you hired her? And you!" She whirled on her agent. "First my coach and now my dad? Have you ever even heard the phrase *conflict of interest*?"

"Is everything okay over here?"

Jack stood behind her dad, his eyes trying to hold on to hers from over her dad's shoulder. He was coming to her rescue again and it made her stomach turn. If he cared, really cared, he would've been there to begin with instead of only showing up to help, only to disappear again a moment later just like he always did.

She was sick of it, sick of him, sick of everything.

"No, but it doesn't matter. I'm out of here."

Indy stormed forward, her dad and her agent pulling apart just in time to get out of her way. Most of the people in the lobby stared in their direction, fascinated by the sudden outburst, but she ignored them as she moved down a hallway through to the back of the hotel. There was a small courtyard lined with a large fence and trees, the cherry blossoms still flourishing even as the calendar moved toward summer.

"Indy!"

Jack. He followed her. He never called her that. She'd always been Indiana to him before.

"Are you all right?" he asked.

She crossed her arms and hugged herself tightly but kept silent, willing herself not to cry.

"Just tell me you're all right."

"I'm all right," she muttered. Seconds ticked away, but she didn't hear him leave, so she turned to face him. He was leaning against the outer wall of the hotel, arms crossed, studying her. "I swear to you, I'm fine, Jack. You can go."

"What if I don't want to go?" he asked, pushing off the wall and taking a step closer. "What if I want to stay here with you? Can I stay?"

She saw the moment when his expression shifted, moving from concern to something else, something she'd only seen glimpses of over the last few weeks when he'd allow the wall he built up between them to slip.

"Why do you want to stay?" she asked, no louder than a whisper, terrified the sound of her voice would break the moment.

He took slow, measured steps until he was just inches away from her. "A few days ago, a beautiful woman called me a coward and she was right."

"She was?"

"You were, and I should have done this a long time ago."

It was a soft brush of the lips at first, and then that fire, that intensity and passion that had swirled and built between them in the last few weeks, came bubbling to the surface as their mouths caressed each other, tongues dancing slowly.

He brought her close, pulling her body gently into his, but she had other ideas. She pushed up against him, one hand twisting into the cotton of his shirt, the other caressing the back of his neck, keeping him close.

When they finally broke apart, he buried his face into her hair, inhaling deeply. They breathed each other in for a moment until he ended the silence. "Is this really what you want?"

"Yes," she said, wrapping her arms around his shoulders, pushing up on her toes to brush their lips together again.

Pulling back, their eyes locked and he lifted a hand to her cheek, stroking his thumb over the line of her jaw. "Fuck it," he said as he drew her mouth to his again and they lost themselves in each other.

Chapter 26

THERE WAS TOO MUCH TIME TO KILL. PENNY GLANCED DOWN at her watch, the gift Rolex sent in anticipation of her signing yet another endorsement contract. It was heavy on her wrist and nicer than anything she'd ever owned, but in that moment, all it did was reinforce the fact it was only six o'clock. Though she needed her rest before her match tomorrow against Lutrova, she couldn't reasonably go to bed before eight. Any earlier than that and she'd be wide awake at some ungodly hour the next morning.

So instead of sitting around, staring at the walls of her room or watching random French television shows, she wandered down to the lobby, hoping the hustle and bustle would make the minutes tick by faster. At least, that's what she told herself.

She settled into a chair next to a large pillar. She would be well hidden and still have a view of the lobby. Of course, her motives for sitting there had nothing to do with the possibility of seeing Alex coming back to the hotel after his hitting session. The television mounted on the lobby wall was airing his press conference from earlier in the day and she couldn't tear her eyes away.

"Last time, my opponent gave me some chances and I took advantage of them," he said. "We've played each other a lot over the years, so neither of us will be surprised by the other. It'll be a matter of executing, and hopefully I'll be able to do that."

"Alex, much has been said about your relationship with American star Penny Harrison," the reporter began before Alex interrupted him.

"I'm only going to say this once, so pay attention," he said, glaring daggers into the press pool. "Penny Harrison is the most genuinely good person I've ever met. She inspires me every single day to be a better man, and she's definitely too good for the likes of me. Now, does anyone have any actual tennis questions? No? Fine, then we're done." He stood, knocking his chair over, and marched off camera, the reporters shouting after him.

Her heart swelled against her rib cage. She knew he meant every word of it, and she wanted desperately to forgive him, but it was too much. She couldn't keep opening herself up only to be blasted by another disaster. She was not going to make that mistake again.

Glancing around the lobby, she wondered if he'd returned, then she shook her head at how completely ridiculous she was being. She should go back to her room, put on a movie, and try to zone out before going to bed. Sitting there waiting for him to come back, especially since she had zero intention of talking to him, was pathetic.

She started for the elevator bay when she caught a quick glimpse of sandy-blond hair at the other end of the lobby, heading straight for the hotel bar.

Backtracking in that direction, she saw Alex taking a seat at the bar, the bartender pouring a drink into a shot glass. She watched, her heart rising into her throat, as a woman took a seat on the stool beside him and ordered a drink. Tennis tournaments were notorious for attracting groupies. Alex looked up and glanced at the woman, took in her long legs, the deep-cut neckline of her dress, and the clear invitation in her pouted lips and half-lidded eyes before turning away, studying his drink even more carefully than before. The woman took the hint and sauntered away toward a table of players at the other end of the bar.

Relief swept through Penny, but then she shook herself back to reality. It didn't matter if he hooked up with a random woman.

It wasn't any of her business, not anymore.

Alex still hadn't taken a sip of his drink; he stared at it like he was looking for answers. He shouldn't be drinking. His next-round match was early tomorrow morning, even before hers. Her instincts screamed at her to go to him, to figure out whatever it was that drove him there in the first place. Except, she was the reason he was sitting at that bar, and there was nothing she could do to help. Penny felt another piece of her heart crack.

She pulled her phone from her pocket and shot off a quick

message to Dom. He and Alex weren't only coach and athlete. They were friends. Dom would know what to do.

Then she raced to the elevators and pressed the call button, but her patience wore out quickly. She pushed open the door to the stairwell and sprinted up the six flights of stairs to her floor. Her breath came short and quick as she scanned her key and fell into her room, the sound of the door slamming behind her heavy and satisfying. Curling onto her bed, she let go, dry sobs wrenching from her throat as she struggled to breathe.

She hugged herself, shoulders shaking with the heavy emotions spilling out of her, but no tears came. She didn't know how long she lay there, rolled into a tight knot of anguish, but eventually her breathing slowed and her muscles relaxed.

Enough.

It was enough now.

Her pain could wait until later; after all, it wasn't going anywhere anytime soon.

She woke with her mind fixed on one thing: beating Zina Lutrova. There were no nagging injuries to fuss over, no sudden hitches in her game to tweak. She was ready and it was time to go out and win. Dressing quickly, she eyed the velvet box sitting on her dresser. Alex said the necklace was for luck, and she'd need all the luck she could get.

"Morning," Dom said when she answered the door. "Ready to go?"

"What are you doing here? Shouldn't you be at Alex's match? He didn't...please tell me he didn't withdraw."

"No, he sent me away, said I should be with you this morning, so here I am."

"Oh, okay," she said, pushing Alex's thoughtfulness out of her mind. "Let's go, then."

The players' lounge where she and Dom had breakfast was practically empty. Alex's match was on the television, but she was determined not to watch. She would find out how he did later.

"Last night," Dom said, drawing her attention away from her oatmeal, "you did the right thing by texting me."

"It was nothing."

"It wasn't nothing. A lot of people would've left him there to drown his sorrows and throw away his chances at this tournament. You're one of the best people I know, Penny. You don't deserve what's been happening to you the last couple of days, but don't let it get to you, okay?"

"I'm not. I promise. I'm ready for this."

"Good," he said, taking her at her word. "Okay, one last time. Game plan."

"Attack her backhand, make her move as much as possible and keep at her with the velocity. No letting up or getting cute, just keep at her."

"Good." He took a bite of his grapefruit. "She's expecting an aggressive game, but honestly, I don't think she can handle it. No one attacks her like you do."

Penny took a sip of her orange juice, not quite as sure as he seemed to be. "Well, we'll see, won't we?"

"I'm sure of it. As sure as I've ever been of anything in my entire career. You're better than her, Penny. I know it, you know it, and maybe most importantly, she knows it."

"Thanks, Dom."

"I mean it," he said, though she didn't need that reassurance. He never said anything he didn't mean. "And don't thank me. Prove me right."

It was overcast and gloomy by match time. Court Philipe Chartier was the premier court at Roland-Garros. The stands could hold more than 14,000 fans, and every seat was filled. The media was billing this match as the real championship, declaring over and over again that whoever won would be the clear favorite to take home the title at the end of the fortnight in Paris.

Lutrova won the toss and chose to serve first.

Excellent, Penny thought, she would have the first chance to break. She bounced up and down, getting used to the clay surface, testing with little shuffle steps how it would play during the match.

The umpire climbed to his chair overlooking the court. After a brief warm-up, silence reigned in the sold-out stadium, but the hum of anticipation was nearly palpable on the court.

Lutrova bounced the ball at her feet before bringing her arms together and tossing it into the air. Just as it reached the pinnacle of its rise, she slammed her racket head through it, sending a low-lying rocket of a serve across the court. Reacting instinctively, Penny stepped into the shot, returning the ball so fast that Lutrova barely had time to recover her feet. The ball bounced in and then slammed into the wall behind the service line.

For a moment, the stadium remained silent, stunned by the speed and perfection of the point.

"Zéro-quinze," the umpire said, and the crowd finally applauded, cheering the statement she made with that shot.

She was there to win.

Penny stared across the court. Zina met her eyes and Penny let the corner of her mouth lift up in the smallest of smirks. That return, that was what Dom wanted when he brought in Alex to train with her. He wanted her to take Zina's best weapon, her serve, and shove it back down her throat. The hurt of the last few days hadn't faded, but lifting her hand to the neckline of her shirt, she pressed against the coin through the material. Alex had helped her get here, and she wasn't going to let that go to waste.

Three more serves and three more short points later and Penny had the lead.

"Jeu, Harrison."

She turned to the box behind her. Dom, Jack, Indy, and Jasmine were all sitting in the front row.

"You go, girl," Indy said, loud enough for her to hear even over the buzz of the crowd.

Penny held out her racket to the ball boy, who placed three balls on it as options for her serve. She tucked one beneath her skirt and let another fall back to the ground in his direction before she approached the baseline.

Lutrova was on the other side of the net, bent at the waist, racket spinning in her hands, poised on the balls of her feet.

Her forehead was creased, blond eyebrows knit together, face pinched in concentration.

Penny would go right at her, like she and Dom discussed. It was time to see if the best player in the world could handle her game. She coiled her body, every muscle tensing, then releasing. The serve was perfectly placed, right where the lines crossed in the center of the court. It whistled past Lutrova before pounding once again into the wall lining the backcourt.

"Quinze-zéro."

The match was a whirlwind as they went back and forth. The Lutrova she'd beaten in Madrid was nowhere to be found. The Russian superstar had won two tournaments since then and was at the top of her game. Her shots were crisp and accurate. They exchanged blows, making each other race around the court.

Penny served, a screaming line drive down the center of the court. Lutrova fired a return, and it began again, a rally from the baselines. Penny sent a slice backhand, short and spinning, into the clay, and Lutrova came storming up to the net. A forehand rocketed into the far corner and Penny raced after it, letting her last step fail, sliding across the clay, legs fully extended as she swung into a winner down the line. Her momentum died and she stopped in a full split before popping up into the air and back onto her feet. The crowd erupted.

"Jeu. Harrison remporte le premier set, 6–4."

Sitting in her chair, she placed her racket beside her and downed half a bottle of electrolyte-infused water before burying her face in her towel, wiping off the layer of sweat. She allowed herself a huge grin while the terry cloth shielded her from the cameras.

Lutrova called for the trainer between sets and was having her legs rubbed down. Maybe it was an excuse for dropping the first set, getting the trainer out there, making everyone believe she was hurt, so Penny would let her guard down in the second set. Whatever game she was playing wasn't going to work. Dom was right; she was better than Lutrova, she was better than the best player in the world. And that meant—shaking her head, she cleared out those thoughts. She could think about that after the tournament was over. Right now, it was time to finish off this match.

The chair umpire called them back, and Penny leapt to her feet, striding quickly out to the baseline, getting her muscles loose for the second set. This was in stark contrast to Zina, who stood up slowly and walked across her side of the court, examining her racket as if it might tell her how to win the match.

Only about a half hour later, it was clear whatever advice Lutrova's racket gave her was crap.

Penny waited in the corner of the court for a serve that would never arrive as Lutrova buried her shot into the bottom of the net and yet another double fault brought Penny within one game of victory.

"Jeu. Harrison conduit le second set, 5–4."

For a moment she let her focus slip away and she listened to the crowd cheering. Turning to her box, she saw they were all yelling wildly.

"Let's go, Pen," Jack yelled. "Finish it."

She stepped up to the baseline.

"S'il vous plaît, soyez tranquille," the umpire said as she prepared to serve, and the crowd quieted, but only a fraction.

With a small groan, she sliced her serve, putting an arching spin on it. Lutrova sat back on the shot, handcuffed for a split second by the angle and the change of speed. She shuffle-stepped and swung, but mishit, sending a soft lob over the net. Penny sprinted forward, feet light as she sped up to the net, getting her racket under the ball just in time. A quick flick of her wrist sent it back over the net. The ball bounced once and then again before Zina could reach it.

As Penny tried to stop, her toe slid into a divot; her ankle twisted and then rolled under. She caught herself with her other foot, but a sharp, blistering pain shot up her leg and then back down again before settling on the inside of her ankle. She tried to put her weight on it. Bad idea. A murmur of concern went through the crowd, but she blocked them out as she lifted her foot off the ground immediately.

Shit, that was a lot of pain. Way too much pain, more pain than she'd ever been in before. A sliver of panic went through her and she tried to fight it down. Maybe it was just a tweak, maybe she'd be fine.

She tested it again.

Nope. Definitely not just a tweak.

Fuck.

Thankful the last shot brought her near the sidelines, she hopped quickly over to her chair and looked up to the umpire to call for a trainer, but he'd anticipated her request and was waving a member of the tour's medical staff in from the edge of the court—the same man who'd worked on Lutrova's legs before the start of the set.

Before she could react, her sneaker and sock were lying on the ground and gentle, well-trained hands were examining her ankle, checking the range of motion—almost none—and the amount of discomfort—a lot—and then he asked, "Do you want to continue playing?"

Withdrawing hadn't even crossed her mind. How could it? It had all happened so quickly, but she was not going to give up. A forfeit wouldn't just mean a loss. It would practically hand this tournament championship to Lutrova. She wasn't going to let that happen. Even if she couldn't play her next match, she wasn't going to give her rival a free pass to the next round. She glanced around quickly and saw the Russian girl standing off to the side, watching intently, a brief flash of victory in her gaze. Oh, hell no.

"Wrap it and give me my racket."

"It's a pretty bad sprain, could be worse than that. It might be your Achilles. I can't tell for sure unless you get a scan."

Penny raised an eyebrow and the trainer gave up.

"Fine, but it's against my recommendation."

"Fine," she agreed, and winced as he reached for his bag and jostled her ankle in the process. Her hand came up to her throat and she pulled at the chain secured around her neck. The penny slipped out and she held it in her palm for a second. It was warm from resting against her skin, and she began to breathe slowly, closing her eyes and letting her mind go blank. Like lying on the court with Alex, her hand wrapped in his.

The trainer wrapped her ankle tightly. He had to—it was the only way to stabilize the joint. And as she slid her sneaker back on, she bit her lip to keep from crying out.

Tucking the necklace back inside her shirt, she checked the scoreboard quickly. She was three points away from the win and she had to get those points as fast as possible. She had to get the next three serves past Lutrova, because there was no way her ankle would stand a rally. She had to keep the ball away from her, nothing into the body and definitely nothing off-speed. It would have to be three serves. Three aces. That was the only way.

This was going to hurt.

A lot.

She stood and the crowd went from eerily silent to a slow but steady rise into a roar.

She was going to play and they loved her for it.

Trying to minimize her limp as she moved to the baseline, she took a ball from the ball boy and breathed deeply, focusing instead on the feeling of the penny against her skin.

With a small prayer that the joint wouldn't give out, she pushed down into the ground and then up and out, lining the ball dead center as hard as she could and let out a shrieking wail as she did at the pain.

"Trente-zéro."

The crowd erupted. She could feel them willing her to victory. "Allez, Penny!" someone shouted from the stands over the general roar, and then several others echoed him. "Allez!"

Pressing her lips together, she shuffled her feet, keeping the weight on one foot. The ball boy ran to her and placed one on her racket. Lutrova inched up in front of the baseline, clearly anticipating a softer serve this time.

"That's a mistake," Penny whispered to herself before tossing the ball into the air, using every ounce of power she had to send the ball hard, straight, and flat down the center of the court.

"Quarante-zéro," the chair umpire said, but his voice was nearly drowned out by the crowd's approval, shouts, and whistles and the pounding of thousands of hands together.

Match point. She had match point, and her ankle hurt so much it was actually pulsing inside her sneaker. The pain made it impossible to hold her focus, and the sounds from the crowd started to invade her ears—a blur of voices and noise that was actually helping distract her from the throbbing in her foot. One more, just one more.

Lutrova wasn't having a great match, but she had to know what was coming now. She set up for the next serve a step behind the baseline, near the center of the court, cutting off the easiest route for an ace. What Lutrova didn't know was that over the last month or so, Penny had learned something important. The easiest path wasn't always the right one.

She launched her serve, a high kicker, skidding off the edge of the service line, spinning up and away.

"Jeu, set et match, Harrison: 6–4, 6–4."

The stadium practically exploded around her, but Penny couldn't move. She was frozen at the baseline, weight leaning entirely on her good ankle, using her racket to try to balance. She didn't want to take a step, but she had to. The match was over; she needed to shake her opponent's hand. She stared down at the court for a moment to catch her breath, willing the pain to go away, when another set of sneakers invaded her vision.

"Good match," Lutrova said, extending her hand. She'd come all the way over from her side of the court. If Penny didn't know better and the pain wasn't totally clouding her judgment, she'd have thought it was a sign of respect.

Nodding, Penny took her hand and shook it firmly. "Good match."

A moment later, the trainer walked out to her, clucking his tongue in disapproval as he helped her off the court, forcing her to skip the on-the-court interview. He muttered something about stubborn girls who don't know what's good for them, but Penny ignored him in favor of listening to the crowd cheer before they made it into the tunnel.

"Penny," a voice echoed against the concrete of the hallway, followed by the pounding of feet against the ground. "I've got it from here, mate."

The trainer glanced at her, confirming it was all right to leave her with him. She nodded and stood on one leg as he switched places with Alex. He wrapped his arm around her waist and she hooked hers over his shoulders, but before he could lead her down the hallway, she pressed herself into him and rested her head against his chest. He held her tightly, pressing a kiss into her hair, and then she pulled back, nodding to a changing room a few feet away. Once inside, he led her to a table and helped her onto it. She lifted her leg up onto the padded tabletop to keep her ankle elevated.

The trainer *tsked* at her, but she ignored him. "Could you give us a minute?"

He left the room, but Alex stayed a few steps away. He

was still in his match clothes, the black-on-black look he'd started wearing during the *Athlete Weekly* photo shoot. Tennis's very own rebel. He ran a hand through his hair.

"Did you win?" Penny asked.

"Yeah, I did," he said, but then shook his head. "What were you thinking?" She snorted, uninterested in his disapproval. "It was bloody incredible. I was in a press conference when I heard what happened. I ran over here as fast as I could, knocked over a few reporters come to think of it." He took her hands in his and squeezed gently. "Are you okay?"

She was in too much pain to lie. "My ankle hurts," she admitted in a wild understatement.

Alex's hands cupped her cheeks, his thumbs stroking against her skin softly over the line of her jaw, down to her throat. His index finger hooked into the gold chain at her neck and he tugged. "You wore it." His voice held disbelief and awe.

"For luck," Penny said, swallowing roughly, trying to find the voice to say the words she wanted to say. "But really, I needed *you*. I didn't realize how much until I was out there all alone and it felt like my ankle was going to fall off and I just needed you."

"Yeah?" He leaned forward, resting his forehead against hers.

"Yeah."

His free hand brushed back a strand of hair that fell loose from her braid. "I fired Caroline. I know you said it didn't matter, but she published that last picture without my permission, and I swear to you, love, I never want to hurt you again." He bent his head to hers, pressing a soft kiss against her lips. "I am so bloody sorry."

"I know," she said, pulling away just enough to get the words out. "I . . . I can't go through that again, Alex. I need you to promise me we're in this together, you and me, or not at all. Please."

"I swear it. I promise. I—"

His words were cut off as Dom, Jack, Indy, and Jasmine all poured in through the doorway, words of censure and congratulations spilling over one another. She smiled at them but felt Alex lean away, putting some space between them. Her attention snapped back to him and she took his hand.

"Don't leave," she said, tightening her grip.

He raised her hand to his lips. "I won't."

They still had so much unsaid between them, so many things to talk about and work through, but for now, she just needed *him*.

Maybe forever and suddenly, that wasn't scary at all.

Epilogue

HE SHOULD HAVE BEEN SLEEPING. HE NEEDED REST IF HE wanted to be at the top of his game. The biggest match of his life was tomorrow. Alex raised his head from the pillows and glanced at his phone.

Correction, *today.*

There were worse places to sleep the night before the French Open final, a king-sized bed in a five-star hotel with the girl of his dreams beside him and the Eiffel Tower in the distance just becoming visible as the sun began to glow orange and pink on the horizon.

But if he let himself sleep, he'd be missing out on an even better view than a Paris sunrise. The long line of her back, the wild locks of her hair spread across the pillow, the smattering of freckles on the curve of her shoulder, the gentle fall and rise of her body beneath the sheets.

Penny was absolutely gorgeous, always, but there was

something especially fascinating about her when she slept, when the strength and stoicism and grace she carried herself with fell to the wayside and she was finally able to simply *be.*

The contrast was even more noticeable in the last week, when the reality set in that she wasn't just hurt, but *injured.* That her run at the French Open was over and any hope of playing Wimbledon was reliant on the vagaries of how fast her body would recover. Four to six weeks, according to the doctor, but that two-week gray area would be the difference between fighting for her first major championship or not.

She was devastated by the possibility even if she wasn't letting it show. He knew, because he'd been there before. But instead of wallowing, she channeled it into supporting him. After she went down with an injury, all he'd wanted to do was wrap her in his arms, get her on a plane, and fly off to somewhere, anywhere, where the world could disappear around them and she wouldn't have to think about tennis or how her body had betrayed her.

But that wasn't their world and she'd never want that anyway.

He was still competing, still carving a path through the men's draw. And she showed up to every match, sat beside Dom, and cheered as hard as she could through it all. It was her voice he could hear echoing over the crowd after a tough point, pulling him through when his body felt like it couldn't give any more. And she was the first face he saw when he clinched his spot in the final two nights ago, the relief and joy coursing through him immediately coalescing into the heady mix of love and lust he could never fully control around her.

Alex reached out, letting just the tip of his finger hook

beneath the gold of the chain around her neck, tugging gently to lift the coin that served as a lucky charm into his hand. It was warm from her body heat and he closed his fist around it, careful not to pull too hard.

God, he loved her, and he wanted her in ways he never imagined before.

He could see it, all laid out ahead of them, a ring and a wedding, an entire room in their house dedicated to their trophies. No, two rooms, one for him and one for her.

A life together.

But not yet.

He knew he was in deeper than she was, had known that since Australia, when he woke up to find the sheets beside him cold even though his body was still burning from her touch. He'd never been a particularly patient man, but for Penny, he would wait, and while he waited he'd spend every day proving himself. He'd fucked up and it was a miracle she'd forgiven him. He wouldn't make that mistake again.

He'd never loved anything more, not even tennis. He used to think winning was everything, that it could cure any ill and that he'd do anything to experience it again, but with her beside him, winning was nothing but an afterthought. Hell, he'd trade places with her in a second if he could, swap his healthy Achilles for her partially torn one. She was the best in the world, and she deserved a chance to prove it on the biggest stage.

She let out a soft sigh and then rolled over slowly, even in her semiconscious state still careful not to put pressure on her ankle as she moved. She reached for him and he shifted closer as her hand landed gently on his chest and her head tucked in against his shoulder.

"You need to sleep," she murmured, the words a soft kiss against his skin as she settled against his side, their legs tangling together.

"Mm-hmm," he hummed, even as the slide of her body along his banished any thought of it. His hands found her waist and he pulled her even closer, then slid his hand up to cup her breast, filling his palm, loving the way her breath caught when he brushed his calloused thumb over the rise of flesh.

"Alex," she murmured contentedly.

His name on her lips drew a smile as he lowered his head to trace the line of her jaw with his mouth. He trailed his hand in a deliberate path, knowingly scraping the calloused tips of his fingers over her smooth skin and reveling in every goose bump that rose against them.

"What were you saying about sleep?" he said, his voice raspy.

"Overrated," she said, and he was going to tease her about her sudden change of opinion when her hand sifted through his hair, tightening around the strands, and she gave it a sharp tug.

"Fuck," he groaned, his body reacting instantly, his hips canting into hers while her sweet mouth found the cords of his neck, knowing she'd leave a mark, one he'd be happy to sport on Chartier later today.

"Yes," she said.

"C'mere, love," he said, gripping at her hip as he marveled at the way she fit just right against him as he guided her to turn over, her back to his front. He propped himself up on an elbow behind her and she took his cues easily, lifting her thigh over his as he slid between her legs.

She tossed her head against his shoulder, the silk of her hair spilling against his chest. She reached back between them, her hand sliding over him. Alex had always prided himself on his control, on his ability to draw out his own pleasure while he made sure his partner went first, at least once or twice, before him, but Penny tested every ounce of restraint he had—in bed, on the court, everywhere.

"Hang on," he ground out from between clenched teeth, and rolled away from her, patting blindly at the nightstand before finding the foil packet, the last one in the strip he'd fished out of his luggage earlier that night.

Alex knew he could live a hundred years and never hear anything better than the way Penny said his name as her body pulled him in and she arched against him.

He kept his grip firm around her thigh—her ankle was still fragile and there was no need for her to do any of the work, not when he had strength enough for the both of them. He was just getting lost in her, but he knew the signs, a fine sheen of sweat on her skin, her thighs shaking, the curl of her toes against the back of his calf, her breath coming hard and fast.

"Close, love?" he asked, though he already knew the answer, and that hand on her thigh slid between her legs to get her there faster, because he was already barreling toward the end, and if he couldn't hold out, at the very least he wanted her to take him with her.

A sweet keening sound lit from her throat as she tensed and then released into a shaking, incoherent, beautiful mess in his arms as he lost his rhythm, his hips rutting wildly before he fell right behind her.

He held her close as they both came down from their incredible shared high.

The sun was pouring into their room now; any thought of sleep fled as she slid from his arms and limped gracefully toward the en suite, the light and shadows playing against her curves as he watched in fascination.

"Well," she said, stopping at the doorway and looking back over her shoulder, "if you're not going to sleep..." She trailed off and then, with a wicked grin, disappeared into the bathroom.

And as he stumbled out of the bed to follow her, he knew, no matter what happened later on the court, he'd already won.

ACKNOWLEDGMENTS

I've started to get used to the idea that for the foreseeable future I will find myself in places and working on projects that I never expected or looked for. The opportunity to breathe new life into my debut novel was so far-fetched I never even thought to dream about it, but the road a publishing career takes is never without its detours, and I am so proud to bring this book back to readers after all this time.

None of this would have happened without my editor Alice Jerman. I'm so deeply grateful for her faith in me and her belief in my work. It's a rare thing in this industry to find someone who shares your vision and understands your voice, but when you do, that's when writing a book can become a truly magical experience. Working with Alice has brought that magic back for me in a major way. With her comes an entire team of dedicated professionals without whom this book would not shine the way it does. Their dedication to editorial excellence, author care, and desire to serve an audience that has been neglected for far too long is second to none. First to Lisa Yoskowitz for steering the ship and for making me feel so at home at Requited; and everyone who had a hand in bringing this book to life: Alex

Houdeshell, Sasha Illingworth, Sandra Chiu, Jen Graham, Jonathan Lopes, Emilie Polster, Annie McDonnell, Caroline Clouse, Kerianne Steinberg, Cheryl Lew, Emilie Polster, Savannah Kennelly, Christie Michel, and Tuesday Hadden.

And to Brittani Hilles, at Lavender PR, for keeping me sane throughout it all. Thank you for shaping the sheer chaos of these past few months into such a smooth, exciting journey!

A good agent makes you feel like you're about to take over the world; a great agent helps you actually do it, and I am fortunate enough to have a truly great agent. Alice Sutherland-Hawes continues to be my most fervent advocate, a fierce negotiator, a consummate professional, and a true ally in this most difficult of industries. I, quite literally, could not do this without her and truly would not want to.

As exciting as it is to look forward right now, for this book I also need to look back and thank Michelle Wolfson, Lisa Rutherford, and Melanie Murray-Downing, because I would not be here now if you had not believed in Penny, Indy, and Jasmine first. Fourteen years ago, you found me in the slush pile and made my dreams come true. I will be forever thankful to you all for it.

Author life is often very isolating, just you and the world you've built in your head and the voices of people who feel real, but are simply figments of your imagination. In the last decade and change I've been lucky enough to find friendships that have kept me sane. I wish I could do more to thank you than simply list you all here, but it's a start: Dahlia Adler, Jenn Alvarado, Christian Berkey, Mark Benson, Romily Bernard, Livia Blackburne, Jessica Burkhart, Sona Charaipotra,

Victor Correa, Nadine Jolie Courtney, Tom Franz, Angi Griffee, Cheryl Harvey, Michelle Heaney, Sarah Henning, E.K. Johnston, Colleen Korte, Phil Kordula, Sasha Laurens, Katie Locke, Emily Lloyd-Jones, Alexa Martin, Tabitha Martin, Elizabeth May, Brian Methven, Alexandra Monir, Miel Moreland, Katarina Odette, Margaret Owen, Megan Paasch, Joe Pfeffer, Ashley Poston, Cassie Raker, Mary Reiser, Bonnie Rubin, Tara Sim, Amy Tintera, Rosiee Thor, Diana Urban, Jean Ward, and Sara Waxelbaum.

And finally, as always, to my family. I love you all so very much, but this year especially to my grandma, Jennie Hennessy, who always made sure to tell me she was very proud of me. I miss her every day.

The story continues in

Wildcard

Chapter 1

INDY HAD GRASS STAINS ON HER ELBOWS AND A GIGANTIC bruise blooming on her knee, but neither could stop her wild smile as she high-fived Jasmine with a satisfying *thwack*.

She and her doubles partner were at the top of their game and had absolutely dominated their training session, two separate entities moving around the court as one seamless unit. They were so ready for Wimbledon.

"Nice one," Dom called from the sidelines, actually standing up and applauding, his broad smile slipping over his perpetually tanned features. But he then turned his attention to their training partners, two young men who were regulars on the Challenger circuit, standing flat-footed and winded, grumbling to each other in low tones.

"And what the holy hell do you two think you're doing?" Dom barked at them.

Indy couldn't help but smirk at Jas as they listened to Dom's lecture.

"Last I checked, this was the Outer Banks Tennis Club. Did you think they'd be easy pickings?" he asked, gesturing toward them with a sweep of his arm. "They took the best doubles team in the world to three sets. Indy just kicked the shit out of the entire field in Bari. You're lucky to be on the same court as them. Get out of here. I'm sick of the sight of you."

The young men trudged off the court still muttering, and Dom's eyes narrowed. "Changed my mind. Three tours. Want to make it four?"

The taller one nudged the smaller with his elbow as they both shook their heads and said, "No, Coach."

"Good. Get lost."

They took off down the path at a measured jog, conserving their energy for the three laps of the entire facility, a circuitous route that would take them through the maze of forty-five practice courts, finishing up with a sprint across the sandy beach that lined the property.

Jasmine raised her eyebrows toward Indy, who smiled back. In her short time at OBX, she'd endured Dom's wrath enough to simply enjoy when someone else was his target.

"Ladies, that's enough for this morning," Dom called over to them. "Cool down. Indy, get some ice on that knee before it blows up like a balloon."

She'd taken a little tumble during that last rally, but it didn't even sting.

"It's fine," she said, glancing down at it. "I bruise easy."

"Okay, then, video analysis after lunch," he said before leaving them for his next training session.

Indy grabbed her water bottle and swished a mouthful before spitting it out. Too much water would weigh her down for the rest of the day, but she had to stay hydrated under the hot North Carolina sun as the weather shifted from a warm spring toward what promised to be a humid summer. Though, if she had her way, most of that summer would be spent a long way away, on courts around the world, starting with the grass lawns of Wimbledon. She envisioned herself there as she swung her arms around in slow circles, letting those muscles slowly recover from the intense workout she'd just put in, before moving farther down her body, twisting and bending at her core, then lunging and reaching for her legs.

"Better every day," Jasmine said as they left the court and headed toward the locker room for a shower and a fresh set of clothes.

Indy nodded, pulling her long blond hair free from its ponytail and running her hands through the sweaty locks. "I just wish they would make a decision."

"They" were the Lawn Tennis Association, or LTA, the English equivalent to the USTA and the people in charge of her fate for the next month or so. It was within their power to grant wild card entries to the Championships at Wimbledon. After she and Jasmine pushed the number one doubles team in the world to a third-set tiebreaker, it made sense that they'd be granted a wild card into the main doubles draw, but sometimes sense had very little to do with what went on in professional tennis. They would be headed there regardless, both of them attempting to qualify for the singles tournament, but the rest was out of Indy's control and patience had never been one of her virtues.

"It should happen soon, maybe tomorrow," Jasmine said as they entered the locker room; the buzz of dozens of girls echoing off the tile floors and metal lockers soon faded. Since their return from France, the atmosphere at OBX had been strange, to say the least. Indy was used to it. She'd been an outsider from the moment she arrived, but her stomach twisted for Jasmine, who'd spent her entire career training inside the high fences of the best tennis club in the world. The other girl didn't know how to handle the silent glares and fervent whispers that followed them everywhere. "Ignore them," Indy said, "they're just jealous."

Jasmine sighed heavily. "Like I was when you first got here."

Indy shook her head, not letting Jasmine go back down that road. She'd moved on. "To be fair, I can be a massive pain in the ass."

And that did the trick. Jasmine laughed. "Yeah, you can be, and *speaking* of asses, how are things with you-know-who?"

"'Speaking of asses'?" Indy asked, wrinkling her nose, the rest of the question not registering fully.

Jasmine grinned wickedly. "He has a really, really nice one or haven't you noticed?"

For half a second, Indy indulged in the memory of exactly how nice Jack Harrison's ass was and the noise he made when she'd had her hands on it, but then reality set in. Looking around quickly to make sure they were alone, Indy shook her head. "Not here."

Jasmine stared at her, unimpressed, and then whispered, "You're not going to be able to keep the secret forever."

"I know," Indy said quietly.

"Have you talked to her?" Jasmine asked, thankfully changing the subject. She nodded toward Penny's empty locker while grabbing her shower kit from her own.

"Yeah," Indy said, wrinkling her nose. "She's pissed off that she can't train."

"Sucks," Jasmine said before walking off to the shower room.

"Totally," Indy agreed. She'd never missed tennis because of an injury before, but just talking to Penny on the phone told her all she needed to know. She could hear the longing in her voice to get back on the court, to do something. But, in true Penny fashion, she hadn't wallowed for too long. She'd gushed about being able to spend time with Alex in England and how PT was a bitch but going well. And she'd even hyped her up for Wimbledon qualifying because she knew how hard Indy was working, knew how hard it was to build herself back up after her mom died and how shitty it was that her dad really only cared about Caroline Morneau. And all the while Indy sat there biting her tongue and trying desperately not to let it slip about Jack.

God, she was a shitty friend.

A little more than a month ago, Penny and Jasmine hadn't even known she existed, and somehow they'd become her closest friends. Now she was lying to one and asking the other to lie for her.

Jasmine was right, she needed to come clean, and she would, if she could only work up the courage to do it.

The hot water was heaven after the morning workout. Indy took her time, letting her muscles recover as much as they could, because she'd need them again during that afternoon's singles training. She knew that building up her endurance to pursue both was even more grueling than she'd imagined. And she'd imagined a lot.

The locker room was blissfully empty as she emerged from the showers. Jasmine had headed to lunch with her parents, the facility's founders. So she could get ready in peace. She left her hair alone, knowing the warm air outside would make it curl, and pulled on a pair of white terry cloth shorts, then a bronze T-shirt with the Nike swoosh blazoned across the chest in black. The shirt was a gift from Penny, who had more Nike merchandise than she knew what to do with after signing a lucrative sponsorship deal to become the face of their tennis line. Indy smiled to herself, knowing that one day soon, she'd have her own sponsorship deal. Caroline had said as much over and over again since they'd returned from France. She had made contact with all the big tennis outfitters, and it was just a matter of waiting for the best deal and negotiating terms that brought in the most money for the most exposure.

Stepping into the sunshine, she shouldered her bag and turned toward the OBX video room to keep cool while analyzing some of her own play from the past week, when a shadow crossed over her path, a large body falling into step with her, close but not touching, their strides matching.

"Jack," she said, glancing up at him sideways, a small smile threatening at the corners of her mouth.

"Indiana," he said, echoing back her name, sending a shiver down her spine. He was the only one she didn't mind calling her that, the only person who made the name she'd hated since forever sound so, so good.

They walked together in silence, turning the corner that separated the courts from the residential area of the complex, but her steps were suddenly cut off when Jack slid his arm around her waist and pulled her into a shady walkway between buildings. Her heart leapt as he gently guided her back into the wall, his eyes boring into hers.

Walls were their thing. Their first real kiss had been against a wall in a random hallway at Roland-Garros, their second pressed against the wall of their hotel in Paris, and now that they were back in North Carolina, they'd found any excuse to push each other against a wall and kiss until they were gasping for air and their bodies begged for relief. Now Jack's lips trailed from her temple, using the wall behind her as an anchor before bending his head to hers. Pushing up onto her toes, Indy met him halfway. She'd never been so grateful for every millimeter of her five feet ten inches as she was when she was kissing Jack. She fit perfectly against him.

She pulled away to draw a breath. "My favorite part of the day," she murmured, and he answered with a soft chuckle.

"Mine too." His hands slid through her hair, twisting it around his fingers, then he cradled the back of her head, drew her mouth firmly against his.

Indy brought her hands to his torso, gripping his T-shirt, letting her palms press against the cut of muscle that disappeared into his cargo shorts. His mouth fell open just enough to allow her tongue to slide in, deepening the kiss, before letting her teeth nip at his bottom lip. A groan rumbled in his throat as he pressed even closer, his body full length against hers.

He wrenched his lips from hers, trailing his mouth over the line of her jaw to the spot just behind her ear. "You feel incredible," he said, his voice husky, before diving in for more.

It was her turn to gasp, and her head fell back, scraping against the rough wall, as she arched into him. No one had ever kissed her there before. Jack smiled against her skin as her fingertips dug into his sides, and she let a moan slip free as he focused his attention on that spot, his teeth sharp against it, then soothing that small pain with a flick of his tongue. Her hands scrambled to get purchase against his shoulders, desperate for some leverage, anything to help her press her body against his. Then he was gone, his hand out of her hair, his mouth away from her neck and his body inches, then feet, from hers. Indy blinked at him, trying to figure out what had happened, when the voices echoing down the pathway toward them finally reached her ears.

He was already lifting her bag from where it had fallen on the ground, and she desperately ran her fingers through her hair, knowing he'd made an unholy mess of it.

"You're fine," he muttered, handing her the bag, keeping the distance between them as a group of junior boys stomped past, none giving them a second glance.

"You have good ears," Indy said finally, biting her lip at the close call. If those boys had seen them, the news would have spread like wildfire through the OBX campus and everyone would have known by the end of the day. And they couldn't have that. She was a young tennis pro on the verge of breaking out; he was an up-and-coming agent. The last thing either of their careers needed was the heightened publicity of a controversial relationship, even if Jack Harrison was far more of a gentleman than any guy she'd ever met. Sometimes, a little too much of a gentleman, truth be told.

Jack shrugged, and he glanced back over his shoulder again before facing her fully. "I'm sorry about this."

She reached out and took his hand. "We agreed," she said, entwining their fingers, "it's just between us for now. It makes sense for both of us." Pressing his lips together in a thin line, he nodded, but she knew he wasn't entirely convinced. Hell, she wasn't entirely convinced. "You said you were okay with it."

"I just wish it were different," he said, tugging her closer, pressing a soft kiss to her forehead. He released her hands and dropped his to her hips, the edges of his thumbs brushing against her hip bones in slow circles, sending shivers over her skin.

"Me too." She wanted to scream it from the rooftops that this amazing guy was hers. That he had deep green eyes that lit up at her touch and a smile that brightened whenever he looked at her. That he was brilliant in ways she couldn't even fathom, with a degree from Harvard to prove it. That he'd fought their attraction for so long because of an ingrained sense of honor, like one of those heroes in a fairy tale, except Jack was real, flesh and blood.

"Have you thought at least...maybe we should tell

Penny?" Indy asked, her guilt from earlier creeping back in even as her fingertips landed on his forearms, gently stroking up to his elbows and back down to his wrists. Maybe Jack would have some answers there.

Jack let out a heavy breath. "Penny has a lot on her plate right now."

"I know. I just feel funny keeping it from her. And Jasmine knows. I would feel bad if Penny found out from someone who wasn't us."

"You think she'd tell her?"

Indy considered for a moment and shook her head. "I don't think so, not on purpose anyway, but secrets have a way of getting out, one way or another."

"If you're uncomfortable, Indiana, then the rest of it doesn't matter. If you want to tell Penny or tell everyone, that's what we'll do."

"No, I...that's not what I mean. I don't need a supportive..." She hesitated, almost using the word *boyfriend*, but that didn't really fit, did it? Not if they were keeping it a secret. "I need your honest opinion."

He leaned back, looking her in the eye. "Honest? Honestly, my sister doesn't do well with change. It freaks her out, and right now, I'm not sure that the idea of you and me will go over that well. On the other hand, if we don't tell her and she finds out?"

"She'll be pissed."

"Yep."

"We could tell her in London."

Jack considered for a moment and then nodded. "Face-to-face instead of over the phone."

"There's always FaceTime," she said, though her stomach twisted at the thought of telling her at all. She wasn't really sure if she wanted to know what Penny, the only girl who'd made an effort to befriend her when she first arrived at OBX, would think if she found out she and Jack were together and they'd both lied about it.

"There's that," he said, sounding just as hesitant as she was.

Indy shook her head. They should do it in person. They should have done it before they left Paris, but Penny had been so devastated after she had to withdraw from the tournament that it hadn't felt like the right time then either. "In London. We'll be there in less than a week. We'll tell her then."

"Okay, in London," he agreed.

They stood together for a moment, just breathing each other in, until Jack leaned away, checking his phone. "I should go. I have a meeting with a potential new client this afternoon and I've got to prep."

Indy snorted a laugh. "Right, like you don't already have a complete profile worked up, along with potential sponsors to contact if they sign."

"You know me so well," he said with a smile, peering around the building and checking the pathway for any more unwanted spectators. "I'll go this way."

Indy nodded back in the opposite direction. "And I'll go that way."

He hesitated for a second and then leaned in for one more kiss, quick and fierce, that sent a current of white-hot electricity through her. Then he was gone.

She adjusted her bag over her shoulder and headed toward the video room. She'd only have about half the time for vid analysis that she originally planned for. But as she pressed her fingertips against that spot on her neck lightly, recalling the feel of his mouth and the way her entire body was lit on fire by his touch, it was totally worth it.

"Are you sure that is a good idea?" rang a voice from just a few steps behind her, the French accent giving its owner away, if the superiority and condescension weren't enough of a clue. Indy spun around and came face-to-face with Caroline Morneau, her agent. Tall, blond, perfectly put together in a silk blouse and linen skirt, she somehow looked completely cool and calm despite the blazing sun. She was in town before they all left for England, mostly to go over her plans for Indy's future off the court.

Words of denial formed on Indy's tongue, but she knew it was useless. Caroline had clearly seen them. Shit.

"Good idea or not, it's none of your business."

Raising her eyes to the sky and shaking her head, Caroline said, "*You* are my business, Indiana."

"How many times do I have to say it? Don't call me that, and my *tennis* is your business," Indy corrected. "Keep your nose out of everything else."

"It is not that simple," Caroline insisted, her voice inching up in pitch.

"It really is." She turned and walked away, wanting to look back, hoping that Caroline's brow was furrowed and her hands were on her hips, mouth twisted in aggravation. But looking back would ruin the moment. Even though Indy had gotten the last word, Caroline now had the upper hand, and it was only a matter of time before she pressed her advantage.

Madison More

JENNIFER IACOPELLI

is the author of *Game, Set, Match*; *Break the Fall*; and *Finding Her Edge*, as seen on Netflix. She co-edited the anthology *Out of Our League* with Dahlia Adler. She lives in New York and invites you to visit her at jenniferiacopelli.com.

RAISING READERS

Books Build Bright Futures

Thank you for reading this book and for being a reader of books in general. As a author, I am so grateful to share being part of a community of readers with you and I hope you will join me in passing our love of books on to the next generation of readers.

Did you know that reading for enjoyment is the single biggest predictor of a child's future happiness and success?

More than family circumstances, parents' educational background, or income reading impacts a child's future academic performance, emotional well-being communication skills, economic security, ambition, and happiness.

Studies show that kids reading for enjoyment in the US is in rapid decline:

- In 2012, 53% of 9-year-olds read almost every day. Just 10 years later, in 2022, the number had fallen to 39%.
- In 2012, 27% of 13-year-olds read for fun daily. By 2023, that number was just 14%.

Together, we can commit to **Raising Readers** and change this trend. How?

- Read to children in your life daily.
- Model reading as a fun activity.
- Reduce screen time.
- Start a family, school, or community book club.
- Visit bookstores and libraries regularly.
- Listen to audiobooks.
- Read the book before you see the movie.
- Encourage your child to read aloud to a pet or stuffed animal.
- Give books as gifts.
- Donate books to families and communities in need.

BOB1217

Books build bright futures, and **Raising Readers** is our shared responsibility.

For more information, visit **JoinRaisingReaders.com**

Sources: National Endowment for the Arts, National Assessment of Educational Progress, WorldBookDay.org, Nielsen BookData's 2023 "Understanding the Children's Book Consumer"